Julian Hawthorne

An American penman : From the diary of Inspector Byrnes

Julian Hawthorne

An American penman : From the diary of Inspector Byrnes

ISBN/EAN: 9783337197711

Printed in Europe, USA, Canada, Australia, Japan

Cover: Foto ©Andreas Hilbeck / pixelio.de

More available books at **www.hansebooks.com**

AN AMERICAN PENMAN

AN AMERICAN PENMAN

FROM THE DIARY OF
INSPECTOR BYRNES

BY

JULIAN HAWTHORNE

AUTHOR OF "A TRAGIC MYSTERY," AND "THE
GREAT BANK ROBBERY."

CASSELL & COMPANY, LIMITED,
LONDON, PARIS, NEW YORK AND MELBOURNE.

CONTENTS.

PAGE.

CHAPTER XII.

CHAPTER XIII.

CHAPTER XIV.

CHAPTER XV.

CHAPTER XVI.

CHAPTER XVII.

CHAPTER XVIII.

CHAPTER XIX.

CHAPTER XX.

CHAPTER XXI.

CHAPTER XXII.

CHAPTER XXIII.

CHAPTER XXIV

AN AMERICAN PENMAN.

CHAPTER I.

A PRISONER.

IN October, New York ceases to be deserted : the shutters of her mansions open, her fashionable avenues and corners are thronged with the returning throng of those who have sought change amidst the mountains, on the seashore, and across the seas ; the shops recover from the dullness and lethargy of the heated term, and their windows sparkle and glow with alluring merchandise ; friends greet one another on the street, exchange congratulations on their improved appearance, and forecast the pleasures of the winter season ; the theaters light their lamps and display their placards, and the actors and actresses bloom out in gorgeous raiment, and elaborate fresh " gags " for the delectation of the gallery ; the ministers of the gospel, or of whatever modern philosophy stands in the place thereof, don their black robes and ascend their pulpits, and, contemplating their congregations, perhaps wonder whether fresh air and sunshine have not done more for the general morality and good-humor than can be ascribed to their own most eloquent sermons ; the *café* at Delmonico's is crowded with nondescript *nouveaux riches* from half-past six to eight ; and the dining-saloon of the same immortal establishment, from eleven o'clock till midnight, is bewildering with the beauty and aristocracy of Murray Hill, discussing their after-theater oysters and champagne.   The clubs are full, and redolent of club-gossip and club disputes and scandals ; and down on Wall Street the stock brokers are settling themselves to their winter's work, each with the resolve to boom himself, beggar his neighbor, and be quoted on 'Change as the latest Napoleon of finance.   The perennial tribe of pickpockets, burglars, bank sneaks, confidence men, and forgers are also on hand, prepared to put in practice the schemes they have been hatching during the summer, and wishing, no doubt, that the police and detective-office would drop asleep for a few months, and allow them to work their will upon a defenseless and incorrigibly heedless public.

But the observer who would betake himself to Mulberry Street, and, ascending the broad stone steps of the Central Office, cast an eye over the various departments, and note the preoccupation of the chief, the diligence of the employés, the discipline of the patrol and roundsmen, and the ceaseless movement and energy apparent on all sides, would speedily become convinced that the hope of the rogues was predestined to disappointment. Every year the municipal control over the criminal population becomes more nearly complete, and the various "gangs" that attempt to gather headway are more surely and irrevocably broken up and dispersed. If the prevention of crime in New York be not better than its cure, at all events it bids fair to achieve results that are practically as good.

Some seven or eight years ago, however, the ascendency of the police over the thieves was a good deal less palpable than it is to-day. The man who, perhaps more than any other individual, has been recognized as responsible for the better order of things, had at that time but lately been instated in his position of authority ; and the measures which he has so successfully carried out were then but purposes for the most part unrealized. At the moment when this story begins, the new inspector of the Detective Bureau, Thomas Byrnes, was sitting in his office, engaged in conversation with a young man whose face was well known on the street, where he filled a responsible position in his father's banking house, and was regarded as the latter's destined successor in the great business of Vanderblick & Co.

The inspector himself had scarcely reached the prime of life, and looked, at the first glance, younger than his years ; but a more careful observation revealed a certain solidity and repose of manner, based upon a settled character and a strong will, which in many a much older man are conspicuous by their absence. He had already, during his brief term of office, achieved more than one signal victory over the forces of disorder ; and those who feared law-breakers were already beginning to look to him as to a man both able and willing to afford them the protection which they had almost accustomed themselves to consider apocryphal.

His interlocutor on this occasion had the kind, intelligent, good-humored face and bearing of one who has passed his first novitiate in the great money market of America, and has not yet been sobered and stiffened by the rebuffs and calamities which not one in ten thousand can hope to escape. He was of good height and figure, with light hair and a handsome mustache, but his clothes bore the stamp of excellent tailoring, and were worn with the careless ease of one whose tailor's bills afford him no anxiety.

"How long," the inspector was saying, "have you noticed this sort of thing?"

"So far as we can make out," replied young Mr. Vanderblick, "it has been under way all summer. Of course, that is only our surmise : but there are a good many small circumstances that conspire to support it. The bank has been watched for two or three months past—there can be no doubt of that. Persons have come in to cash checks and to buy drafts, and have seemed desirous to engage the clerks in conversation. The transactions, thus far, have been legitimate, it is true, but still there was something in the way they were conducted which tended to make us suspicious. But, as I was saying, it was only yesterday that we came upon any thing tangible. A party came in—a pale man, with dark side-whiskers, and looking as much as any thing like a suburban clergyman strayed from his pulpit, and wanted to sell a five hundred dollar bond of the —— Railroad. It so happened that the clerk for that department of the business was out : and the clerk who was temporarily in his place, expecting him back every minute, thought it would be as well to wait for him : so he took the bond, which seemed to be all right, and told the applicant that he would be attended to presently."

" Did the applicant give his name ? " inquired the inspector.

" He did not : the transaction had not got so far. The clerk took the number and specification of the bond, meanwhile asking the applicant to be seated ; but he seemed uneasy, walked up and down, looked at his watch, and finally said that he was obliged to keep an appointment, and would come again later. So he went off."

" Taking the bond with him ? "

" Yes. The clerk did not feel authorized to retain it."

" Well ? "

" Well, a few minuets later, the other clerk came in, was told about the affair, and shown the number of the bond. He referred to the lists, and became persuaded there was something irregular. He laid the matter before my father, and it was investigated.

The result was that the bond turned out to be forged."

" How did you arrive at that conviction ?"

" Why, the fact is," replied the young banker, with some signs of hesitation, "the fact is—though this is in confidence—that we have been engaged lately, in rather extensive transactions with the bonds of this very railroad. The stock, as you may be aware, is largely held in Europe ; and, by the way, we came near accepting as partner in the transaction a former Russian friend of mine, a certain Count Fedovsky, who, however, proved to be a man of straw just in time to save us from an awkward predicament. Well, it naturally happened that a great many of these bonds were passing through our hands at the time ; and among them, curiously enough, was found the very one of which this was a fraudulent reproduction. It was a lucky escape."

" It would have been still more lucky if you had kept the forgery," the inspector remarked. "One is sometimes able to find out, from the character of the work, something about the forgers. Can the clerk identify the man ?"

" He thinks he can. But, of course, he might easily alter his appearance somewhat. He kept his hat on—a soft black felt—and wore it low down on his forehead."

" Well, Mr. Vanderblick," said the inspector, " there does not seem to be much to go upon ; but I will have investigations made, and see what can be done.   If I get any results, I will communicate with you."

" The affair is not of so much importance in itself," returned the other, rising and taking his hat, " but from another point of view it may be.   I have heard it suggested that there is a big scheme on foot to float a lot of forged paper of high denominations."

"You have heard that ? " said the inspector, looking up with a dry smile : " are you in the habit of believing all you hear, Mr. Vanderblick ? "

" Oh, I only mentioned it as a rumor," the young man hastened to reply.

" A rumor of that kind is apt to do more harm than good," said the detective, in a grave tone. "I think you would consult your own interest, as well as that of others, by not giving it your countenance."

Mr. Vanderblick murmured something inarticulate, and took his leave with some signs of embarrassment, leaving the inspector to his meditations. " How can people expect us to protect them," said the latter to himself ; " if they will insist on gossiping in and out of season like a parcel of schoolgirls ! If we had to deal with the thieves alone, we should have little to complain of : but when the persons the thieves are after are the first to give them the alarm, what chance is there left for us ? I wish I had that young man under my tuition for a month or two ! I'll wager he would learn to talk less and to think more.   He has heard something about this forgery business, and instead of guarding it like a fatal secret, and thus allowing the rogues to suppose that they are not suspected, and encouraging them to run their heads into the trap, he runs about cackling with his mouth wide open, and it is not his fault if our friends the forgers don't give us the slip. However," concluded the inspector, taking a cigar from his pocket, and lighting it with the resigned sigh of a philosopher, " it's no use grumbling. It always has been this way, and it always will be : and we have got to take all the blame and make the best of it."

At this juncture, there was a loud knock at the door.

" Come in !" quoth the inspector, blowing out a cloud of smoke, and crossing one knee over the other.

The door opened, and there entered two officers, leading between them a tall young man, dressed in a suit of clothes of fashionable cut, but rather light for the season. He was ghastly pale, and seemed to be under the influence of an irrepressible nervous agitation. Nevertheless, his face was of so manly and straightforward an aspect, and his bearing, though marked by physical weakness, had so little of the cowering air of the timid criminal, or of the braggadocio of the bold one, that the inspector was immediately struck by it, and told himself that this could be no ordinary case.

The group already described was followed by a fourth person, possessing no marked characteristics, who was evidently the complainant.

The inspector assumed the impassive air of the man of routine, and, straightening himself in his chair, inquired of the officers what they had to report.

"This man here," replied one of the officers, "told us to arrest this prisoner on a charge of highway robbery. We didn't see the affair, and don't know nothing about it, except from him. He's a bank messenger, and was going along Nassau Street, when some one run into him; the next moment his box — show his box, Jack."

The other officer produced from under his cloak a tin box, such as is used by bankers for the transmission of securities from one point to another.

"The next moment he felt some one grab his box," continued the speaker, "and when he turned round, he saw this man on the ground, with the box under him. He caught hold of him, and hollered for the police, and I heard him, and took the prisoner into custody. That's all I know about it, inspector."

The inspector now turned to the complainant. "What is your name?" he asked.

"Philip Jackson, sir."

"What is your occupation?"

"Employé of Vanderblick's bank, sir, — messenger."

At this reply, the prisoner gave a slight start, which the inspector noted, without seeming to do so.

"What is your version of this affair?" he said to the messenger.

"Mr. Vanderblick gave me that box, sir, to carry down to a place on Broad Street, and he told me to be very careful, for there was a large amount of securities in it. Well, I started down Nassau Street, which was pretty crowded then, sir, owing to the gentlemen going out to their lunch; and I was about a block off Wall Street when a big chap came along, and just as he got up to me, he gave a lurch, and tumbled right into me, most knocking me over. I sort of staggered back, and then I felt a jerk from behind, and away went the box. I didn't see who'd got it at first, for the reason that the big fellow hit out at me, and caught me one on the side of the head, knocking me down. As soon as I recovered myself, I saw this man flat on the ground, with his arms round the box. So I caught on to him, till the officer came along, and then I handed him over."

The inspector's eyes were next directed upon the prisoner, who returned the glance firmly, though he swayed slightly as he stood, and evidently kept himself erect only by an effort. His hair, which was soft and curly, was disordered and matted with blood, which also stained his collar and coat.

"How was this man wounded?" demanded the inspector of the officers. "Did he resist arrest?"

"No, sir. He came quiet enough, only saying he was innocent. He got that lick before we got hold of him."

" Let him sit down ! "

A chair was brought, and the prisoner dropped into it with an involuntary groan of relief. At the same time he bent his head to the inspector, in silent acknowledgment of his humanity.

" Who are you ? " the chief of detectives asked.

" I am a Russian. My name is Ivan Fedovsky."

" How long have you been in New York ? "

" About eight months."

" Have you any thing to say about this charge against you ? "

" The witness has told the truth, as far as he knows it. But he knows only a part of the truth. I am not guilty of what he charges."

This was said with an accent of such sincerity and earnestness, that the inspector, whose ear, by long practice, had become as quick to detect the various intonations of the criminal voice as is that of a musician to catch a false note, was impressed and interested. But, on the other hand, he had just heard the name of Fedovsky alluded to in no very complimentary manner by young Vanderblick, and he proceeded with due caution.

" Tell your story your own way," he said carelessly.

" I was walking down Nassau Street about noon," began Fedovsky, who, like many educated Russians, spoke English with fluency and good accent, " and presently I noticed a man walking in front of me, with a box under his arm. It was that man," he added, indicating the messenger, " and the box was the one which has been produced. I remember it passed through my mind that the box probably was one of those in which bank securities are carried from one place to another, and I thought how great was the risk of such a method of transmission. The next moment I saw a large, heavily built man coming toward me at a quick pace ; he gave one look at this man, and then looked away, but he walked straight at him, and ran into him with great force. This man—the messenger—staggered, slipped on the curb, and almost fell. The big man called out something, and made a blow at him, knocking him down. At the same moment, from a doorway, I saw a person in a black coat, with a soft black hat on, glide out, and snatch the box from the messenger's hold. As soon as he had taken it, he turned, and started toward me ; instinctively I stretched out my hand and caught him by the collar of his coat. He tried to wrench himself away, and when he found he could not, he thrust one hand into the pocket of his coat, and I thought he was going to produce some weapon. I let go of his collar, and seized the box with both hands, and dragged it away from him. Then I felt a stunning blow on the back of my head. I felt myself falling, but I kept hold of the box, and fell upon it. I remember nothing else, until I came to myself, and found that I was under arrest. Then I was brought here."

This story was told slowly, owing to the physical weakness of the speaker, and his recurring pauses to gain strength to proceed ; and his voice was low, and sometimes sank away almost to a whisper. But it was a straightforward story, and told with a clearness and sincerity of manner that had their effect. The inspector listened closely to every word of it, and wrote something down on a bit of paper in front of him. After a few moments' consideration, he said :

" Could you describe the man who snatched the box ? "

" I think I should know him again," replied the other, " and I had an impression that I had seen him somewhere before—I couldn't remember where. He was rather tall, and had full dark whiskers."

" Do you think he was the man who struck you ? "

" It could not have been he. He was in front of me at the time I fell, and I was struck from behind. He made no movement to strike."

" It was the large man, then ? "

" Possibly ; but I don't think so. I think he went to the other side of the street just as I seized the man in black."

" Jackson," said the inspector sharply, turning to the messenger, " was it you who gave this blow ? "

" No, sir," replied Jackson promptly, " I never hit anybody."

" Did you see the blow struck ? "

" I can't say I did, sir."

" If he was a thief, he must have been struck by

some one who wished to capture or stop him. Has any such person appeared?"

"Not that I know of, sir."

"But if his story is true, it is reasonable to suppose that he was attacked by one of a gang of thieves. The blow must have come from some one. The thing must be inquired into." He spoke to the officers. "Find out who were the witnesses of this affair, and have them brought here. Meanwhile you will be detained," he added, to the prisoner, "and —"

"He has fainted, inspector," said one of the policemen ; and so it proved.

CHAPTER II.

THE inspector immediately directed that the prisoner should be subjected to a medical examination, and every thing necessary done towards his recovery. Meanwhile, several witnesses were obtained, and their testimony taken.

This testimony tended to confirm the prisoner's version of the occurrence. One or two of the witnesses had seen the box snatched by the dark-whiskered individual: another had seen the prisoner wrestling with the latter; and one had seen him struck by a man who ran up from behind. Every thing seemed to point to the conclusion that his accusation and arrest had been a mistake, and that the really guilty parties had escaped. Orders were issued to use every means to apprehend the parties in question; but they had obtained a long start of their pursuers, and there was not much prospect of overtaking them.

This investigation occupied two or three hours. By the time it was over, word was brought to the inspector that the prisoner was in a state of extreme emaciation, and was apparently suffering from starvation. The wound on his head, though cutting deeply into the scalp, had not fractured the skull, and there was every probability of its healing under proper treatment.

"Let him be taken to the hospital," said the inspector, "and see that he is kindly cared for ; and when he is sufficiently recovered, let him be brought here again."

Four or five days passed away, when word was brought to the inspector that the patient, Ivan Fedovsky, was well enough to leave the hospital. A detective sergeant was immediately dispatched thither, and returned in the course of an hour, bringing Fedovsky with him. The officer then retired, leaving him and the inspector alone together.

"So you are able to be about again, are you ?" demanded the other cheerfully, motioning his visitor to a chair. "I'm glad it was no worse."

"Thanks to you," replied the other, in a voice that betrayed the sincerity of his feeling. "I am practically myself again. I thank you heartily—"

"Well, well, that's all right : I wanted to say to you that my inquiries have satisfied me that you were wrongly accused. And that instead of attempting a robbery, you met with your misfortune while in the act of performing a gallant and disinterested deed. So far as this office was concerned in the affair, I wish to express my regret : but when our men are directed to make an arrest in such a case, they are bound to do so. You would probably not have been brought here at all, however, had you, at the time of your arrest, named any person who knew you. Since, as you told me, you have resided for several months in New York. I should have thought this would have occurred to you."

The young man colored faintly, but he met the inspector's eyes firmly. "It did occur to me," he said, "but circumstances rendered it impossible for me to adopt that course. There is no one in this city, among the many with whom I have been acquainted, to whom I cared to look for help. But that fact," he added, in an unsteady voice, "makes me feel your kindness the more : for you are a stranger, and you hold a position which one does not usually connect with offices of humanity." As he ended, tears rolled down his face, and his mouth twitched.

"Oh, you are not to think that even men in our business have no bowels of compassion," replied the inspector, with a smile. "Our immediate object is the suppression of crime and criminals, it is true : but that implies that we have at heart the welfare of honest and unfortunate persons. You are to feel under no special obligations to us. We do our duty, as well as circumstances permit."

"If you have done only your duty, at any rate you have done it in a way I can never forget," returned the other, struggling to compose himself. "You must pardon my weakness, Inspector Byrnes," he presently added : "but I have passed through a terrible ordeal, and I have not the strength, either of mind or body, that belongs to me." After another pause, he said, "There is no one in this city to whom I feel able to speak freely, except to yourself. But I would like to tell you, in confidence, the story of my life, so that you may not think that your kindness has been thrown away upon a common vagabond."

"As I already have told you," was the reply, "I am satisfied of your integrity. There is no need of your telling me any thing that would add to your suffering."

"It will be a relief rather than a pain to ·speak to you," the other answered, "and it is the only acknowledgment I can make of my indebtedness to you. As for the accident that brought me here, I have cause to be thankful for it, rather than to regret it : it saved me from a fatal folly—what I now feel would have been a crime. You will better understand that when I come to it in the course of my story. But have you a little time at your disposal ? "

For reply, the inspector touched a bell. A sergeant appeared.

"I am engaged," the inspector said. "Admit no one, except on business that can not be postponed. Now, sir," he added, when the officer had withdrawn ; "I am ready to listen to you."

Fedovsky began his story in a hesitating and uncertain manner : but, as he proceeded, the narrative gained strength and color, and at times rose to the height of dramatic interest. It was the history of a life, strange and not uneventful, and doubtless it owed something of its interest to the style and personality of the narrator. But it would take too long to reproduce it in his very words, even were that otherwise practicable ; and the convenience of the reader will best be consulted by putting Fedovsky in the third person. Certain unimportant digressions will thus be avoided, and, on the other hand, certain points will be elucidated which were not sufficiently defined in the original narrative.

* * * * * * * *

A man takes to gambling for either one of three reasons : either from natural predilection : or because he hopes to recoup himself promptly for a desperate loss of money : or because he has tried and wearied of all other forms of excitement, and has only this left to him.

The young Russian gentleman known as Count Fedovsky might have been classed under the third of these divisions. He was not by nature specially inclined to games of chance ; and after two or three years of aimless and rather extravagant life in European capitals, he still had plenty of money. But his mental and moral palate had become somewhat callous to ordinary forms of amusement and dissipation, and he felt the need of a stronger stimulus. It occurred to him one day that he had not yet tried the spell of the cards and the green cloth; and, acting, as he was wont to do, on the spur of the moment, he packed his trunks (or ordered his valet to do so) and took tickets on the next train for Monaco.

Up to this point in his career, Count Fedovsky had been in many respects a favorite of fortune. He was the only son of one of the wealthy members of the Russian nobility. He had received an excellent education, and was familiar, from his childhood up, with the principal European languages. His father had been an influential officer of the Imperial government, with a long line of Cossack ancestry behind him ; he had been high in favor with the Czar, and was saturated with all the prejudices and traditions of the autocratic idea. His mother was a beautiful, indolent and amiable woman, who had indulged her son without stint, and, if he disobeyed her, contented herself with punishing her serfs, who, for their part, were so fond of their young master, that they generally suffered without complaining.

When the count was about twenty years of age, he fell desperately in love with a young girl whom it was impossible he should marry. She was not of his rank in the first place, and there were other reasons of a politic character against the match. On the other hand, she returned the young fellow's passion, and in mind and body they seemed eminently suited to each other. The count's mother, whose conceptions of morality were those of her race and generation, would not have been averse from allowing the lovers to indulge their affection without the intervention of legal and ecclesiastical formalities : but her son, whose best and purest emotions were concerned in the affair, had the rare magnanimity to decline any such compromise. Vera should be his wife, or nothing ! It was in vain to argue with him : and as his will had never before been crossed, he became very difficult to manage. At length the mother, apprehensive lest her boy should run off and get married in spite of her, was fain to reveal the state of affairs to her husband. She wrote him a letter on the subject, and the old autocrat arrived from St. Petersburg three days later.

His course was marked by promptness and decision. He had an interview with his son, in which he put before him in terse language the magnitude of his folly, and then informed him that he must prepare to return with him the next week to St. Petersburg, where an official position awaited him. Refusing to listen to any persuasions or entreaties, he ordered the young man to his room, locked the door upon him, and, getting into his carriage, drove to the residence of the unfortunate Vera. To her parents, who were poor people, he gave a brief epitome of the situation, and ended by proposing that their daughter should be immediately united in the bonds of matrimony to a certain enterprising man, the overseer of one of his estates. By way of facilitating this arrangement, he placed in the parents' hands the sum of fifty thousand roubles, as dower for the bride. The parents did not dare to offer any objection, even if they were otherwise disposed to do so ; and the marriage was actually an accomplished fact before the end of the week. The young count, on learning the truth, went to his father, and informed him that, since it was now impossible that he should ever be happy, he intended to take leave of his life ; at the same moment he snatched up a pistol from the table, and placed the muzzle against his forehead. The father sat unmoved, his eyes fixed sternly upon the youth. The latter drew his breath for the last time, turned pale, set his teeth, and pulled the trigger. No explosion followed ; the sagacious old noble had taken the precaution (knowing his son's impulsive temperament) to draw the charge. He now rose from his seat, took the useless weapon from the boy's unnerved hand, and forced him into a chair.

" Come," he said, in a kindly tone, " I have hopes of you after all. You have proved to me that you possess courage and determination ; and as for the girl, you have attempted to lay down your life for her sake, and no man can do more. Thanks to my foresight, however, instead of being a useless dead body, you are still alive, and with a fine career before you. Do not regret the irrevocable : that is the part of a coward and an imbecile, which you are not. To-morrow you return with me to the capital. I will put you on the road to preferment : with your abilities, and my influence, there is no height too lofty for your ambition to aim at. Be a man henceforth, and live in the world of men. You are my son : you already have my affection : deserve likewise my respect and esteem ! "

The autocrat carried his point ; such men generally do. But it was a lethargic and indifferent youth that he took with him to St. Petersburg. The disappointed lover, though he had his life, placed no value on it and took no interest in it. For some months, this negative state of mind continued, and neither the gayeties nor the occupations of the capital sufficed to dispel it. Gradually, however, time began to produce its inevitable effect : and probably, had things continued in their ordinary course, young Count Fedovsky would have become the man of routine, forms, and authority that the old count was before him. But, as fate would have it, an incident occurred which completely altered the course of his life. On entering his father's room one morning, he found him lying on the floor, dead from a stroke of the heart.

Count Fedovsky at once dispatched a messenger to his mother with the news ; and, on her arrival at St. Petersburg, the funeral was solemnized with all due pomp and ceremony. The young man then obtained an indefinite leave of absence from his official duties, and returned with his mother to his estate, heir to a large fortune. The shock of the sudden death of his father, for whom he had begun to feel a sentiment somewhat warmer than respect, enhanced what had grown to be the habitual gravity of his demeanor; but, in some concealed chamber of his heart, there may have lurked an anticipation of a possible future happiness with Vera. If such were the case, the hope was destined to be frustrated. Upon instituting enquiries with regard to his former lady-love, it was discovered that her husband had retired from the management of the estate, and that there was an impression that his control of it had been more remarkable for astuteness than for honesty. Whither he had gone no one could say; but, wherever it might be, he had taken his wife with him.

This was doubtless depressing news for the count; and he seemed to lack energy or inclination to take a new departure in life. He settled indolently down on his estate, and betook himself to a desultory course of reading and dreaming. His mother was his only companion: her health was beginning to give way, and she placed all her dependence on him. He remained at her side, leading an existence that scarcely differed save in name from imprisonment, during no less than four years. During that time, from his twenty-first to near the end of his twenty-sixth year, he was never visited by an impulse to escape, to see the world, to mingle with men and women, to achieve any worthy ambition, or in any manner to vary his environment. The instincts of youth seemed to be dead within him.

About the end of the fourth year his mother died. Her death had not been unexpected, but it left the count with a sense of loneliness that surprised himself. He had not realized how much she had been to him, nor how large a void her departure would leave. He wandered about his great house, restless, moody and disconsolate. One night he had a vivid dream that he met Vera, and that she was in some sort of peril. It was the first time he had dreamt of her since their parting. It produced an exaggerated impression upon him. After brooding over it for a week, he took a sudden resolution. He determined to leave his home and travel about the world, and not to return until he had found Vera or settled all doubts as to her fate.

This new purpose in life acted upon his dormant nature like a charm. He became alert and active. He summoned his stewards and business agents, and made arrangements for a prolonged absence. He neither knew nor cared whither he was going, nor what length of time might elapse before his return. His mind was full of vague schemes and anticipations. He was busy all day, ate heartily, and at night slept soundly. He was surprised to find himself happy and eager. The long-repressed energy of his nature came rushing forth with all the impetus of so many passionless years. He felt as if he had been asleep for a century, and had awakened with the strength and capacities of a giant. Although the thought of Vera was the ostensible cause of this change in him, it can not be held accountable for the whole or the greater part of it. The time had come for him to take a new step, and his dream of finding his lost love was but a pretext for taking it. Once launched upon the world, with his fortune, his ample education, and the warm blood of his youth, it was not likely that he would ever again relapse—Vera or no Vera—into the old moody and lethargic state from which he was now emancipated.

He took only one companion with him on his journey This was an English servant, a man some ten or a dozen years older than himself, of approved faithfulness and sagacity. This fellow, Tom Bolan by name, was a personage of various accomplishments. He had begun life as a sailor, and was an adept at all kinds of trades—was a carpenter, locksmith, tailor, painter, and glazier. In addition to this, he had in some way acquired a speaking acquaintance with the French and Italian languages, could play an excellent tune on the fiddle, and could dance a hornpipe or a fandango to admiration. After making a number of voyages, he found himself stranded in New York, and, by way of variety, he strolled into a large livery stable, where he made himself so agreeable, and showed himself so handy, that he was forthwith engaged as hostler; and, during his three or four years' discharge of his duties, obtained a very good knowledge of horseflesh and all thereto appertaining. The stable gave accommodation to horses of private gentlemen, and one of the latter, to whose steed Tom had been ministering, took a fancy to the clever youth, and engaged him as his own groom and attendant. With his new master he subsequently visited Europe,

and made the rounds there ; but, while on a visit
to St. Petersburg, the master was taken ill with
pneumonia and died, and Tom was thrown upon
the world with a few hundred dollars in his pocket,
and an unusual share of worldly experience. With
such a capital he could not be at a loss ; and, after
serving for a few months as waiter in one of the
fashionable restaurants, he attracted the favorable
notice of no less a personage than the old Count
Fedovsky himself, and presently found himself an
inmate of that nobleman's city establishment. Here
he acted in various capacities, chiefly as valet and
table-servant, and gave complete satisfaction. It
was sometime after his establishment there that the
old count brought his son to the capital. Tom
immediately conceived an immense affection for the
young man, which grew so marked that the father
formally made him over to Fedovsky junior, and
he became the latter's confidential attendant and
factotum. He stood by him during all those lonely
and gloomy years, never losing his own spirits, and
doing much toward keeping those of his master
from falling into still lower deeps ; and, when
the count set forth upon his journey into the
unknown, it was a matter of course as well as of
necessity that faithful Tom should go with him.

The two companions, on leaving the center of
Muscovite civilization, shaped their course for
London, in which every Russian finds a greater or
less degree of interest. The count had excellent letters of introduction, as well as practically

unlimited letters of credit ; and, as a consequence, he was at once received into the best society. After passing a season or two in the world's city, seeing the sights, riding in Rotten Row, dining with the aristocracy, listening to debates in Parliament, boating on the Thames, betting at the Derby and Ascot, and following all this up with a couple of months' shooting on the northern moors, Count Fedovsky bade farewell to his English friends, and crossed the channel to Paris, where he soon found himself agreeably at home. The life of the boulevards, the cafés and the theaters amused him : in the young men of Parisian society he found charming companions, and he made his first studies in some of the mysteries and eccentricities of the feminine nature. But how different were all the women he met from Vera ! And in what corner of the universe had she hidden herself?

From Paris he traveled to Dresden, Berlin and Vienna : thence, again, to Rome, Florence, Naples and Venice : he made excursions into Sweden and Norway, and even penetrated into Turkey, Roumania and Palestine. In the following June he returned again to London : and the succeeding two years were passed more or less after the same fashion. He became a recognized figure among the well-to-do idlers of Europe; and he was still so young and handsome that it was a matter of continual surprise to those who knew him that he did not either marry, or form a liaison with one or other of the many women who would have needed but little urging to associate themselves with so wealthy and attractive a personage. Perhaps Fedovsky himself would have found it difficult to explain his own indifference. It was not a premeditated or deliberate indifference. He had no idea of steeling his heart against the charms of the other sex. Neither, on the other hand, could it be said that the loss of Vera still affected him to such a degree that he was powerless to appreciate any one else. It was now more than seven years since Vera's marriage, and Fedovsky was, after all, like other human beings ; an impression, however strong, could not remain with him forever. Nevertheless, up to the time he set out for Monaco, he had met with no woman who could take Vera's place.

CHAPTER III.

MR. WILLIAMS.

MONACO—or, to be more accurate, Monte Carlo —is as beautiful as it is famous, and that is giving it high praise. Before the gambling palace was erected by M. Blanc, the place was little visited by tourists, because the Cornice Road passed on the cliffs above it at such an altitude that no one, unless he were furnished with a parachute, ever thought of taking more than a passing glance at it from his carriage-window, as it lay far below him in the blue Mediterranean. Subsequently, a railroad was built to it along the shore of the sea ; and then M. Blanc, by establishing his business there, made it one of the head-quarters of wealthy and frivolous Europe.

It is all very well to protest, but gambling is the normal expression of a certain quality in human nature, just as love-making and fighting are, and all the laws framed by abstract morality must remain powerless to suppress it. If it be shut out from one place it will appear in another, and, were the whole universe freed from it, it would still have its impregnable abiding-place in the hearts of its votaries.

Accordingly, though Baden-Baden knows it no longer, it flourishes with more than its pristine luxuriance in the tiny Italian principality ; and, if the prince should forbid it there, it would still be practiced in the center of Africa or in the remote recesses of Chinese Tartary.

Meanwhile, Monte Carlo is a very charming habitation for it. No doubt, indeed, a person who is suddenly making or losing a fortune may not be especially awake to the beauties of natural scenery ; but a large proportion of the visitors do not make gambling their principal occupation ; they merely look on, or play with chance as children play with a toy, instead of engaging in a life and death battle with the wild goddess whose secrets no human being has resolved. Gambling is always dissipation, but, when taken in moderation, it temporarily stimulates and amuses the mind, as small quantities of alcohol do the physical system, and leaves no serious dilapidation behind it. And one may be immensely amused at Monte Carlo without once winning or losing so much as a five-franc piece.

In planning his visit, however, Fedovsky had no such temperate intentions. He meant to find out all there was in gambling, and to spare neither time nor expense in the investigation. It was an entirely deliberate step on his part, for he had not what is called the gambler's instinct ; his mind was so constituted as to prefer law and method to accident ; and suspense and uncertainty, which for many possess inexhaustible fascination, seemed rather

stupid and wearisome to him. But he had read
and heard that people have been driven mad by
unexpected successes at play, and have blown out
their brains under the despair of sudden and total
ruin ; and, as he believed himself capable of feeling
all the emotions incident to humanity, and had been,
nevertheless, for a long time barren of any emotion
to speak of, he was resolved not to give so fairly
promising a stimulus the go-by. He was devoured
with *ennui*, in short, and deemed no sacrifice too
great to dispel it.

He gave Tom orders to pack his trunks accordingly, and—being at the time in Paris—proceeded
by ·rail to Marseilles and thence by steamer to
Genoa. From Genoa, with which he was already
familiar, it was no long journey to Monte Carlo
and he arrived there in due course and without
incident.   A comfortable suite of rooms at the best
hotel had already been engaged by telegraph ; and
in the course of twelve hours after arrival, the
ingenuity of the English valet, assisted by his
master's excellent taste, and the contents of the
trunks, had made them look homelike and comfortable. This done, and before approaching the green
tables, the young count sallied forth to explore the
features and surroundings of the scene of his proposed experiment.

It was certainly a lovely spot, where great natural
advantages had been enhanced by art, and were
enriched by historic association. On the one hand
rose the immense mass of the maritime Alps,

mounting tier above tier to the sky, green with ver-
dure and stern with precipices; on the other,
bosomed upon the broad blue expanse, lay the rocky
promontory, with its vertical sides which had so
often defied the assaults of war, and which, mere
bowlder though it was, contained a kingdom that
had been ruled by one hereditary race of kings since
the dawn of European history. Upon this basis of
rock and shore rose an agreeable medley of archi-
tecture, modern and mediæval, elegant and picturesque, interspersed with beautiful gardens in
luxuriant cultivation, broad white roads, winding
paths, and charming embowered nooks and coigns of
vantage. The Casino and the adjoining buildings
were separated from the citadel of Monaco by some
two miles of curving road, along which diligences
plied constantly, bearing visitors to and fro. Every-
where well-dressed people were strolling about, all
apparently in a holiday humor, and with nothing on
earth to do except to enjoy themselves. The hotels
were close to the Casino, and in the immediate
neighborhood were a number of pretty villas, owned
or rented by private persons. Altogether it was a
fairy-like place—a sort of enchanted domain, where
every thing seemed happy and prosperous, but
beneath the fair outside of which you dimly felt the
presence of evil influence, which could in a moment
—for such as came under the evil spell—cause the
phantom beauty and good cheer to vanish, leaving
in their place a grisly desert peopled by demons and
lost souls.

Count Fedovsky strolled about with the others, and admired the view, and quietly observed his associates, and matured his impressions of the place ; and it impressed him favorably. It was not at all like any of the great capitals to which he was accustomed. There was no society, in the ordinary sense of the word. Not that there were not plenty of people who were in society when they were at home ; but this was a species of communism : a person was expected to wear decent clothes and not to create an uproar ; but nobody cared who anybody was, where he came from, or whither he went when he went away. It was not good form to be over-inquisitive about the antecedents and worldly circumstances of the individual who happened to sit opposite you at dinner, or beside you at the gaming table ; he might be the Czarevitch, or he might be a convict newly escaped from the hulks ; and in either case he would prefer to postpone any discussion of the fact. If he smoked good cigars, did not eat with his knife or his fingers, and lost or won his money with tolerable composure, it was the utmost that any body could require of him.

As regarded the women, the case was similar, though with such modifications as are inseparable from the sex. The man of the world does not much mind temporary association with almost any variety or grade of men ; but he is necessarily more circumspect with women. A woman may appear every thing that the most fastidious taste can demand ; and yet, if she be away from the surroundings proper to her, which afford the only means of really fixing her social standing, she will be regarded with wary eyes. No doubt, women who never leave their own private circle may be just as deficient on the moral side as the most unmistakable adventuress : but people are obliged to form their judgments of one another according to certain conventional rules, in default of mutual transparency.

There were a great many attractive women at Monte Carlo ; but Fedovsky did not happen to meet with any whom he knew, and he lacked the enterprise to introduce himself. Nor did any of his male acquaintances appear amidst the crowd ; he had no one except Tom to converse with for several days. During this time he did not enter the Casino. But at the end of a week, when the novelty of the scenery had worn off, and he was beginning to feel bored again, he made up his mind to begin the experiment he had set out to accomplish. He strolled into the Salon de Jeu one afternoon, and stood with a cigarette between his fingers, contemplating the scene at one of the *Rouge et Noir* tables. The players seemed interested, and made a good deal of noise. There were orders to the croupiers, protests, comments, and disputes. Piles of gold and silver appeared, disappeared, and shifted their position upon the board in a manner to make one's head swim, while the revolving bowl in the center kept the fateful ball whirling, upon the destination of whose incalculable career so many million francs are yearly lost and won. It was the game of a lifetime concentrated into an hour or a minute. If only the interest and excitement were correspondingly intensified, Fedovsky could not but admit that it would be worth playing.

A gentleman who was standing on the opposite side of the table, looking on like Fedovsky, put his hand in his pocket, reached forward, and placed a gold louis on the red. Black came up at the next round; the gentleman smiled, and turned away; as he did so, his eye caught that of Fedovsky, which happened to be fixed upon him.

A humorous, half-deprecating expression passed over the stranger's face, and he swung his shoulders a little, as much as to say, "Any man may be a fool occasionally." A few minutes later, the movement of the shifting crowd brought the two men together, and the stranger, noticing that Fedovsky was exploring his pockets for a match, silently extended toward him his own newly-lighted cigar.

The count bowed and availed himself of the courtesy, and then returned the cigar with an acknowledgment. The other merely nodded good-humoredly, and they drifted apart again. But ten minutes later, Fedovsky was lounging on the outskirts of the *Trente et Quarante* board, when the person immediately in front of him turned suddenly, and came in contact with him. It was the gentleman who had just furnished him with a light.

"I beg your pardon!" said the count, in French.

"Not at all," replied the stranger. "My fault."

"I trust you have been more fortunate here," said the count, nodding toward the table.

The stranger glanced at him rather keenly for a moment, as if to satisfy himself that the person addressing him was the right sort of man to talk with. Apparently the examination was reassuring, for he answered, in an affable tone, "Oh, I don't do much playing here. I throw away a louis or two, when I come in, just to pay for my entertainment, but that's all. You don't seem to take much interest in it, either?"

"I haven't tried it yet," the count replied; "but I came here to see what it is like; it seems to interest many people."

"Oh, yes," said the other, "it's exciting, no doubt, when you get into it. But, for my part, I made my money by hard work, and I'd rather spend it for something more permanently valuable than an hour's excitement."

At this speech, the count, in his turn, subjected his interlocutor to a brief scrutiny. He was well dressed, though he wore his clothes rather carelessly; his figure was slight, and a trifle above the medium height; his face and eyes were keen, grave and intelligent, and when he smiled, his expression was very agreeable. He might have been five-and-thirty years of age.

"You are a foreigner, I presume?" said the count, politely.

"Well, we're all foreigners here, for the most part, I suppose," returned the other with a laugh. "Monaco is something like my country in that respect : only they don't take out naturalization papers here.   I am an American ; " and as he spoke he handed a card to the count, on which was engraved the name and address, " George Williams, 15 West 41st St., New York."

"Oh, you are from the United States," said the count, in English ; "then we may speak in your language."

"And whom have I the pleasure of addressing ?" Mr. Williams inquired.

"Pardon me—I had forgotten," said the count, producing his card-case.   "I am a Russian, but, like many Russians, I have much admiration for American institutions."

"Well, our institutions are all right on paper," Mr. Williams replied, " but, somehow or other, they don't always work out quite right in practice. However, I guess our form of government is a touch beyond despotism, anyhow.   You're not a Nihilist, are you ? "

"Not a bit of one," answered Fedovsky, smiling ; "but I feel the necessity for greater civil freedom, if Russia is ever to become truly great."   The young count had often expressed similar opinions before, perhaps showing rather less judgment than right feeling in so doing ; for Europe is full of ears and tongues, and the spies of the Czar sometimes turn up in the most unexpected places.   But, during his long period of solitary existence on his estate, he had read and meditated much on questions of political science, and had come to adopt very liberal views, which his observation of the working of other European governments had served to confirm. Had his attitude been known at the Russian court, it would undoubtedly have cost him dear.

Mr. Williams, however, was not a Russian spy, and he assented freely enough to the count's remarks, though evincing no special inclination to enter into a discussion of the subject. "You Russians," he observed, "are a curious mixture. The only Russians we see have so much money that they don't know how to spend it : and the only ones we hear about are either trying to blow up the Czar, or are being exiled to Siberia."

"I hope to escape Siberia, at any rate," returned the count, good-naturedly ; "and as for the money, if all accounts be true, M. Blanc will soon disembarrass me of any superfluity."

"As to that, it's none of my business," said the American, "but if I was in your place, I'd let the tables alone. If you want to lose your money, take a hand at poker with a friend, and lose it to him. However, that's your lookout. Good-day, sir."

He walked off, with the careless, sauntering step that was characteristic of him, and Fedovsky was left to his own devices. At first, he was somewhat inclined to follow the keen-eyed American's counsel ; and he perhaps would have done so, had **there** been a friend of his at hand who was ready and able to gamble with him.   But no one answering that description was accessible, and besides, he had agreed with himself to gamble at Monte Carlo, and he meant to do it.   Presently, therefore, on a chair being vacated at the table, he occupied the retiring player's place, and laid his first stake upon the table.   He had with him gold and bank-notes to the amount of about twenty thousand francs.   He played all the afternoon and well into the evening, and, after several vicissitudes, one of which brought him within a few hundred francs of being cleaned out, he left the table with thirty-five thousand francs in his pockets, and a vague suspicion that he had been rather bored than otherwise.   At the mention of Mr. George Williams, the attention of Inspector Byrnes, which had hitherto been somewhat lax, at once became earnest, and he interrupted the narrator to ask him several questions as to the appearance and behavior of the individual in question.   Thereafter he listened much more closely to the story, and took a good many notes, though with what object Fedovsky was unable to divine.   No subsequent mention of Mr. Williams was allowed to pass without remark and analysis.   Meanwhile, the young Russian continued his story.

CHAPTER IV

THE next morning Fedovsky met Williams in the garden overlooking the sea, and after greeting each other, and strolling about together for awhile, they came to a seat beneath some palm trees, commanding an exquisite prospect of the azure bay, with triangular-sailed boats flitting about, and sat down there. After a pause, the American said :

" Did you keep it up long, yesterday ? "

" Longer than was altogether pleasant, I believe. I expected to lose, and stayed on for that purpose: but, though I came near it once, I picked up again, and left off richer than I began. I shall try again to-day."

" Well," said Williams, tipping his hat back from his broad forehead, and fixing his eyes on the blue line of the horizon, " I was rewarded for my abstention by a very pleasant experience. I met one of the most charming women, last night, that I ever remember seeing."

" I congratulate you ! " said the count, amiably.

" By the way, she was a country-woman of yours, too."

" Ah, really ! what was her name ? "

" Princess Volgorouki was what they called her. There was something more to it, but I could never get the hang of these Russian names. But she did things in very good style.   She lives in one of those villas near the hotel.   She comes here every winter, but she seems to know very few people.   There was some old Italian diplomat there, and his wife. We had some caravan tea, and a drop of wine, with a cigarette or two afterward.   She is a widow, but quite young still, and as handsome as a picture. The latter part of the evening we sat down and had a game of cards.   There wasn't much money on it, but, for all that, it beat the Casino hollow."

" It must have been very pleasant," responded Fedovsky, who felt no very ardent desire to make the acquaintance of any of his own country people. He had been considering, during the last few hours, the project of making a journey to the United States, and, perhaps, taking up his permanent residence there.   Tom had given him favorable accounts of the country, and his reading had made him familiar with its history and characteristics. It would not be difficult for him to dispose of his estates on terms sufficient to provide him with an ample competence ; and he might fairly anticipate that the great Western Republic would prove novel and interesting enough to take the place of Mount Carlo as a cure of *ennui*.   In view of this scheme, he regarded his meeting with the American tourist as a possibly convenient circumstance.   Mr.

Williams evidently belonged to the better class of people in his own country, and could put him in the way of beginning his American career at the right end.

" Have you ever thought of returning to New York before long ? " he inquired, after a pause.

" If you had asked me yesterday, I might have said yes," was the reply. " But, now, I don't know. I want to see a little more of the princess. One don't often come across a woman really worth knowing, and it would be a pity not to improve the opportunity."

" I begin to suspect that you are a little smitten," said Fedovsky, smiling.

" Oh, I admit it ! " returned the American humorously. " So would you be, if you saw her. The time you spend with a woman like that is not wasted. I'm going again this evening."

" I wish you all success," said the count: " for myself, I mean to try once more the fascinations of the green cloth."

" You will get tired of your evening's amusement before I shall of mine," rejoined the other: and having lighted a cigar, he arose and strolled away. He had made no offer to introduce Fedovsky to the princess, nor had Fedovsky been sufficiently interested to ask the favor : but enough had been said to make her a subject of thought in the young Russian's mind, and to suggest to him that he might sometime feel inclined to make an effort toward becoming acquainted with her. For the present however, he was content to let the matter drop, and to return to the Casino.

He took with him, on this occasion, no less a sum than fifty thousand francs, and he played stakes of a thousand francs at a time. At first he was successful ; but after a few hours, his luck changed, and he lost every stake. Not to dwell upon this episode, which has only an indirect bearing upon our story, he ultimately lost the whole sum he had with him, and rose from the table with an empty purse. Indeed, when, on his way out, he stopped in the café to buy a packet of cigarettes, he discovered that he had not the money to pay for it. It was a new sensation, and he turned away with a laugh. As he did so, his eye caught the figure of Mr. Williams, who was standing at a little distance, smoking his customary cigar. Upon recognizing the count, he advanced toward him with a " Well, how are you getting along ?"

" To tell you the truth," replied Fedovsky, " I am in want of something to smoke. May I ask you to oblige me with a cigarette ? "

"I don't carry cigarettes," answered the American, apparently somewhat puzzled at the request, " but if a cigar will do—" he drew forth his cigar case.

" Cigars are not my usual form of tobacco," said the other : " however, since you are so kind, I will make an exception this evening,—it is an exceptional evening certainly."

" Oh, I guess I know what is the matter." remarked Williams, lifting his eyebrows with an arch expression. "You forgot to put any change in your pocket. I came in here to get a glass of brandy and water before turning in. It would be a favor if you'd join me ; and we'll have some cigarettes at the same time. Come on ! "

He led the count to a table, where a waiter soon supplied their wants. In the chat which ensued, Fedovsky gave an account of his adventure. Williams listened without making any comment, and finally said, "Well, I suppose ten thousand dollars more or less is nothing to you, but if you go on at that rate, it's only a question of time. I hope you won't be offended .at my talking, count : but I'm an older man than you are, and I've known what it was to be without a cent in the world. Have you any idea how long you are going to keep this thing up ? "

" I haven't thought seriously about the matter at all," the count answered. "The amusement is all I have considered. I shall take my ups and downs for awhile, and then have done with it."

" If I were you," said the American, " I'd have done with it now, and come and see the princess. She would cure your *ennui* in no time."

" She may not be such a philanthropist as you suppose."

" Would you like me to ask her permission to bring you ? " inquired the American.

" Thank you very much ; I may be able to avail myself of your kindness later. The fact is, I have been on my good behavior so long, that I wanted a change. It has been a relief to get away from people I know, and from having to talk small-talk with ladies. But no doubt I shall want to get back to it again before long, and then I shall remind you of your offer."

"That's all right," said Williams, in his careless, affable way. "Please yourself! Will you have another glass? Well, then, I'll say good-night, for I'm an early bird, and like to be in bed before midnight."

When the count was left alone, he told himself, as he sauntered along the broad, white road to his quarters, that Mr. Williams was quite right, and that he was making a fool of himself. However large a man's fortune may be, fifty thousand francs is a large sum to throw away in one evening. At that rate it would not take him till next spring to become a pauper. He had nothing to show for the money, and the amount of amusement and excitement he had derived from the transaction might certainly have been had at a lower figure. Why not decide that the experiment was a failure, and stop right here?

He reflected, however, that he had scarcely as yet given the experiment a fair trial. To be really satisfactory, it ought to be carried to a more decisive issue, one way or the other. He must either break the bank, or come within a measurable distance of breaking himself. To leave off at this stage would look like timidity. He would play for a day or two more, and play in earnest ; and then, if the invitation still held good, he would be presented to the princess. Perhaps, after all, she would turn out to be the true providential cause of his coming to Monte Carlo. But at this idea, Fedovsky smiled, and shook his head slightly. He was a little skeptical as to the power of woman to heal all ills.

At his rooms he found Tom, his English valet, waiting as usual to assist him in his preparations for the night. The relations between the master and man were, as has been intimated, easy and almost familiar.

Fedovsky flung his empty pocket-book down on the table. "There are my winnings for the evening," he remarked. *A la guerre comme à la guerre!*"

Tom took up the purse and opened it. "Not the price of a 'alf pint left!" he said.

"I even had to borrow a cigarette from a man whom I had hardly seen twice."

"The American gent you spoke of, sir?"

"Mr. Williams—yes. And he was kind enough to advise me to let gambling alone."

"That's because he didn't know you, sir."

"Why, what would you have done in his place?"

"Well, sir, I'd may be have told you I'd invented a system to beat the bank every time, and have offered to go shares with you in it."

"Hem! I hope you haven't invented any such system, Thomas?"

"I saw a little of the game while I was in New

York, sir.   There was a place kept by a cove down on Fourth Street, where I learned a thing or two about the cards.   He was a fraud, that fellow was ; I'd like to see him again ! "

" My American friend here apparently has no system, except to avoid the Casino. He has offered, as an inducement to me to desist, to introduce me to a charming Russian princess with whom he has become acquainted."

At this information, Thomas pursed up his lips and knit his brows.

" I understand you," said his master, smiling. " You think she is some adventuress.   It is quite likely. Still, Mr. Williams does not look like a fool ; he certainly must have seen something of the world.   I doubt if he could be taken in by any ordinary sharper, male or female."

" As regards women, there's never no telling what may happen," said Tom sententiously. " She might be doing business with him, for the matter of that."

" How do you mean ? "

" They might be running a private gambling concern of their own, sir.   She stays at home and does the fine lady, and he goes about and ropes in the dupes.   That ain't an uncommon dodge, and it's as likely to be played here as anywhere.   It wouldn't take 'em long to find out that you had money ; and as a matter of course, they'd rather have the picking of you themselves than let the Casino get it all."

The count was amused by this suggestion. " You

are a cynic, Tom," he said, " and cynics always exaggerate, and are generally mistaken. However, this idea of yours about the princess and Mr. Wil-liams arouses my curiosity, and almost decides me to go there and inspect the *ménage*. I don't believe a word of your theory, but, if it were true, it would be something new, and worth all the money they could make it cost me. Meanwhile, I am going to bed. Wake me at eight."

" I was going to ask you, sir," said Tom, with some hesitation, " whether you would want me to-morrow afternoon and evening ? I thought I'd like to take a bit of an outing, sir."

" By all means," replied the count, good-natur-edly, " only be back by eleven."

" That I will, sir, and thank you ! Good-night, sir ; " and so they parted.

The next day the count returned to the *Trente et Quarante* table, and, by making his bets the maximum sum of twelve thousand francs each time, he succeeded, in the course of three hours, in losing one hundred thousand francs. This was equal to about half his yearly income. Somewhat aroused by this bad luck, and determined to retrieve it, he went back to his hotel, and, having drawn a check for three hundred thousand francs, cashed it in the office, and made his way once more to the Casino. He played recklessly, and by nine o'clock only nine thousand francs were left. He paused at that point, and left the table, feeling that matters were getting beyond a joke. In three days he had lost nearly half a million. This was nearly all that he had brought with him for the season. Of course there were untouched resources in Russia, which he could obtain by notifying his agents there ; but he was inclined to call a halt for the present. He could admit that the experience was developing an exciting element, but the excitement was prevailing too much on one side.

As he left the room, and passed through the one devoted to *Rouge et Noir*, he noticed a crowd round one of the tables there, acting as if something of special interest were going on. He forbore to investigate the matter, however, and went into the open air. The sea was calm ; the moon was shining across it ; the garden was full of fragrance. As he neared the drive, a lady passed him in a low phaeton, accompanied by an elderly woman, apparently a companion. The moonlight fell on her face, revealing her features with soft distinctness. It was a beautiful face, though the expression was weary and sad. But neither its sadness nor its beauty was the cause of the effect which the sight of it produced upon Fedovsky. The blood burned in his cheeks, then rushed back upon his heart, and left him in a tremble. For a few moments he remained in a bewildered condition, incapable of reflection or judgment. Then he told himself that he must have been mistaken. And, yet, how could he be mistaken? In all his life, he had met with no face resembling hers ; and considering that seven years had elapsed since he met her last, and that the surroundings were now so different from then, and that the encounter had been so unexpected, the wonder was that he had recognized her at all. She had not seen him ; but he was as certain as he was of his own existence that the woman who had passed him in the moonlight was the woman whom he had loved in his youth, and had lost, and had left his home to seek throughout the world. She was Vera, and no other.

CHAPTER V.

BY the time Fedovsky had made up his mind that he was not mistaken, it was quite too late to think of overtaking the carriage ; he had lost her again in the moment of finding her. He reflected, however, that she must be stopping at Monte Carlo, and that he would have ample opportunities of meeting her again. There was at all events, nothing more to be done to-night.

He had intended to go straight to his hotel ; but this incident had so completely turned the current of his thoughts that he postponed his purpose, and sat down on a bench to think the matter over. Would Vera care to meet him ? Was she still living with the roguish overseer to whom she had been compelled to unite herself ? Had she left him ? or was he dead ? From the glimpse he had obtained of her, Fedovsky was inclined to think that she must have become accustomed to a much more luxurious mode of living than formerly. Her phaeton was sumptuously appointed, the horses which drew it were of fine breed and carefully kept ; the coachman and footman were dressed in handsome livery. In a word, she had the appearance of being a wealthy woman, whereas the overseer, after all allowance had been made for his speculations, must still have been a comparatively poor man. How, then, was Vera's appearance to be explained ?

The longer Fedovsky contemplated this question the less inclined did he feel to press for an answer to it. A great many things may happen to a beautiful woman in the course of seven years. And the fact that her worldly circumstances had improved was not necessarily an indication that she was improved in all other respects. There might be passages in Vera's later life which it would be painful to know. The count was no longer an inexperienced and emotional boy, but a man of the world ; and he did not conceal from himself the fact that he had, after all, known Vera only superficially. He had loved her for her beauty, for her voice, for her sweet behavior, and because she loved him ; and perhaps most of all, because of the opposition which had been made to their union. But of her inward mental and moral constitution, he had known little ; indeed, at her age, these qualities could not have been developed to any recognizable degree. Her career since they had been separated had not—in its beginning at all events—been such as to call out what was best in her. So, upon the whole, it might be the part of prudence not to risk an unwelcome discovery.

There was, also, her own side of the matter

to be considered. She might have many reasons for not wishing to meet Fedovsky. In any case it would not be becoming to intrude himself upon her without warning. She must be allowed the option of receiving him or not. And if she consented, then it would be time enough to decide whether he should avail himself of her consent.

This attitude of mind towards the only woman he had ever cared for, and whose memory had kept him away from all other women, could have surprised no one more than it did Fedovsky himself. The real secret was, not the possible change in Vera, but the actual change in himself. He was no longer the same man : he could no longer feel as he had once done. If he loved her now it would be not because she was the same woman, but because she also was different, and because her difference was adapted to his.

It was in a depressed and unsettled frame of mind that Fedovsky arose from his bench and went homeward. He was half resolved to leave Monte Carlo the next morning and get as far away from it as possible—to America, perhaps. And yet what a lame conclusion of his wanderings would it be to turn back from the goal of them just as it was within his reach ! Then he thought of his losses at the gaming-table, and the recollection annoyed him afresh. He had been a fool, and he marveled at his folly. Plainly, the first thing to be done was to arrange to get a fresh supply of money. He must write to his agents and instruct them to send him new credits. He would remain where he was until these arrived and then go. If, in the meanwhile, chance brought about a meeting between him and Vera well and good. If not he would accept it as an indication that the meeting was undesirable, and would give up all thought of her. Upon this conclusion he entered his hotel.

Tom was not there to receive him ; but it was not yet eleven o'clock, and he recollected that he had given him leave of absence until that hour. He sat down at his writing-table, and wrote his letters to his agents. As he was sealing them up, Tom came in. The faithful valet wore a contented expression on his square, cheerful visage, in marked contrast with the troubled and distraught aspect of his master.

" Beg pardon, sir," he said on seeing the latter, " hope I'm not late ? "

" You are before your time," was the reply. " I want these letters to go by the early post to-morrow. Don't forget it, for they are important."

Tom took the letters, and after glancing at their addresses, gazed upon the count with a significant expression.

" Yes, we shall need some more money," the latter said : " and when it comes, I mean to leave here—perhaps we shall go to America. I've had enough of it."

" Well, sir, I'm glad to hear you say so."

" And how have you enjoyed yourself this afternoon, Tom ? "

"Very well, sir, thanks to you. By the way, I ran across something a bit queer, too."

"What was that ?"

"You may recollect that chap I was speaking to you about—the one that did me out of some cash at cards, in New York ?"

The count nodded.

"Well, sir, I wouldn't want to take my ' davy ' to it, for it's some time since then ; but I'm pretty moderate sure that I saw that fellow again this evening. He was got up in good style, and he'd cut off his beard ; but he's got the same eyes and nose, and the same way of getting about on his legs. I might be mistaken, but I think it's my man."

"I fancy you are mistaken. What should he be doing here ?"

"The same old game, sir. That's a game you can play anywhere. He'd get in with one or two others of the same sort, and do the respectable business. There's always plenty of fish in a place like this for them as knows how to catch 'em."

"Well, you had better keep clear of him in any case. You could prove nothing against him, even if you were certain of his identity ; and we don't want any disturbances here. Meanwhile, you may as well post those letters to-night. I have money to last us till they are answered : but I don't care to stay here any longer than is necessary."

"Trust me, sir," replied the valet cheerfully. " I've got all I want out of this place, and the sooner we're away from it, the better I'm suited."

The following day dragged along rather stupidly. Fedovsky did not leave the hotel until as late an hour as possible : he could not keep the thought of Vera out of his mind. Having forbidden himself the Casino, he had no object to look forward to ; he had already explored all the natural attractions of the region ; there were no books or society to divert his mind : and altogether, the prospects for the week or more during which he must wait for his remittances were decidedly dismal. He had never been so bored in his life.

He spent the forenoon wandering about the gardens. It was a fine day, and the offing was alive with little pleasure boats voyaging to and fro. This gave him an idea, and after lunch he hired one of the small vessels, and went out sailing. He was not much of a mariner, but it was better than nothing, and he kept at it till dinner-time. He lingered over that meal, and consumed an extra bottle of claret. Then he lit a cigarette, and went out once more. His steps turned of themselves toward the Casino, and he would probably have ended by going there in sheer self-defense, had not something occurred to prevent it.

This occurrence began with the appearance of Mr. Williams. Fedovsky was so glad to see him that his pleasure was plainly expressed in his greeting. The American was like the shadow of a rock in a desert to the forlorn young nobleman.

" Well," the former said, with his slow smile and keen look, " I've been hearing about you ! "

"Ah!" returned Fedovsky, with an illogical misgiving as to Vera in his mind.

"Yes; they say, to put it mildly, that you didn't break the bank last night."

"Oh, that's it," said the other, feeling relieved. "Yes, it's true I had a little bad luck, and I mean to follow your advice for the future. I have forsworn the green cloth."

"My advice, if you remember, didn't stop at counseling you to keep out of the Casino. I proposed that you should go somewhere else." And, as Fedovsky looked a little puzzled, he added, "To the princess's, you know. She's in town still, and I venture to say she will be glad to see you."

The princess had quite slipped out of Fedovsky's mind. He recollected her now, and he was just in the mood to accept Williams's suggestion. It would help him to get through at least one evening, and it might conceivably lead to further entertainment. Nothing, at all events, could well be more wearisome than the sort of life he was leading at present.

"I shall be very glad to be presented," he said, "and I am at your service whenever you please."

"Come along, then," said the other; "there is no time like the present, and I was just on my way to call on her."

The count took his arm, and they walked along together till they reached a pretty villa not far from the hotel. The door was opened by a footman, to whom Williams gave his card and that of Fedovsky.

In a few minutes the man returned and said that the princess would receive them.

The room where they sat down was beautifully furnished, and showed the influence of a taste which not only possessed the means of gratifying itself, but which had been trained in the best æsthetic school. The colors were quiet, but well chosen : the ornaments few, but unique and aptly arranged. The chairs and lounges were luxurious, without being conspicuous ; the drapery of the windows was graceful and soft. It was just dusk ; in a moment a servant entered and lit the lamps. These shed a subdued light through the apartment, which was reflected from an antique beveled mirror over the mantelpiece, and sparkled on the gold handle of a paper-knife on the table, and upon the rim of an agate vase on a bracket on the wall. A delicate perfume was also manifest in the atmosphere of the room, unobtrusive, but sufficient to render breathing a conscious pleasure. There was a piano in one corner, standing open, with the stool in front of it, as if some one had just been touching the keys. The harmony still seemed to linger in the room, and to impress itself upon the inanimate objects contained there.

All this, and more, Fedovsky had leisure to notice before the princess made her appearance. It was different from what he had anticipated, and the effect upon him was the more pleasing. The woman who lived amid such surroundings could not but be refined and cultivated ; and she must, also, possess an individuality that distinguished her from the general mob of people of birth and breeding.   Fedovsky even imagined that he could divine something of the character of his hostess from the aspect and order of her household possessions ; and, if his impression were correct, she must surely be a woman whom it would be a privilege to know. And she was a Russian, too.

The silken curtain that hung before the door was drawn aside, and the hostess entered.   The shades over the lamps threw the light downward, so that, as she stood on the threshold, her face was shadowed ; and all that could be clearly discerned was a rather tall, slender figure in an evening dress of black satin, with bare white arms and throat, and the glitter of an ornament on her wrist and on her bosom.   After a moment's pause, she advanced toward the count, who had risen to his feet on her first entrance.   There was something in the supple undulation of her gait that brought back a long-vanished impression to his mind.   He divined what had happened before he knew it.

"Good-evening, princess," said Mr. Williams, getting up and stepping towards them. "This is the gentleman you told me I might bring here. Count Fedovsky, this is Princess Volgorouki. As you are compatriots already, I presume it won't take you long to get acquainted."

Hereupon, Mr. Williams seemed to vanish into air, although, as a matter of fact, he simply retired a few steps and resumed his chair. But Fedovsky was conscious only of the woman who had come nearer to him and laid her hand in his. It was a soft, slender hand, but with a nervous life in it that made each of the supple fingers eloquent. He looked in her face and saw large dark hazel eyes meeting his own ; a vivid face, oval, with a broad brow crowned with auburn hair. In that mellow light it looked as fresh and blooming as it had done in the old days when it had been his ideal of all that was lovely and lovable in woman-hood ; and yet there was something in the expression that told of years and of experience—of things in which her former love had had no part, and which had changed her from what he had known into something which he did not know. But, however changed, the strength of the bond which had once bound her to him still made itself felt ; he could not look upon her with indifference. Destiny had brought them together once more : surely, then, they belonged to each other. The world might know her as the wealthy Princess Volgo-rouki ; but, to Fedovsky, she was and must remain the Vera of his youth.

CHAPTER VI.

A MYSTERY.

THESE thoughts passed through the count's mind in an instant. The next instant the princess gave him his cue. "I am most happy," she said, in the melodious voice he knew so well, "to make the acquaintance of the Count Fedovsky "

It was evident, then, that she did not wish their American friend to be made privy to the past relations between them. Before him, at all events, they were to act as if they were really the strangers to each other that he must suppose them to be. That she desired this secrecy was interpreted by Fedovsky as a good sign. It pointed to a prospect that their former relations were to be hereafter recalled, if not renewed. And, as a moment's reflection showed him, Vera must have been prepared for this interview : it was no sudden surprise to her, as it had been to him. Mr. Williams had of course mentioned his name to her some time before ; and she had had his card for five minutes before presenting herself. She had considered what course to pursue, and it was for him to follow her lead.

He uttered a few conventional words, therefore, and the first shock of the meeting was over.

In the conversation which ensued, and which was carried on in French, Mr. Williams took part : and it was of a sufficiently commonplace character. But, if the things that were said were devoid of special interest, the inner significance of it all was deeply interesting to Fedovsky. He heard meanings in the tones of Vera's voice that seemed to him as plain as speech would have been. She spoke with her looks, with her movements, with her pauses, with her swift smiles and glances. He responded in like manner : it was like a beautiful symbolic play. They renewed their past : they indicated the vicissitudes that had taken place, they foreshadowed what might be to come, and all without speaking a single explanatory word. It was not a narration of events that they were conveying to each other, but of mutual and emotional growth and change. Fedovsky was rejoiced, though scarcely surprised, to find that their relative attitude remained nearly the same. The boy that he once was could not have known how to love the woman that she was now ; but that woman was singularly adapted to harmonize with the finished man of the world that he had become. What mattered the minor details ? They had taken a long plunge beneath the waters of life and had now found each other again, at a great distance, indeed, from their former place, but not less united than before in sympathy and feeling.

From what few remarks about herself the princess actually let fall, Fedovsky gathered that she had married Prince Volgorouki about five years before. If this were the case, it followed that her first husband, the rascally overseer, must have died soon after his disappearance from Russia. What were the events that brought about the second union. Fedovsky could only conjecture. He surmised that some painful passages must have taken place. Be that as it might, they were over now, and she was free again,—free and wealthy. There would be ample opportunity to determine what he and she were to be to each other in the future.

After this situation had lasted about an hour, Mr. Williams inquired whether Signor and Madame Strogello were expected that evening. The princess replied that she had sent them no special invitation, but remarked that they might come if the suggestion were made to them. The personages in question were the Italian diplomatist and his wife, of whom Williams had previously spoken to Fedovsky. Williams now offered to go and bring them, to which Vera, after a glance at the count, offered no objection. In truth, they were both eager to embrace the opportunity of private communion which the American's temporary absence would afford them.

Williams took his hat and went off, promising to return shortly. When he was gone, Vera left her chair, and seated herself beside Fedovsky on the lounge. She was perceptibly moved, and, for a few

moments, she looked at him intently, without saying any thing, her bosom rising and falling with an
uneven motion.

"I thank you," she said at length, "for not having
permitted Mr. Williams to suspect that we have
known each other before. Never let him—or any
one else—suspect it. You will know the reasons
later." She broke off, and folded her hands ner-
vously in her lap. "Oh, is it really you!" she
exclaimed, her voice falling almost to a whisper.

"And are you glad to see me?" demanded the
count.

"Glad!—if you could only know!— And yet,
perhaps I ought not to be glad. So much has happened! If we had only met sooner! It seems so
strange now,—so   " She broke off again
and looked away. "Tell me, have you married?"
she asked suddenly, fixing her eyes upon him.

Fedovsky shook his head. "I have met but
one woman whom I should have wished to marry,"
he replied. "I am not a man of many fancies."

"Ah, do not blame me—I have not been
happy!" said she, with a deprecating gesture of
her hand. As she made the movement, Fedovsky
noticed upon her finger a peculiar ring,—a signet
of antique workmanship, set in massive gold. It
was the same ring that he had given her as a
pledge of their betrothal more than seven years
before. She had kept it, through all changes, ever
since. It was a trifle, perhaps, but its effect upon
him was deep. It made him feel as if, after all and

through all, he had never quite lost his hold upon her heart.

"A woman like me can do little to control her own fate," she continued. "You know how I was forced into that first marriage. Yet I did not yield even then, until I had been made to believe that you, too, had been persuaded to give yourself to another. That thought left me indifferent to every thing. I hoped to die; but death does not come merely because we believe ourselves ready to take leave of life. That man drew me down from unhappiness to degradation. After the revelation of his rascality I became reckless; I ceased to regret or to think, and tried to exist only for the passing moment. In those days I forgot—or fancied that I had forgotten—that I had ever known you."

Her voice faltered,—how vividly Fedovsky recollected that tremulous sinking note,—and tears glistened in her eyes. But in a moment, with a swiftness that was characteristic of all her movements, mental and physical, she recovered herself and went on.

"If that had continued much longer, I don't know what I might have become. But it came to an end—so suddenly that I could not myself realize that it was really ended—I thought that I should awake and find all the old trouble still there. One does not soon get over having been the wife of a—thief!

"He was shot in attempting to make an escape . . no! I can not even now speak of that dreadful affair ; and nothing in it was more dreadful than my joy that it had happened. For there was no doubt that the man had loved me, with such love as was in him. If he had hated me, I think I should have felt less miserable. But, at all events, I was free, and at first I could see nothing that was not delightful in my freedom. I had a few thousand roubles and some jewelry,—enough to live on for a while. But of course I should have starved to death at last, or come to some. worse end, had I not met with a far better fortune than I ever hoped for or deserved."

"It must have been then that I dreamed you were in peril," muttered Fedovsky, who sat with his head leaning on his hand, painfully absorbed in this recital.

"I had advertised to give singing lessons," she continued. "For a long time there had been no response ; but, on the very morning that I had resolved to cease incurring what seemed a fruitless expense, I received a letter from the secretary of the Prince Volgorouki. I went to his hotel, and was admitted to an interview with him. He was a venerable old man, with a noble face. He asked me about myself : I told him what I could ; I could not bring myself to tell him all. He seemed satisfied, and told me that he wished me to train a little girl—his grand-daughter. She was the only descendant left to him,—his wife and his only daughter were dead. The arrangements were made, and I entered his household in that capac-

ity.   The little girl was in delicate health ; we
traveled from place to place ; in summer we went
for a month or two to Moscow ; but the winter was
spent in Italy and along the Mediterranean coast.
One spring we staid in the south too long, and the
child caught the fever.   I took care of her ; I loved
the little thing.   But in the autumn she died.   The
Prince was broken down by her death.   When I
spoke of taking leave of him, he would not hear of
my going.   I was truly sorry for him, but I told
him that I could not stay.   At last he asked me if
I would marry him.   He said he had not long to
live—that he did not expect me to love him ; that
he himself was too old and broken to think of the
love of passion ; but that he had grown to depend
upon my presence, and that I was associated in his
mind with his grand-child ; and that to give me
his name would be but a slight return for the comfort of having me with him.   Such an offer was
too honorable and too delicate to be turned aside ;
but I felt that he had a right to know, first, what
my past life had been ; and I told him all that I
had not told before.   He heard me through, looking at me all the time with his great eyes ; and
then he said that I must still be his wife.   He lived
for three years after that, and I was a faithful wife
to him, and he treated me always with tenderness
and respect.   He died eighteen months ago, and
his will enabled me to live in independence for the
rest of my life, as you see.   But there are few people whom I know, and it is only within a few

months that I have come back to the world at all."

This story was told with occasional lapses and interruptions ; sometimes she seemed lost in recollections ; sometimes she spoke with her intent gaze fixed upon her listener's face ; sometimes she passed one white hand over the other, or interlaced her fingers and drew them slowly apart. But at the end she rose suddenly and walked up the room and back, pressing her handkerchief to her eyes, her rich dress rustling as she stepped. These reminiscences of the past, combined with the present situation, had evidently wrought her up to a high pitch.

" Well, we have met at last," said Fedovsky, at length; "but, of all places in the world, I should least have expected to find you here."

" I have ceased being surprised at myself—at what happens to me, or at what I do," was her reply. " My career has taught me one thing—that I can not control either events or actions. It is not what I expect, or what I wish, that occurs, but something different. If you had sent me word that you intended coming here, I should have told you not to come."

" Why so ? Do you fear any harm from me ? "

" That is not the reason. But harm may come."

" I don't understand," said Fedovsky.

" The best I can hope is, that you never will."

" Are you in any trouble ? Can I help you ? "

" Can any human being ever help another ? I doubt it. Here are we two, alone together in this room.   It seems as if we might do any thing that we chose.   What is to prevent my speaking a few words to you—a dozen words would be enough—and then putting my hand in yours, and leaving the house and the country forever?"

"Do it!" exclaimed Fedovsky, with energy. "Whatever the trouble may be, come! Trust to me!"

He rose to his feet as he spoke, and held out his hands.

She bent her head a little, and looked at him from beneath her brows, which were unusually broad and high.   The color in her cheeks, which had till now been faint, deepened and spread.   She was visibly moved, and seemed to be wavering on the brink of a decision.   She was an imaginative as well as a passionate woman, and such women are capable of daring and unprecedented acts ; but she also possessed a cold and critical intellect, and this was usually able to counterbalance the other elements of her nature.   The only way to control her was to give her no time to reflect.   Fedovsky made the mistake of omitting to press his advantage. He was in earnest, but he was not arbitrary and despotic enough.   The moment of indecision passed without his repeating and following up his appeal. He should have caught her in his arms, and hurried her beyond her discretion, until it was too late for her to retreat.   But the habit of indifference, which he had acquired during the later years, operated even now when he was not indifferent ; and so he lost

her.   Indeed, he was so entirely in the dark as to
what motives and considerations were operating in
her mind, that it is small wonder he failed to act
decisively.

"How can you be sure that I may trust you?"
she said, turning away.   "Circumstances would
affect you, as they do all other human beings.   I
can trust no one.   I shall stay here.   You are free
to go or stay, as you please."

"I shall stay," he replied.   "If you will not tell
me what constrains you, I shall do my best to find
out for myself.   And when I know all I shall repeat
what I have said.   I care more for you than for any
circumstances."

"Here come my guests," she said, as the bell
sounded.   "You and I are strangers again.   These
people bore me, but they are the only ones I happen to know here.   A little gossip, a little tea, a
little card-playing—those are my diversions."

She laughed, with a sort of melancholy mockery;
and the door opened to admit Signor and Madame
Strogello, followed by Mr. Williams.

CHAPTER VII.

SIGNOR STROGELLO was a large-bodied, smooth-faced, elderly personage, with a round head covered with short gray hair, a pair of very shiny spectacles on his small aquiline nose, and a thin-lipped mouth, which was constantly working itself into the semblance of a courteous and complaisant smile. He was full of polite little bows and gestures, and seemed to be inspired with an unfailing fund of gayety and sociability. He wore a dress-coat faced with satin, with the blue and red ribbon of some order in the button-hole, and a white waist-coat with three buttons formed each of a single carbuncle ; a fourth sparkled in the center of his shirt front. His hands were thick and rather short, but the stubby fingers were decorated with a number of rings. Madame Strogello was a tall and angular woman of about forty years of age, gaunt and harsh of feature, and of taciturn and reticent behavior. Her eyes were small, black and observant : her dress was sumptuous rather than tasteful. This couple entered arm-in-arm, and after making their obeisance to the hostess, and being presented to the count, they proceeded to enter upon the social duties of the evening. Mr. Williams and Madame Strogello gradually drew apart with the princess, while the Italian diplomat devoted himself to the count.

Fedovsky soon discovered that his interlocutor was a well-informed and entertaining individual. He had visited most of the capitals of Europe, and mentioned familiarly the names of the great personages there. "Yes, I have lived a busy and interesting life," he said : "I have mingled much in affairs, and with the men who conduct the destiny of empires. But, as old age comes on, I discover that the true pleasures of life are to be found within the social and domestic circle. The relations are not less varied and amusing, and they are far more sincere and genuine. The results of our activity may be less widespread and sensational ; but are they less effective—are they less vital ? Every thing is relative ; and doubtless the simple peasant, who looks back upon his little round of duties and obligations, faithfully and cheerfully performed, experiences a contentment that might well be envied by the Napoleons and Bismarcks of history, who have wrestled with the great world, and who, sooner or later, sustain defeat, disappointment, or humiliation. It has been said that war and diplomacy are like a game of chess : I concede it, but I add that a game of chess or of cards is like diplomacy and war, with all the harsher and coarser features eliminated, and only the abstract elements remaining."

"There is no reason, however," remarked Fedovsky, who was amused at this grandiloquence, "why the abstract and the actual should not both be enjoyed. Napoleon and Bismarck need not postpone chess and cards until they have ceased to direct the affairs of Europe."

"No doubt," returned Signor Strogello, "the greater may include the less ; but I only intended to convey that the retired statesman may renew, in the harmless social diversion of the card-table, the pleasures and vicissitudes of his public career."

"The most ardent statesman might find excitement at Monte Carlo, I should suppose," Fedovsky observed. " M. Blanc seems to make a very effective deputy Providence."

"For myself," said the Italian, "I confess I care nothing for gambling—for the public gambling of the Casino, that is to say. In the social circle, it is another matter: no one objects to winning or losing a few hundred francs with friends. But perhaps you are of an opposite opinion."

"To tell the truth, I don't know that I have come to any final conclusions about the matter," said Fedovsky, smiling. "I came here to find out what gambling was like. I found it was a good deal like burning bank-notes in a candle, or throwing gold into the sea. My curiosity is satisfied, and that is the end of it, so far as I am concerned."

"Exactly ! But as regards the social and friendly game, that, I presume, is not included in your very reasonable antipathy to the excesses of the public gaming-table ?"

"Well, I suppose not ; but I repeat that I know little or nothing about cards, and I doubt if I have ever played a dozen games in my life."

"Then, my dear count, I assure you that you have missed a great resource and pleasure. It will give me genuine gratification to be the means of introducing you to it."

"I shall be very happy," replied Fedovsky, politely. But politeness was not the true—or, at any rate, the only—cause of his assent. His nerves and emotions were in a state of unusual excitement, and he felt a pressing need for some distraction. Cards would serve, in default of any thing better, and he was in a mood to use them for all they were worth. His thoughts were dwelling with such intensity upon his recent interview with Vera, that he would have submitted even to a surgical operation as a means of abating their concentration.

The proposition to have a little game was made, and met with a favorable acceptance from the company. A table was drawn out, the cloth removed, and a servant dispatched for a pack of cards, there being, apparently, none in the house. Vera, somewhat to Fedovsky's relief, excused herself from playing, and the other four took their places, Fedovsky having Madame Strogello as a partner ; the signor himself, though taking part with Mr. Williams against him, acting as his benevolent instructor. After some discussion, the game finally decided on was poker, as being at once easily learned and interesting, and one in which each player played for his own hand. No chips were to be had, so Mr. Williams rapidly cut up little squares of paper of different colors to meet the need of the moment. While all this was going on, Vera employed herself in making tea, which she did after the Russian recipe, and capital tea it was. Signor Strogello produced a packet of cigarettes, which were smoked by all present, except Mr. Williams, who asked permission to light a cigar. Tea and tobacco are admirable social stimuli, and the party were soon chatting together with freedom and animation. Half a dozen hands were played, during which Fedovsky's instruction proceeded ; then he declared himself prepared to attempt the contest on his own unaided responsibility.

"You'd better not be too rash," Williams remarked as he dealt out the cards. " Poker is easy enough in one way ; but there's a good deal to be learned, after you know all the rules. Isn't that so, signor ?"

" I can affirm it with confidence," the latter replied. " Yes, I would counsel M. le Comte not to venture any thing this evening. We should be taking an advantage."

" That is easily arranged," remarked Madame Strogello. " We can play for one franc points, or even for the chips only."

" Yes, yes ! That will be best ! " exclaimed her husband and Mr. Williams.

" I beg to object," returned the count decidedly. " All we want is a little amusement, and there is no amusement in playing for bits of paper. It is said that fortune assists the tyro. Come, I will wager that I get the better of you ! Let us say ten francs for the white chips and twenty for the red. *Allons!* I challenge you all ! "

He looked up laughingly, and, as he did so, caught the eye of Vera, who was standing behind Madame Strogello, and was fixing a strangely intent gaze upon him. Her straight eyebrows were contracted slightly, and her lips were pressed together. The look startled Fedovsky a little, though he could not comprehend the significance of it. He supposed that she, like himself, was secretly preoccupied with their late conversation. But it was to escape thought that he was now engaged ; and, with an effort, he looked away and turned his mind upon the game. The others had, with more or less reluctance and deprecation, accepted his proposal. They began to play.

The tyro's luck, which Fedovsky had invoked, certainly seemed to attend him. He threw himself into the game, and his success was remarkable. In the course of an hour, the majority of the chips were piled in front of him. Williams twisted his mustachios and shrugged his shoulders humorously : Signor Strogello politely felicitated himself on the proficiency of his pupil. Madame declared, rather plaintively, that she was convinced M. le Comte was making a fool of them, and that he was in fact a poker-player of long standing, and ripe experience. As for Vera, she retired to the piano in the corner of the room, and began to play, and sing in an undertone. The delicious harmonies of her voice welled and trembled through the apartment, and disturbed Fedovsky not a little ; for it reminded him of passionate and happy days now gone by forever. He became excited, and demanded higher play

" I will play more carefully," he said, " and then I shall be sure to lose ! And in order to set things straight the quicker, let me raise the chips to one and two hundred francs each. Madame Strogello shall acknowledge that I am an even greater ignoramus than I profess myself to be ! "

" Whether you are a poker-player or not, at any rate you re a born gambler," Williams observed, as he shuffled the cards. " You have missed your vocation, count. But you must excuse me from taking a hand in any such game as you propose. I'm not a millionaire, and two hundred francs a point is beyond a joke. Call it twenty-five and fifty, and I'll try you."

" Whatever you please," Fedovsky replied. "You know better what is customary than I do."

Williams dealt the cards, and each player took up his hand. Meanwhile the princess had left the piano, and come forward to the table. She stood near Fedovsky, in such a position that he was aware of her proximity, but could not see her. Suddenly she stooped, and picked up one of the paper chips from the floor.

"This is yours, I think," she said. "You just dropped it."

"Thank you!" said Fedovsky. She placed the chip on the table beside him. He glanced at it, and saw that something was written on it in pencil. He looked again: it was a single word, in the Russian character,—"Beware!"

The princess returned to the piano, and began playing again.

Whatever may have been the purpose of this singular act of hers, its only effect was to throw Fedovsky still further off his balance. It did not occur to him that the warning could have any other reference than to something personal between him and her. Had he unwittingly offended her in any way? Was he perpetrating some ignorant blunder? As for the game, it was so entirely a subordinate matter with him—a mere expedient for suppressing anxiety and suspense—that he did not take it into consideration at all. In a quieter or colder mood, or anywhere else than in Vera's own house, he might have been on his guard against his company: but, under the circumstances, he simply thought nothing about them.

He slipped the chip into his pocket, and the game went on, and, for awhile, still continued to favor him, and also, though to a less extent, Madame Strogello; until most of the chips were

divided between him and her. It was now again
Williams's deal. When Fedovsky took up his cards,
he saw at once that he had an excellent hand, and
he began to bet upon it.

Madame Strogello also seemed to be satisfied
with her hand, and she raised him. He answered
by a bet of fifty. She replied, and so it went on
for half a dozen times. At length Fedovsky became
impatient, and raised his bet to five hundred francs.
There was a chorus of surprise and remonstrance.
" Better keep it down," said Williams :   " Madame
knows what she is about, as a general thing. There
are two thousand up now."

" Madame shall decide," returned Fedovsky,
with a bow.

" I suppose I must take it, then," she remarked,
after another look at her cards. The betting continued, the others looking on with silent interest.
Proceeding by such long leaps, the amount at
stake increased rapidly. In less than five minutes
there were over twenty thousand francs on the
table. Fedovsky had reached the limit of the cash
in his possession. He called. The antagonists dis-
played their cards. Fedovsky had the king, queen,
knave, ten, and nine of hearts. Madame Strogello
had the ace, king, queen, knave, and ten of diamonds.

CHAPTER VIII

As the game ended, the princess struck a loud chord on the piano, and rose. Fedovsky rose, also, with a laugh, and said : " I offer my felicitations to Madame Strogello, and I thank you all for an agreeable evening."

" But, my dear, I protest you should not have done it," exclaimed the signor to his wife. " M. le Comte will think we wish to pillage him ! A royal flush is a thing that comes so seldom ! You should not have permitted him to involve himself."

" Not at all ! Madame simply yielded to my persistence," Fedovsky said. " I should have been very sorry had the game turned out otherwise. As it is, I may bid you adieu with a light conscience ; and I may hope—with the princess's permission— to see you again."

He bowed towards Vera as he spoke. She made no reply, and, though her face was turned upon him, it was expressionless and cold. Something had apparently offended her. Fedovsky could not imagine what it was. Was it that he had urged her to go away with him ? That seemed impossible.	The more inasmuch as she herself had actually suggested the idea to him.	Was she displeased because he had played, in her house, for such high stakes?	That might be the case ; and yet, it would surely have been easy for her to have intimated as much beforehand.	Or had his failure to divine the meaning of her " Beware !" offended her?	All these questions passed through his mind in a moment of time, and left him as wise as he was before.

" Ah, you shall be given your revenge undoubtedly," Signor Strogello said ; " for my part, I shall not be easy until you have had it.	The princess is so kind and hospitable that I could almost affirm beforehand that she will let us assemble here again —is it not so, charming lady ? "

" I shall depend upon seeing all of you again— the sooner the better," returned the princess, with what appeared to Fedovsky an almost sarcastic formality.	He had intended to find a pretext for remaining after the others had gone, or for coming at some hour when he might find her alone : but her manner discouraged him.	It occurred to him, however, that he could write her a letter, in which he could enlarge upon topics of mutual interest, and ask an explanation of her demeanor ; and this project partly consoled him for his discomfiture. He was the first to take his leave ; and so perturbed had he been, that it was only after he found himself in the cool open air, that he remembered he had again lost his last franc, and that he would not be able to get any more until his remittances arrived. This was awkward, and, incidentally, it would stand in the way of his encountering his new friends the next evening at the princess's. Moreover, his bill at the hotel must amount to a thousand francs or more, and there was no telling how soon it might be presented. The idea of being dunned for a bill that he could not pay was new to Fedovsky, and amused and annoyed him at the same time. Fortunately, there were several millions yet to be drawn on, and his poverty was only for the moment. He was determined to be caught in no such tight place again. He would go to America at the first opportunity ; and, before going, he would make a fresh and resolute effort to persuade Vera to go with him. And he felt confident that he would succeed.

He was not destined to remain much longer in this conviction. On going up to his rooms, he found Tom awaiting him.

" Glad to see you back, sir," said the faithful valet. " The letters has come, sir."

" The letters ? What letters ? "

" The letters with the money in them, sir."

" Already ? Why, that's impossible ! They can hardly have received my letters, yet. It must be something else."

" They're from the agents, anyhow, sir," returned the other. " You can see that for yourself by the handwriting on the envelope."

Fedovsky looked at them. Certainly, they were

from his agents.   But they were posted on the same
day that he wrote to them.   It was an unusual
thing for them to address him except at stated sea-
sons, or in reply to communications from him.
There must be some special news.   What could it be ?

He sat down, opened one of the letters, and began to read it.   Tom, who was quietly observing
him, saw his face change almost at once.   He set
his lips, his brows lowered, and the blood gradually forsook his cheeks.   As he read on, slight
twitchings and contractions passed across his features.   He finished the first letter, laid it down
without any remark, and then took up the other,
which he opened with impassive deliberation.   He
read it through more rapidly than the other, and
then placed it also on the table.   After sitting in
silent thought for a few minutes, he took a cigarette and lit it, and turned to his valet.

"Tom," he said, "when did I pay you your
wages last ?"

"First of the month, sir.   Two weeks back."

"Have you any of them left ?"

* That I have, sir !   The whole of 'em."

"I'm glad to hear it.   I may not be able to pay
you any more for some time to come.   And, meanwhile, my good fellow, you will have to look out for
another place."

"Me, sir ?   Not if I knows it !   Beg pardon, sir,
but I don't go into any service but yours.   If
you're suited, I am ; wages no object.   What's
wrong, sir ?"

" Why, these letters tell me that I haven't a copeck in the world that I can call my own. Both my estates have been confiscated by the government. I am accused—and found guilty too, it seems—of plotting against the czar, of treasonable language, of neglecting to report myself to the authorities, and of I don't know what else. As to the neglect not to report, there may be something in that ; but I was given to understand that the authorities had consented to excuse me. At all events, here I am, no better than a detected swindler ; for I have my hotel-bill yet to pay, and I don't know whether the contents of my trunks will satisfy the landlord's claims. So, as I said before, you must be looking out for another place. You can depend on me for giving you a good character."

" It would be a pretty poor character I'd have if I was to leave you at a time like this, sir," Tom replied, with an attempt to disguise emotion under a garb of cheerfulness. "As for the hotel-bill, you needn't bother yourself about that. I've money enough to pay it, and to take the two of us to America afterwards,—yes, and to make a show after we get there, too. We can get along without your estates, sir, never fear ! "

" You have money ? Where did you get it ? "

" Why, I'll tell you, sir. You may remember you gave me leave of absence the other night ? Well, I didn't tell you what I meant to do ; but I'd set my mind on having a shy at the green cloth myself. I'd thought out a bit of a system that I wanted to try on. Well, the way it turned out, I didn't get my system to work, for the reason that it was the table that the little ball was spinning on that I got into, instead of the one with the cards. It was the first one I come to, anyhow. I'd brought with me eighty francs to play with; but I had a five-franc bit in my waistcoat pocket, and thinks I, " I'll have a go with that first, just for luck. So I put it down on a red place; and the fellow spun the little ball, and up came red sure enough. 'Well,' says I to myself, 'what's good once is good again,' so I just left the ten francs I'd won where it was; and it won again, and made twenty 'Come,' says I 'that isn't bad either,' so I let it go again, and the next minute I was forty francs to the good. Well, twice forty was eighty; I stood to win that on the next throw, and if I lost it would be but five francs at the worst, so I let it alone again, and the red came round again as regular as cock-crow. By that time the folks were beginning to take notice, and a crowd of 'em was looking on. ' This is my lucky day,' thinks I; ' let her go for all she's worth !' Red it was again, and that made six times in a run. 'Will you stop now, Tom?' says I. 'Not if I know myself,' I says; and so the next spin fetched me up to three hundred and twenty francs. 'You're good for a thousand, Tom,' I says; and what did I do but turn my back on the board till he'd spun the ball twice more, and I was worth twelve hundred and eighty francs

With that, somebody says to me : 'Better take it up now,' he says ; 'it's run nine times, and there's luck in odd numbers,' he says. 'Well, then,' says I, 'there's more odd numbers besides nine,' I says, 'and I'll let it stay where it is.' 'You'll lose it,' he says. 'Will you bet on it ?' says I ; but before he could make up his mind to do it, red came again, and twenty-five hundred and sixty francs with it. 'I'll bet you five hundred francs against fifty you lose the next time,' says he. 'Done !' says I, and we puts up the money ; and you should have seen the crowd that was looking on, sir ; and it's my belief I might have got all the bets I wanted. Well I was in that shape, I couldn't lose if I tried, and when the red turned up next time, the crowd just hollered, and there was a woman fainted dead away in her chair. What did I do but put the five hundred I'd won from the feller down on the red along with the rest, and that made five thousand six hundred and twenty francs, and says I, out loud, 'That's my last stake, ladies and gentlemen,' says I, 'and if I win, I'll give the odd two hundred and forty francs to the gentleman here that spins the ball,' I says. So at that they gave a laugh and the fellow he spun the ball with an extra twist, and round she went, and we all looking on like the eyes would pop out of our heads ; and the thing began to slow up ; and the chap I betted with sang out : 'It's black !' he says. 'Wait a bit till she stops,' says I ; and just then she turns into the red and stays there. Well, sir, I raked in my cash, and says I : 'That's good enough for me, ladies and gentlemen, I ain't a hog ; here's my place for any one that wants it.'   And I gave the old croupier the two hundred and forty I'd promised him, and the other eleven thousand 1 stuck in my pockets and off I went ; and some of 'em gave me a hurray   That's my yarn, sir ; and, as things turned out, the only mistake I made was not putting down my whole eighty francs, instead of the five in my waistcoat pocket."

Tom told this story with so much zest and animation that the effect was irresistible, and Fedovsky almost forgot his troubles while he listened to him.   As the valet concluded he thrust his hands into his pockets, and produced several large wads of bank notes, which he spread out on the table.   "There," said he.   "That ain't a million, but it's money, as far as it goes ; and it'll take us to New York, and give us a start when we get there.   It's all yours, sir, provided only you'll take me along with you, sir ; and glad I am of the chance of giving it to you."

"Well, Tom," said the count, after a few minutes' silence, " I will take the money, not as a loan, but as a free gift from one man to another.   I don't know that I shall ever be able to make you any return for it.   But we will go to America, where all men are equal, and you and I will be friends—we have done with master and servant.   If I meet with any good fortune there, you shall share it, as I now share yours ; though, to tell the truth, I think it much more probable that you will make a living than that

I shall, for you can turn your hand to any thing, whereas I am absolutely good for nothing."

"We can do better together, sir, than what either of us could alone," returned Tom, with cheerful confidence. "It's just as easy making money as it is spending it, though at first it may not come in quite so fast as it used to go out, but, to make up for that, there's more fun in making ten dollars than in spending a hundred. What you want, sir, is to get a place as corresponding secretary of a corporation, or foreign clerk to a bank, or may be you'll get into politics, and then there's no telling where you'll stop. And you've met American swells enough in Europe to give you all the lift you need."

" People who are very obliging when one is rich, are not always the same when they know that one is poor," Fedovsky replied, with a touch of the worldly wisdom which he was already beginning to find would be required in his future career; " but we'll try every thing, and perhaps something may turn up a success. I shouldn't wonder if Mr. Williams could give me some good letters of introduction to New York people. It might be worth while to ask him."

"Begging your pardon, sir, before you do that, I'd like to ask you a question," said Tom, with a peculiarly sagacious look. "This evening, a little while after you went out, I was looking out of the window, and I saw you passing by arm-in-arm with a gentleman with a brown mustache. Was that your Mr. Williams?"

"Yes."

"And do you remember my telling you about a chap in New York, who kept a place on Fourth Street, and did me out of some money?"

"Well, what of it?"

"And that I had seen somebody here that put me in mind of him, only he'd shaved off his beard, and was got up in swell style?"

"You don't mean to say—"

"I mean to say that your Mr. Williams is the man I'm talking about! I'll bet a Napoleon to a franc that he's my swindler; and I wouldn't be surprised, sir, if he was after you for a big haul; and if so, no one will be sorrier than he to hear the news in them letters of yours!"

This suggestion was so bewildering to Fedovsky that for several moments he was unable to make any reply to it. "It's preposterous and incredible," he exclaimed at last. "You have made a mistake, depend upon it. Why, Williams, from the very first, advised me to let gambling alone. Besides—"

"It's natural he should want to keep you out of the Casino, so that he might get all you had to throw away for himself. Those fellows spot a man and find out all about him before they speak to him. And then they offer to introduce him to some very nice people, friends of theirs; and you go to a house, and meet a gang, and then one of 'em proposes a little game of cards, and you are agreeable of course ; and at first you win ; but after a while the stakes are raised a bit, and then you lose ; you're lucky if you get away with a penny in your pocket."

Tom had so accurately described the actual course of events, that Fedovsky could not help feeling staggered for an instant ; but he recovered himself promptly.

" The thing is impossible," he repeated emphatically, " and I will tell you the reason. Mr. Williams offered to introduce me to a lady "

" Aha ! that's what I thought—it's the regular game ! " muttered Tom, shaking his head.

" And this lady," continued tne other, with a severe glance, " turned out to be some one whom I already knew, but had lost sight of for several years, —a lady for whom I feel the highest regard and affection. I don't suppose you will tell me that she is a partner of swindlers ? But it was at her house I spent the evening ; and it was there that I lost at cards—entirely by my own fault and volition—all the money I happened to have with me. You have been misled by some accidental resemblance."

" Well, sir, if you know the lady, and can answer for her, of course I've nothing to say to the contrary," Tom replied. " But that don't prove that Williams ain't my man. He may have taken in the lady too. Any way, it might be just as well if you didn't ask him to give you letters of introduction. He's only somebody you picked up in a gambling town, after all."

Fedovsky made no promise; but he followed his valet's counsel, nevertheless. And the more he thought over what had passed between them, the less comfortable did he feel. Except that it was at Vera s house that the episode of the game of poker had taken place, he would have but little difficulty in accepting Tom's theory. That fact was his only security; but was even that conclusive? He had seen or heard nothing of Vera for some years. He knew that she had married a thief. As regarded her subsequent marriage with the prince, he had only her own word for it. She had spoken to him of some trouble—some mysterious bondage—under which she was suffering, and from which she even feared to escape. Might not this bondage involve something of a criminal nature? Indeed, could it be any thing essentially innocent and harmless? Might not Williams have acquired some hold over her, whereby he could compel her to assist him in his schemes of plunder? And then, what was the meaning of her strange behavior, and of the word "Beware" that she had conveyed to him? Was she trying to protect him from a danger which she did not venture more fully to explain?

These reflections made him very uneasy, and he made up his mind to go to her the next day, open his mind to her freely, and prevail upon her, if his surmises were correct, to leave it all and accompany him to America. But fate was too nimble for him. When he went to her house the next day he found it closed, and learned that the Princess Volgorouki

had left town early that morning, and had appointed
no time for her return. Neither Williams nor Signor and Madame Strogello were to be found anywhere ; and inquiry revealed that they too had gone
away, no one knew whither. It had an unpleasant
look ; but Fedovsky kept his misgivings to himself.

———

CHAPTER IX.

RUSSIAN ECCENTRICITY.

AT this point in his story, Fedovsky made a
pause : " I need not," he said, " go into the
details of the last month I spent in Europe. I made
no attempt to recover possession of my lost estates :
that would have been worse than useless. I got my

remaining property together as quickly as possible, and sailed with my valet for New York. On the day of my arrival, I ran across a Mr. Frederic Vanderblick, a young American whom I had met in London a year or two before. He knew nothing of the change in my circumstances, and greeted me with cordiality." He then went on to relate his New York experiences, the substance of which was as follows :—

Mr. Frederick B. Vanderblick was a young New Yorker to the manner born, the son of a wealthy man who had made his money in banking, and intended his son to follow the same profession. As a preliminary step, however, he sent him to Columbia College, and then to Europe, to make "a thorough gentleman " of him and enlarge his mind. The boy was of a sociable, popular and enterprising disposition, full of animal spirits, quick to comprehend the scope and details of a business matter, but somewhat lacking in prudence and sober judgment. He matured rapidly, as such men, so placed, are apt to do, yet without losing his youthful ardor. At twenty-five, he was a boy in conversation and impulses, with the good-natured skepticism and facility of a man-of-the-world of fifty. He looked well, talked well, dressed well, and lived rather too well, considering that his business engagements seldom allowed him to make up in the morning the sleep which his social engagements obliged him to lose over night. But his vigorous constitution had hitherto counteracted the ill effects of this hard treatment: his eyes were bright and his cheeks had color : and after all, if his life ended fifteen years sooner than it ought to have done, he would have lived fifteen years more actively while he was about it. He now occupied, nominally, the post of a clerk in the bank of which his father was president ; but it was understood that, when he had mastered the routine, he was to be taken into partnership and, probably, succeed his father in the supreme control.

Mr. Vanderblick junior took his friend into the directors' parlor, and introduced him to Vanderblick senior with all the honors,—as a particular friend and chum of his while abroad, as a distinguished nobleman of the Russian Empire, and as a sevenfold millionaire,—all of these titles to esteem being enumerated so rapidly, that Fedovsky had no opportunity to modify them ; though he perceived that the last of the three had an especially ingratiating effect upon the old gentleman, who promptly invited the count to dine with him on the following Sunday evening. This tender having been accepted, Mr. Frederic observed that he wanted to show his friend round a little, and desired leave of absence for that purpose. It was immediately and graciously accorded, and, at parting, the venerable president arose to shake his visitor by the hand, and to accompany him to the door,—thereby causing the latter to feel more like an accomplished adventurer than ever.

The two now repaired to the club, where Vanderblick inscribed the count's name in the book and caused him to be presented with a visitor's two-weeks ticket. Then they went into the smoking-room, where a few of the old habitués were ensconced in their easy-chairs, and Vanderblick ordered a bottle of Mumm, and cigars, and introduced the count to those present in the same terms as before, and the party drew their chairs together, and began to converse after the manner of American gentlemen of the clubbable sort.

Finding himself so hospitably entreated, Fedovsky could not but reciprocate, and it was evident that he made a favorable impression on his companions. He talked well, and found that he had a great deal to say that was new and interesting to an American audience. They were particularly concerned to hear about his English experiences, and made inquiries regarding various personages of distinction belonging to that nation. More champagne was ordered : more men dropped in, and ever and anon one or other of them would be invited to join the circle. The conversation became general and voluble, though Fedovsky always remained the central figure. Whatever his present condition may have been, he still had all the reminiscences and feelings of a man of millions, and often, in the genial glow of talk, he would forget for a time all that had lately happened. As often as he recollected the lamentable truth, a shadow would pass over his face, and he would become silent and thoughtful. How would all this end?

At all events, it went on very agreeably. Every body wanted to have a hand in the count's entertainment, and in the course of a few hours he had received invitations enough to keep him busy for a fortnight. These invitations, again, would be certain to lead to others. In one way they would, of course, diminish his expenses. But, on the other hand, it was impossible for a gentleman to associate on equal terms with gentlemen, without spending money as they spent it. For example, Fedovsky felt it incumbent upon him to order a bottle of champagne. Nobody present needed champagne, and Fedovsky would rather have kept the three dollars ; but these considerations were nothing to the purpose. It is such incidental outlays—the taxes of social etiquette—that are inevitable, and constitute a serious strain upon the purses of those whose means are limited. But there was no way of escaping them, except to announce his true financial situation ; and although any thing underhand was very distasteful to him, there nevertheless seemed to be no good reason why he should, at this stage, take these gentlemen into his confidence. He was doing them no harm ; he was not taking more than he was ready to give. In every personal respect, he was all that they took him to be ; and so long as he paid his shot, and borrowed no money, what had he to reproach himself with? It might be urged, to be sure, that if his new friends had been aware of his pecuniary condition, they would not have invited him to dine and sleep at their houses, nor even to become a guest of their club ; they would shun him as an adventurer—that is, as a person aiming to profit himself at their expense. But did he intend to profit himself at their expense ? Well, not in any way that would involve loss to them. All he wanted was to maintain himself for awhile in that social level where the best opportunities for advancement were to be met with. There was nothing dishonest in that. And yet he could not satisfy himself that he was not guilty of maintaining, or acquiescing in, false appearances ; and he determined to do something towards putting himself right as soon as possible.

It was nearly five o'clock, and a good many glasses of champagne had been drunk by every one present, when Vanderblick reminded the count that he was to dine with him and others at Delmonico's, and they had better be thinking of dressing. Accordingly, they arose and bade adieu to the others, and sallied forth into the street, which was reddened but not warmed by the beams of the setting sun. It was only a few blocks to the hotel, and they walked thither arm-in-arm.

"Let me come in and have a look at your rooms," said Vanderblick. "I know the clerk here—he's a good fellow—and if he hasn't got you fixed right, I'll give him the tip, and he'll see that you're suited."

Fedovsky knew not how to object to this polite

offer ; and Vanderblick was as good as his word. He introduced the count to the clerk in the usual style, rather exaggerating his aristocratic and pecuniary recommendations than otherwise, at the rate of, say, a hundred thousand dollars to each glass of champagne he had drunk ; asked the situation of his room, and, on learning that it was pretty far away in the upper regions, insisted upon his being transferred to the second floor, and having a suite of parlor, bed-room and dining-room. This being arranged, and orders having been given to have the trunks removed to the new quarters, Mr. Vanderblick finished up his benefactions by saying, jocosely, " Now, you treat him white, boss, and if he goes back on you, you can come down on me." And so withdrew laughing, with the understanding that they were to meet at Delmonico's in an hour's time.

"Well, sir," said Tom, as he bustled about, opening the trunks and getting out his master's evening clothes, "this is something like, ain't it ? I told you how it would be ; we're all right now, and it won't be long before you're as good as you ever was."

"At the rate we are going now," replied the count, "our suspense will soon be at an end, at all events. I tell you plainly, Tom, that we are going the wrong way to work. We had much better let our true position be known at once, instead of waiting until it is found out. This money of yours is being thrown away, with nothing to show for it.   These rooms alone are enough to ruin us; and yet, unless I tell them that I can't afford it, I can not refuse to occupy them.   I want you to give me leave to make a clean breast of it."

"Don't do it, sir!" replied Tom earnestly: "don't do it!" It'll all come out straight, bless you! You've got those swells to back you up, and you can live here a year without nobody as much as asking to see the color of your money."

"It won't do, Tom," returned the other, shaking his head. "I give you fair warning that I won't run in debt, whatever happens. I shall pay as I go, and when the money comes to an end, I shall go for good."

"Very well, sir: but the money won't come to an end, you may take my word for it. Things are in just the shape I wanted them: and you'll find out I'm right."

Conversations similar to this frequently occurred between the count and his valet, and always with the same result.

At half past six Fedovsky was at Delmonico's, and found Vanderblick awaiting him. They were given a private room, and sat down to dinner with four others, some of whom the count had already met in Europe. When the coffee and cigars were served, the company grouped themselves together sociably, and chatted at their ease.

"I suppose you will do like the rest of our distinguished visitors, count," said a middle-aged gentleman known as Judge Farren. "You will go east, west, north and south, see every thing, and write a book about it."

" Not at all," replied Fedovsky. " I have serious thoughts of settling down here in New York, and taking out naturalization papers."

" Oh, you'll get out of that idea after awhile, when you've seen more of us," rejoined a Mr. Wellesley Brooks, who owned a yacht, and had been educated at Oxford. " Democracy seems all right as a novelty, but a fellow finds it a bore in the end."

" Another thing," said Dr. Warren Beade, a gentleman of thirty, who had already made a fortune in the treatment of diseases by electrical processes. " An American is supposed to have something to do. Of course, Brooks is an exception : but he's an Anglomaniac, and doesn't count. But an adopted citizen, at all events, is expected to occupy himself about something. What do you mean to take up ? "

" I should like to learn how to make a living in any respectable way," said Fedovsky.

At this there was a general laugh.

" You Russian nabobs want the earth," remarked Colonel Jack Oakley, who, with his close-cropped head, red mustache and portly stomach, looked the personification of worldly well-being. " You can't make a living in this country. There isn't money enough in it to pay the bill ! "

" I spoke quite seriously," said Fedovsky quietly.

" And you spoke good sense, too," remarked Vanderblick, coming to the support of his guest.

" You've got the correct American idea. Because a man has got a few millions, more or less, laid by for a wet day, it doesn't follow that he shouldn't learn how to make a few thousands by his own work. That's what my governor always told me, and he was right. I only wish there were more fellows like you ! I'd like to have a few of your sort in our office ! "

"I am open to an engagement," replied the count, " and I am willing to begin on a very moderate salary. As to the millions you talk about, I must say, so far as I am concerned, you are quite off the track. I have very little, and my desire to make money is practical, not theoretic."

This was plain speaking, but it was not the right sort of plainness. Nobody believed it. Some of them knew for a certainty that he had been very rich a few months before, and they never imagined that he could have lost all his possessions in the interval. If Fedovsky had entered into explanations on this point, the effect would have been different. But he had in some measure relieved his conscience, and hoped that it might lead the way, without further revelation, to what he wanted.

"Never mind about the millions, my dear fellow," said Vanderblick, with a laugh. "It's none of our business how poor or rich you may be, so long as you are the good fellow that you will be always. For my part if you were to prove to us that you hadn't money enough in the world to settle your hotel bill, I'd settle it myself, and install you in the guest-chamber at our house.   But, seriously, that's a capital notion of yours—to find out by experience what business is like ; and if you are willing, on sober reflection, to follow it out, it will be a good plan to mention it to my governor at dinner to-morrow."

" I have taken more champagne than is good for me," returned Fedovsky, " but I'm still sober enough to assure you that I mean what I say.   I want to begin at the bottom and work up, and to be treated just the same as any other clerk in the office.   But I rather fancy that your father may have other views."

" What eccentric fellows these Russians are," said Colonel Oakley to Judge Farren, in an under-tone.   " What do you suppose his game is ? "

" Oh, some fad of his," the judge replied.   " He was always queer ; but I knew him in London, and he has twenty millions."

" A fellow can afford to have fads on that cap-ital," said the colonel, with a sigh.   " I would be a bank-clerk myself on the same terms ! "

CHAPTER X

MISS SALLIE VANDERBLICK.

THE dinner party at Mr. Vanderblick's house the next evening was a family affair, and therefore the more a compliment to Fedovsky, who was thus invited, as it were, to consider himself a member of the family circle. The circle consisted of Mr. and Mrs. Vanderblick, Fred, and the daughter of the house, whose name was Sallie. This young lady was twenty years of age, and a very favorable specimen of a New York girl. She was of a delicate, high-bred, spirited aspect, and had evidently had the advantage of the best social and educational training that the resources of modern American civilization can bestow. She had brown hair, a pure white skin ; her eyes were large and somewhat imperious in expression, and her other features, though not strictly regular, were refined, and made up a very beautiful countenance. Her figure was well-proportioned, and had a certain maidenly dignity in its bearing that distinguished her from the average young lady of society. She was self-possessed and not talkative, though, when she did say any thing, it evinced a good mind, well balanced.

She was on a higher intellectual and moral plane than the rest of the family; there were, indeed, still some traces of rusticity in the old people, who had not, in their youth, had the advantage of the training and surroundings that they were able to give their children. Mrs. Vanderblick was pious and rather simple; the old gentleman was a man of force and ability, but with the harshness and brusqueness that often belong to men who have had their own way to make. All of them, young and old, were hospitably disposed toward their distinguished foreign guest.

Fedovsky, on his side, was immediately interested in Sallie. He had seen American girls in Europe; but they had not happened to be of the best class: they were audacious, voluble and conspicuous, rather than independent, self-respecting and intelligent. At table he sat beside this young lady, and addressed to her most of his remarks that were not merely conventional and polite. Her questions were penetrating and stimulating, and her replies to his own inquiries were straightforward and satisfactory. They seemed to draw out what was best in each other.

"Do you like a democracy better than a despotism?" she asked.

"Who does not, except the despots?" returned he.

"But you must have a reason. What is it?"

"Every man should have a hand in the making and administration of the laws by which he is governed," said the count.

"They do not have it here. The constitution says they may, but they do not. Out of every ten men, one will have more authority and ability than the other ; and among ten of these, one is stronger than the others, and so on. The subordinates vote as the leaders tell them ; the leaders act for their own interests ; so our laws are made. A few people really do it all ; and though they are generally clever, they are not generally good ; they want money and power, and they get them at the people's expense. Is not that something like what happens under a despotism? And the despotism has one advantage—that it does not pretend to be what it is not, as our democracy does."

"But you will not deny that you have a free press, which must represent the people, because it depends on them for its existence."

"If you believe what the papers say of one another, they are all false, corrupt and blind. Our people are careless and easy, and put up with the best they can get. I don't think we have much dignity, or conscience, or faith in disinterested goodness. And I think the papers encourage us to have less still."

"But you surely don't mean, Miss Vanderblick, that you prefer a despotism to a democracy?" Fedovsky exclaimed in surprise.

"My preferences can make no difference. One must be more nearly right than the other. I should only like to know which belongs most to human nature ; for that is the one that must win in the end.   Men will never be equal in intellect and energy ; and the most intellectual and energetic men must rule the others.   They can't help doing it, and the others can't help obeying them."

"But take a practical instance.   The Americans are the most enlightened people in the world, and the Russians are mostly barbarians."

"Enlightenment is not necessarily goodness, any more than light is necessarily heat."

"But we must become enlightened ; and is goodness any thing more than enlightened selfishness ? "

"I think it is something entirely different."

"Then you think goodness is more important than enlightenment ? "

"Yes," said she ; "I think that no enlightenment that does not come through goodness is worth having, or will last."

"Are you two talking transcendental politics ? " inquired Fred at this point.   "You mustn't mind her, Fedovsky.   She's an anarchist and crank of the worst type, and will stop at nothing."

Sallie smiled quietly at her brother, and said nothing.   Fedovsky was too sincerely interested to make any conventional protest.   Mrs. Vanderblick observed that tea would be served in the drawing-room, and arose and departed, Sallie following her. The gentlemen, after they had left, sat down again and took out their cigars.

"By the way, father," said Fred, "here's the count wants to make a living. Can you help him ? "

" Fred tells me that you think of becoming an American citizen," said the old gentleman. " Is that really your purpose, sir ? "

" I came here meaning to make it my country," answered the count. " I shall never go back to Russia ; and no other place attracts me."

" And you wish to enter into the life and commerce of New York? Well, all I can say is, you are doing a very good thing.   I'm a banker, and of course I believe in banking.   If you want to invest your money in that business, you would find it as profitable as any that is equally safe."

" It isn't of investments that I was thinking.   I have little or nothing to invest.   I would like to learn the banking business, beginning in the ordinary way, and going on step by step.   As I said to your son yesterday, I literally want to make my own living."

" The long and short of it is, father, that the count is a crank," put in Fred, " and he is bound to ride his hobby in his own way   Now, can we give him a lift ? "

" Well, as to that, I dare say we might find or make a place for him," replied Mr. Vanderblick, with a slow smile.   " We had thoughts of adding a new department to our business, by and by, and that might give an opening.   However, there need be no hurry about it, I suppose.   You will want to get used to our American ways a little—make the acquaintance of some of the men on the Exchange, and so on.   And I presume you will be pretty hard-worked socially for some weeks or months to come. By the time you are ready for us, I dare say we shall be ready for you. And you may perhaps not regret having been given time to take a second thought on the matter, sir. People change their minds sometimes, you know."

Fedovsky thanked his host, and said no more on the subject. The situation was quite as promising as could have been expected, and to push it too rapidly might result in losing the opportunity altogether. For the rest, he was quite willing to adjourn to the drawing-room, and have some more talk with Sallie. She was the only woman, save one, that he had ever met, in whom he felt a rational and genuine interest. There was no particular reason for it ; only there was something in her that was deeply congenial to him, and that he seemed to have been seeking for a long while. The sensation was like what a lost traveler feels, who, just as he is making up his mind that all is over with him, sees a familiar object that assures him he is at the threshold of his own home. It gave him a happiness quite unmeasurable under the circumstances, for the idea of marrying never entered his head, and Sallie was, most likely, not in the least aware that there was any thing out of the common in the matter. She was a nice girl—that was all— and he was glad to know her.

On rejoining the ladies, Fedovsky found that two or three other gentlemen had dropped in, and one of them had taken his seat by Sallie, with the apparent purpose of holding it against all comers. Meanwhile the count himself was seized upon by Mrs. Vanderblick, who, it seems, had taken a great fancy to him, in her own extremely quiet way, and had a number of naïve questions to ask him about the peculiarities of domestic life among the Russians, and how the ladies occupied themselves, and what sort of ministers of the gospel they had there. The young man replied to her curiosity as best he might, though he felt that he was much more likely to astonish and scandalize her than to gratify her. Nothing else of importance occurred during the evening.   But the stranger carried away a pleasant impression of the American family—the first that he had ever entered ; and the smile and the touch of the hand that Sallie gave him at parting sent him back to his hotel with a light heart ; though, regarded from a merely rational point of view, he had no particular cause for self-congratulation.

CHAPTER XI.

COUNT FEDOVSKY, considerably to his own anxiety, found himself established in his career of a man of fashion and distinction in New York. Nothing, indeed, could be easier and smoother than this career outwardly appeared to be ; and Tom, at all events, was entirely content with it. The only serious item of expense that he had to incur was his hotel-bill, which he made a point of settling every week : but he only slept at his rooms, the remainder of his time was spent abroad, as the guest of his numerous hospitable friends. All the principal clubs tendered him invitations, so that he was continually free of some of them : in short, there appeared to be a conspiracy on all sides to bring all New York and its resources of entertainment before him in review, without any thing being asked from him in return except an amiable appreciation of the spectacle. Every body contended for the privilege of defraying his expenses ; and he might have borrowed thousands of dollars without any other effect than that of making the gentlemen who lent to him feel flattered by his kindness in constituting them his banker. Fedovsky was only human, and his vanity was perhaps somewhat inflated by all this popularity and courting; but, in his sober moments, he reminded himself that the character of his reception was based upon the theory that he could, were he so minded, buy up the wealthiest of his entertainers, and that, if his real circumstances were known, a radical alteration might be looked for in the demeanor of all concerned.

Perhaps he would have broken away from it all, but for two considerations. The first was, his expectation (not a very sanguine one) that Mr. Vanderblick, senior, would find him a situation in his bank; and the other, that Sallie Vanderblick had made a decided impression on his heart. It was not easy to see how any good could come of that, either: but, where the emotions and affections are concerned, a very small possibility will be magnified a great many diameters. Probably the count avoided speculating as to the final result of the affair: he felt an earnest pleasure in the girl's society, and confined his thoughts to the passing moment.

One day, while the count and a party of gentlemen—Colonel Jack Oakley, Judge Farren, Wellesley Brooks, and one or two more—were sitting over their cigars at the club, the colonel suggested that they should spend the night in going through the slums and shy neighborhoods, and gilded dens of the city. This is an amusement not uncommon among gentlemen who are at a loss for something definite to do, and affords them the pleasure of imagining that they are doing something toward exploring the secret recesses of human nature ; although, as a matter of fact, there is just as much human nature to be seen (if you will only look for it) in the box at the opera, or in the boudoir of the reigning belle of the season, or at a champagne supper of politicians at Chamberlain's, as in the lowest dive or gaudiest gin-mill in the metropolis.

The colonel's proposition was received with favor by the company, Wellesley Brooks remarking that the count's American education would not be complete until he had seen something of the night-side of New York. Fedovsky had no special liking for the adventure, but neither did he care to combat the will of the majority. Judge Farren supported the idea, and after a little discussion as to ways and means, it was unanimously adopted, and an hour and a place agreed upon for the rendezvous.

The colonel being thoroughly acquainted with the city, and well informed on police matters generally, Fedovsky, when they set out on their expedition, attached himself more especially to him, and kept him busy answering his questions regarding the manner in which the New York detective service was conducted. The colonel was fully competent to explain the general features of the business ; and when, at the count's request, he went on to impart such information as he possessed concerning the leading crimes and criminals of the last few years, Fedovsky was interested.

"But I don't understand," he said, " how—in the case of a crime having been committed, and no traces left—they know whom to suspect. Say that my house is entered and I am robbed, and only find it out the next morning. What would be the first step towards identifying the criminals?"

"Well, they go by common-sense, mostly," the colonel replied. " I've read some books about the way they do it in France, but that isn't our style. They work the thing out, much the same as if it were a sum in arithmetic. In the first place, you see, crimes are generally done by criminals."

"That I am willing to admit," said Fedovsky, smiling.

" By professionals, that's to say. Crimes against property--robbery, burglary, forgery, pocket-picking, sneak-thieving, and so on. With murder it's different ; murder is often done by people that aren't professionals."

"There is no profession of murder? It is a comfort to know that ! "

"Yes ; and for that reason, the job is so often muddled, and found out. Not always, by a good deal : but more often than not. They lose their heads, one way or another, and give themselves away. But a professional thief is another thing. The cleverest of them are pretty clever. They lay their plans a long while beforehand—years before, sometimes ; and they don't strike till every thing's as they want it. And half their plans are about getting away after the thing is done, and covering their tracks."

" Don't they ever betray one another ? "

" The saying is," replied the colonel, " that ' there's honor among thieves.' But experience doesn't say the same thing. But the leaders—the tiptop men—don't let themselves in for that risk. They keep in the background, and direct operations, but they never show themselves. Even the men that work for them don't know who they are. Instructions are transmitted through third parties, but nobody asks or answers any inconvenient questions. They understand that least said is soonest mended. If one of the small men is arrested, he tells nothing about the big men, because he knows nothing. It's a recognized arrangement, and it's to their advantage in the long run."

" But how, then, does one know the big men themselves ? "

" Well, it isn't difficult to know them, in one way. You may know that such and such a man is a thief : but it doesn't follow that you can bring home any particular crime to him. They are always on the lookout for them, though, and sooner or later they get most of them. They must communicate with somebody, and one bit of evidence leads to another. Once a man is suspected he is put under surveillance from then out, and he seldom can keep long out of sight. A record is kept of whom he associates with, where he lives, what journeys he makes, what money he spends, and so on. Then, if any big crime is reported, they first determine whether it was possible or likely that one of these fellows had a hand in it ; and then they put a double watch on him, to see if he shows any signs of having benefited by the affair. "But," concluded the colonel, "there are more ways of following them up than I could tell you."

"What is the most difficult class of criminals to catch?" inquired the count.

"Well, I don't know but the first-class forgers are as difficult as any," returned the other. "They generally have the most brains, and they don't need to expose themselves. The police sometimes have to wait a long time before they can capture them. It is said that there is a man hereabouts now," he continued, after a pause, "who is likely to do more mischief in that line than any body they have dealt with yet, if he isn't stopped in time. He has been arrested more than once, but nothing could ever be proved against him. He is a gentleman in manners and education, and has brains enough to run the United States Treasury ; but a more thorough rascal don't live. He never stops long in one place : and he's been over to Europe several times, traveling quietly and living well, like a retired man of business who wants to amuse himself in an elegant way."

"What is his name?" asked the count.

The colonel shrugged his shoulders. "He has more than one," he said, "if he should ever be caught tripping, every body will know what he calls himself ; but, until then, the less it is repeated the better the chance of catching him will be."

" You seem to be thoroughly posted in police matters," replied Fedovsky ; "how did you acquire your knowledge ?"

The colonel smiled, and said, " The chief of detectives, Inspector Byrnes, is an old friend of mine, and we have often talked about criminals and their methods."

The party had now arrived in the midst of the region where their explorations were to begin ; but it will be unnecessary to follow their movements in detail. The scenes and the persons which they were called upon to contemplate were not of an especially edifying character, nor did any exciting incidents take place. Upon the whole, Fedovsky and his friends were not deeply impressed or stimulated by what they saw ; as for Fedovsky, he had felt a livelier interest when in the presence of the historic scenes of wickedness and violence in Europe,—the blood-stain on the floor of Queen Mary's chamber, the prison room of Raleigh, in the tower of London, the guillotine of the French Revolution, or the battle-field of Waterloo. His imagination failed to respond at the instance of more obscure and vulgar villanies and villains. As a matter of fact, he was bored, and the same might be said of the others. They had overestimated the resources of their new amusement. What was to be done? They could scarcely ask the personages at whom they were called upon to stare to authenticate their reputation by committing a robbery or murder in their presence ; that would involve their becoming mere commonplace witnesses in a police court next morning. At length Wellesley Brooks proposed that they should go to some gambling-house, where they might entertain themselves by "bucking against the tiger."

This was agreed to by the others, and the door of a gambling-house was shortly after reached, where, after some parley with the door-keeper, the party was admitted. A tolerably large gathering was present, and the game was proceeding industriously.

After a moment, Tom, who had accompanied his master, noticed a medium-sized man, with pale face and dark whiskers, standing at one of the gambling-tables. There was something about his appearance that aroused his curiosity, and he began to make his way toward him. Meanwhile, Mr. Wellesley Brooks, who had been searching his pockets, uttered an exclamation of dismay :

"What's up, Wellesley?" inquired the colonel, who was standing near him.

"I've lost my pocket-book, confound it!" exclaimed Brooks. "It was in my hip-pocket,too!"

"You may have left it at that table in the dance-hall," suggested the colonel. "You had it out there, didn't you?"

"I haven't touched it since we started," the other replied. "Some rascal has stolen it."

"And he has left his mark," added the colonel, indicating a neat slit in the side of the pocket, through which the purse had evidently been abstracted. "I think I know when you probably lost it, Brooks. It must have been in the dance-house. Had you a large sum of money in it?"

"A good deal larger than I care to lose in that way," Mr. Brooks replied; "there was over six hundred dollars——"

"I'm to blame for not keeping a sharper look-out."

"It's no matter, I can reimburse myself to-night without going home." He turned to Fedovsky, who happened to be standing next him, and said, "You can let me have six hundred for the evening, can't you, count?"

Now, Fedovsky always made it a rule to carry all his money about him, in order to be prepared for any unlooked-for emergency; but it by no means entered into his intentions to spend it otherwise than with the most careful economy. To lend it was, of course, not quite the same as to spend it; and Brooks was, no doubt, fully able and willing to settle a debt of a hundred times the amount named. But Brooks might imagine that a man of millions, such as he supposed Fedovsky to be, would think as little of six hundred dollars as of six cents, and might forget to repay him on time, or even at all. On the other hand, should he decline to lend Brooks the money, Brooks would be sure to think it very strange, as well as disobliging ; and it might lead to unpleasant suspicions and inquiries. He had but a moment in which to weigh the matter, and the result of his weighing was, that he handed Brooks the sum he asked for. Brooks carelessly nodded his acknowledgments, and turned to the gaming-table, where some of the others of the party were already busy. How little did he imagine that Fedovsky had barely fourteen hundred dollars left in the world !

"Come on, count !" cried Colonel Jack Oakley, plucking him by the sleeve, "you must take a hand with the boys for the good of the house ! I've lost fifty, and I want to see you win it back again. You millionaires are always lucky ! Come on !"

For the first in his life, despite some previous experiences of his, Fedovsky felt the true gambler's instinct. If he had luck, he might, in a few minutes, win money enough to live in comfort for a year or two to come. He had had luck when he did not care for it ; why might he not have it now, when he needed it ? Under this impulse, he moved up to the table, and began to play The game happened to be *Trente et Quarante*

He won, and won, and won again. Then he lost ; but, persuaded that it was but a temporary reverse, he went on playing. His losses continued until, in alarm, he was about to stop ; but at that juncture he had another success. He made a venture large enough to restore all his losses if he won. He lost again, and turned from the table, with a laugh, leaving a thousand dollars of his fourteen hundred behind him.

The other gentlemen laughed also, and rallied him jocosely on his ill-luck. He answered them in the same tone, but with consternation at his heart. Four hundred dollars! And he owed several bills, one or two of them quite large ones. What was to be done? Should he ask Brooks for that six hundred? That could at best only postpone the evil day, and it might hasten it. Should he borrow a thousand or two of some friend? They would gladly lend him all he asked for : but how could he repay them? No—not that!

And to make matters worse, the money that he had thrown away was not his own.

Just then, Tom came up to him. He had been during the last fifteen minutes èngaged in conversation with the pale-faced, dark-whiskered man, in a retired corner, and had not noticed Fedovsky's calamity.

" Here s an odd thing has happened to me, sir," he said, in an undertone. " I've found my only brother, Charley, in this gambling den ; and have learned from his own lips that he is a thief ! "

CHAPTER XII.

AN OPERATION

COUNT FEDOVSKY had never before realized what it is to be ruined. A certain former experience of his abroad had come upon him so suddenly and unexpectedly that it had affected him more as a fiction than a fact; especially as a lucky accident had partly filled the breach. This was a different matter. He had had ample time during the last few months, to reflect upon the meaning of poverty, and now that it was come, he understood it in all its bearings. And not poverty only, but disgrace awaited him. His friends, when the truth was known, would regard him as no better than a swindler. He had not technically cheated them of their money; but he had associated with them under false pretenses, and they could truthfully say that they would not have entertained him as they had done, if they had known that he was penniless. To complete his discomfiture, he learned, on the morning after the visit to the slums, that Wellesley Brooks had been called to Chicago on important business, and might not return till the autumn. He had evidently forgotten all about that little loan.

Tom insisted upon treating the loss of the money as a thing of no very serious importance. He reminded the count that he still had his social position and reputation, which were his best capital, and that it would be easy to take the advantage of them now, of which hitherto he had delayed to avail himself. He could strike for the best thing in sight, and when he had gained possession of it, no one would ask him any questions. A little shrewd management would overcome all difficulties. Fedovsky was willing to admit that this might be true : but he was convinced in his own heart that the sort of shrewd management required was precisely the sort that he had no turn for. Tom was more preoccupied concerning the discovery of his brother than about the disappearance of their friends. He had not seen " Charley " for nearly twenty years ; he had long ago given him up as dead : and now he rose above the surface sound in wind and limb, but, evidently, with a very shady past behind him. Precisely how shady it was, or what the particular shadows were, Tom had not been able to learn ; but that it would not stand scrutiny, Charley had made no attempt to deny. He had told Tom, however, that he was anxious to reform : and upon hearing that his brother was in the service of a Russian millionaire, he had expressed the hope that the nobleman in question might feel disposed to lend him a helping hand. The new disaster to their fortunes of course put that out of the question : but Tom nevertheless seemed to have an idea that Charley might in some way be made a party to their adventures, and that they all would be the better for the addition. Fedovsky thought quite otherwise ; but he announced no opinion upon the matter at present, being too much absorbed with the immediate features of his situation.

His first act was to pay all his outstanding bills; which, as is usually the case, turned out to be rather more numerous, and of somewhat greater amount than he had calculated : insomuch that when he had footed the last one, he found himself with just eighty-four dollars surplus. He intended to vacate his rooms at the hotel the next day, and was about to send for his account, when Tom protested so vigorously that he was obliged to listen to his argument—which was to the effect that the personal property contained in his trunk was worth a hundred times the sum of his indebtedness to the hotel, and might be left in the baggage-room there as earnest of payment; meanwhile, he might take, in a valise, whatever valuables were most readily convertible into cash, together with a change of clothes and linen and evening-dress : he might leave the hotel, as if about to return in a day or two ; and then write word that unforeseen circumstances were detaining him, and that in the interval his rooms might be disposed of. In this manner, he would save his eighty-four dollars, retain a few personal necessaries, and have his baggage conveniently stored. The hotel would have its security, and be content.

While **Fedovsky** was hesitating over the scheme, a note was brought to him by a messenger boy, bearing on the envelope the stamp of Vanderblick's bank. It contained a request to come to dinner that evening, at the Vanderblick's home. There were to be no other guests : Mr. Vanderblick wished to talk to Count Fedovsky about a little matter of business.

" That's your straight tip, sir, at last ! " Tom exclaimed, when the count communicated the contents of the note to him. " He's going to offer you a big salary, and all the chances you want. Let the hotel-bill lay over till you've had your talk with him, and then I'll lay odds it'll never trouble you again."

Fedovsky could not deny that the note gave a more promising aspect to the situation, and he consented to let matters stand over for another twenty-four hours. He appeared at the Vanderblick's at the appointed time, and was received with much cordiality.

During dinner the conversation was chiefly between the young people—Fred Vanderblick, Sallie, and the count. Fred, it appeared, had just bought the yacht formerly owned by Wellesley Brooks, and intended to go on a cruise in it during the summer. Sallie was to be of the party, and both she and her brother expressed an urgent hope that Fedovsky would be of the party. The old gentleman nodded his head humorously and said, " You'd better think twice before you accept, count.

A yacht is pretty close quarters, and you will stand a good chance of getting precious tired of one another before you've done with it !"

The idea of getting tired of Sallie Vanderblick was so obviously preposterous, that Fedovsky could not help thinking that Mr. Vanderblick was not averse to the intimate association which he affected to deprecate.　In plain words, he looked with favor upon the prospect of closer relations between Sallie and Fedovsky.　Sallie was not the young Russian's first love, but, as often happens with second loves, the depth and earnestness of his feeling for her was an equivalent for the magnetic passion of his earlier experience.　With her, he could be happy; without her, life would be irksome.　She seemed, so far as he could judge, to return his regard : if he were to ask her to be his wife, he believed that she would consent.　But how could he ask her?　He could not honorably do so without confessing his poverty, and being poor he had no right to demand that she should unite herself to him. On the other hand, by keeping his poverty secret, he might contrive to marry her, and even secure a dowry with her.　But that would be the act of a common adventurer; and Fedovsky thought he could not be happy unless he remained a gentleman. The difficulty of being happy without being a gentleman is one which some people never seem able to overcome; though it by no means follows that gentlemanhood has the effect of securing them happiness.

After Mrs. and Miss Vanderblick had withdrawn,

the banker drew up his chair. Fred passed the guest the bottle, and the elder man spoke as follows :

"What I wanted to suggest was, a little matter of business, which would, I think, be equally profitable to both of us. As I understand it, you wanted to get some insight into the methods of financial transactions. The plan I have in mind would afford you that, and also enable you to realize a sum which—though it would perhaps be unimportant to you—would still be handsome in itself."

"The ordinary salary of a clerk is all I expect, or desire," put in Fedovsky, who was rendered a little uneasy by this beginning.

"That is all right as a bit of romance," returned the financier, with a smile, "but my proposal is of a practical nature. Besides, even the post of a clerk has duties which could not be at once comprehended by an untrained mind ; and any such contract between us would not, therefore, be, strictly speaking, of a business character."

"What the governor means, old fellow," interposed Fred, with a laugh, "is, that you wouldn't be able to earn your salary. We might pay you one, for fun ; but that, I take it, is not exactly what you want."

"I should certainly wish to render an equivalent for my wages," said Fedovsky, with a sinking heart ; "but are you quite sure that I could not do that ? There must be a beginning to every thing."

"Well, you might start as an office-boy, to be

sure," said Fred, much amused, "and sweep out the rooms in the morning, and put the ledgers out. But even that wouldn't teach you finance. There are stories about office-boys who have risen to be kings of plutocracy, I believe; but I guess the time for them to come true is gone by. You will have to begin at the other end, I'm afraid."

"Shall I proceed?" said the banker politely.

"I'm sure I beg your pardon," returned Fedovsky.

"There is now in the market a certain stock," Mr. Vanderblick continued, lowering his voice and leaning forward on his elbow, "which is in excellent repute, as you will admit when I tell you that it is quoted at about ninety." Here he named the stock, which was that of a well-known railroad largely owned in Europe. "Now," he went on, "circumstances have placed us in a position where we can influence a large portion of this stock. I will not trouble you with any of the technical phraseology of the street. The situation, in plain language, is this: We propose to bring about a heavy fall in the stock in question. In order to do that, it will be necessary to shake the public confidence in it. The way to shake confidence in it is to create a conviction that it is being sold whole-sale,—to bring about a panic, as the phrase is, so that all the small holders will sell for whatever they can get. The public will leap to the conclusion that something is wrong with the road; consequently, such of them as hold any of it will get rid of it as fast as possible, and those who have none will keep clear of it. It will depreciate day by day, and we expect finally to bring it down as low as fifty, and possibly much lower."

" But why should one want to depreciate it ? " demanded Fedovsky, much mystified by this statement. " If, as you say, you control a large amount of it, I should think you would wish it to remain at as high a figure as possible."

" My dear Fedovsky, you wouldn't do even for an office-boy," said Fred, again laughing. " You have your a b c still to learn. In the first place, you must know, to sell stock it isn't necessary to be actually possessed of it. You merely agree to deliver so much of it, at such a price, to such a person, on such a date. Of course you expect to make a profit on the trade. To do that you must have bought it at a less price than you mean to sell it. The person from whom you buy it may be in the same position as you regarding actual possession of it. You put up margins to cover the difference in case of loss, and—"

" We need not enter into all that, Fred," interposed the elder, with a wave of his hand. " Count Fedovsky will understand the essential point at issue without these details, which can only be confusing at first. Of course if I agree to sell you a thousand shares at ninety, to-morrow, and it should alter ten points in the interim, I must have deposited with my broker a sum sufficient to liquidate that difference : that is the ' margin ' But to return to what we were saying. The reason we wish to depreciate the stock will be clear to you in a moment. Though our action in selling has had the effect of changing the market-value of the stock from ninety to fifty or less, this fall has been caused only by loss of confidence ; and in order to re-establish confidence, and thus appreciate the stock, all we need do is to begin buying again as largely as we sold before. We buy when the stock has reached what seems likely to be its lowest point—say forty. We buy all we can get hold of at that price. Perceiving this, the public hastens to buy also, and the stock mounts. We expect to be able to send it up to ninety again, or perhaps one hundred : and then we shall have made the difference between the lowest quotation and the highest—say, sixty points."

"That's business, you know," observed Fred, with a nod of the head.

"But surely somebody must suffer," Fedovsky said. "Somebody must have bought at the high price and sold at the low."

"It's business, all the same," Fred repeated. "You can't deal in stocks without somebody getting the worst of it. They will do the same by you, when their turn comes."

"And now for your part in the affair," continued the banker, finishing his glass of sherry and putting it down. "Let me remark, in passing, that all I have told you is in the strictest confidence. If any information as to our intentions were to leak out, of course the game would be lost. We have been for some time past preparing for this operation, and I impart it to you only because I wish you to take part in it."

"What part is that, Mr. Vanderblick ? " the Russian inquired.

"I wish you to join us in bearing the market —I should say, in depreciating the stock," Mr. Vanderblick replied. " We could, of course, carry out the whole enterprise ourselves : but, for various reasons—our cordial regard for you, and other things—we desire to associate you with us. In short, we shall gain by your co-operation, and there can be no doubt that you will gain by ours. The benefits will be mutual."

" Do you mean that there will be no doubt whatever as to the success of the operation ? " said Fedovsky. " Can you be certain that you will be able to depreciate the stock ? "

" Nothing that has not already happened can be termed absolutely certain," the banker answered. " We can not be absolutely certain, for example, that the sun will rise to-morrow. But for any thing short of absolute certainty I should be willing to vouch. The question of margins would be merely a matter of form. In fact, I should request you to allow us to relieve you of the actual arrangement of those details—to conduct the whole affair on our own responsibility, only crediting you with the profit."

"Still, in case there were a loss, I should be liable for my share of it."

"Even in that very improbable contingency, the amount would be, to you, of no serious consequence. In fact, it is rather with a view to cementing our friendly relations, already so agreeable, than with any idea of dazzling you by a financial operation, that I am moved to offer this suggestion. We wish to do what we can to promote your familiarity with our American institutions and customs. My son and daughter will show you one side of them in their yacht; I am only a man of business, and a chapter of business is all that I can contribute. I venture to hope that you will consider the offer in the same friendly spirit in which it is made."

Fedovsky had no reason to distrust Mr. Vanderblick, who had all the appearance and reputation of a man of wealth and position, and who had certainly treated him well. It did not occur to him to ask why he had been treated so exceptionally well—to speculate as to the possible cause of attentions so marked and persistent. And yet, had he reflected upon the matter, he might have thought it a little odd that an old and cautious financier should admit him, a comparative stranger, to a knowledge of an operation so secret and so vast; and should, in the same breath, as good as assure him that he would be happy to have him for a son-in-law. Had he meditated upon these facts, he might have suspected that his own reputed millions, and the fact that, as a European capitalist, he would be popularly supposed to possess inside information as to the condition of a stock so largely owned in Europe, had something to do with it. And then he might have gone on to inquire why a millionaire like Mr. Vandberblick should so particularly desire to associate other millions with his own. The explanation might be, simply the craving for infinite aggrandizement that characterizes some natures. But it might also be nothing more nor less than a pressing need of fresh capital. Mr. Vanderblick might be in a tight place, and might want Fedovsky to help him out of it.

If Fedovsky had taken this view, the saturnine humor of the situation would doubtless have struck him. But he did not take that view ; he accepted Mr. Vanderblick's words in good faith. And he realized the magnitude of the opportunity offered him. It was not the sort of opportunity that comes to a man more than once in a life-time. Without being called upon to so much as put his hand in his pocket, he might, within a week or so, come into the possession of hundreds of thousands of dollars—he knew not how much. With this money, he would once more be independent ; and during the yachting trip, which would follow immediately after, he might offer his hand and heart to Sallie with a clear conscience. There could scarcely be a fairer prospect of a bright future.

Unfortunately, however, the conditions were such as Fedovsky could not bring himself to accept. It was not the financial immorality of the transaction alone that influenced him ; he might have swallowed Mr. Vanderblick's assurance that, if not legitimate in the abstract, it was made so by custom. What he could not face was the possibility, remote though it was, that he might be called upon to pay up his margins. He knew that he could never pay them under any circumstances; and that fact settled the matter in his own mind,— he must decline the banker's proposition. How to decline it, and what the effect of his refusal would be, were other questions. Mr. Vanderblick could not feel otherwise than hurt and offended; and in order to salve the old gentleman's feelings, Fedovsky would be constrained to acquaint him with the truth about himself. In so doing he would bid farewell, in the same breath, to fortune and to love.

"Well, how does the thing sound to you, old fellow?" said Fred, clapping his hand on his shoulder. "Will you take a hand?"

"I am much obliged and flattered by your offer," Fedovsky replied, bowing to the banker, "and I will sleep upon it. You shall have my answer to-morrow."

"I am the more pleased that you do not answer heedlessly," the other responded. "Shall we join the ladies?"

The old man's tone was cheerful and polite; but as he turned away to lower the gas-burner, his furrowed visage wore an expression of anxiety and gloom.

CHAPTER XIII.

FEDOVSKY did not remain long after dinner. When he and the other gentlemen went into the dining-room, he had no clear plan of conduct mapped out for himself. He had told the banker that he would give him an answer on the morrow, merely to gain time. Perhaps he was chiefly actuated by the consideration that if he told the truth then and there, it would prevent his seeing Sallie again : and he felt that he could not part from her in any such abrupt fashion. His love for her had grown imperceptibly and unconsciously, but it was none the less strong on that account, and now that events promised to erect a permanent barrier between him and her, he found that he loved her greatly more than he had hitherto realized.

As he entered the room, and his eyes encountered hers, he suddenly resolved that she was the person to whom, and to whom alone, he was bound to make his confession. She must be aware that he loved her : she had perhaps allowed herself to think that she might love him : and therefore he owed her every thing that he had to give. But he could not disclose himself in that drawing-room.

They must have some degree of privacy. He sat down beside her and said :

" You ride out in the park in the mornings, do you not ? "

" Yes, I never miss my horseback exercise when I can help it."

" You will be out to-morrow, then ? "

" I expect to be."

" At what hour ? "

" I usually start about ten o'clock."

" Does any one go with you ? "

" Only the groom—Duffy," she answered blushing slightly, as she recognized the drift of his questions.

" I shall ride in the park myself to-morrow," he said. " I shall be on the east side after ten o'clock."

She bent her head, but made no audible reply. A few minutes later, Fedovsky took his departure. As he left the house, he told himself that it would be a long time before he entered it again. He walked home, to save car-fare, and because he would have to pay for the hire of a horse the next day.

The morning was fair and mild, the beginning of a perfect day of early summer. At ten o'clock Fedovsky was at the northern end of the park, and rode down along the eastern road at an easy gallop. About half a mile from the southern boundary he saw a lady advancing toward him at a canter. He reined in his horse, and, as she drew near, he lifted his hat and wheeled about to accompany her.

A ride on horseback is often selected, as the *mise en scéne* of a lovers' meeting, or avowal of passion. But in the case of explanations of a delicate and embarrassing character, it is open to certain practical drawbacks. The horses do not always enter into the situation ; and, by their unforeseen divagations and caracoles, sometimes interrupt a sentence at an inconvenient point. If Fedovsky was sensible of this difficulty, he was too much in earnest to be overcome by it : and Sallie, if she missed a word or two here and there, paid such close attention to what he said that the gist of it by no means escaped her.

"I wished to speak to you alone, Miss Sallie," he said, "because I have to bid you farewell, and I could not do that with other people looking on."

"Good-by—in what sense?" Sallie asked, startled by an exordium so different from what she had anticipated. "Are you called back to Russia ?"

"No; and I may not even leave New York. But I can not see you any more."

"What do you mean, Count Fedovsky?"

"I mean what is in no respect to my credit or advantage. You know that I have the reputation of being a very rich man. I was rich, six months ago. But, a few weeks before I sailed for New York, I was ruined, partly by folly of my own, and partly by the action of the Russian government,

which confiscated my estates. I landed here with
only a few thousand dollars. I have been trying,
since I came here, to find some way to earn a living and support myself. I have not denied the
reports of my wealth, and, in that negative way,
I have encouraged them. I intended no dishonesty
by that, but only to maintain a position from which
I could more readily take advantage of opportunities. But it was dishonest, and the reason I
know it is, that it has given me the opportunity to
know and to love you. I do love you, honestly
and with my whole heart ; but I have approached
you under false pretenses : and perhaps I have
caused you unhappiness."

He stopped, and they rode on in silence. Then
Sallie slowly turned her head and looked at him.

" Am I the first woman you ever loved ? " she
asked.

" No. There was one other—eight years ago,"
replied he.

She touched her horse with the whip, and they
galloped on for a hundred yards. Then she drew
her rein, and said, " Well, I have never cared for
any one before. You are the first, Count Fedovsky."

The young man's face flushed red, and his eyes
kindled. " I can't tell you that I'm sorry," he said
at length. " I can't feel an atom of unhappiness
in me ! I have misled you and others : I can no
longer visit you : I have disturbed your peace of
mind : and yet I am only happy—because you love

me ! But I can do something—I can do every thing, now ! I feel the strength for it. I will not lose you ! "

" I am happy, too ! " she said quickly ; and at the same moment the tears gathered in her eyes and her lips trembled.

They rode on side by side. Fedovsky was so deeply moved that he could not speak. He almost longed for the ride to be at an end, in order that he might grapple with his poverty and conquer it. " Your family will not take this as you have done," he said at last."

" You have not told them, have you ? "

" Not yet."

" Well, I will tell them. And I will tell them that we love each other, too."

" There can be no engagement between us," said Fedovsky. " I have no right to ask or allow that. You must promise nothing."

" A promise is nothing in itself," she replied. " There would be no good in my keeping a promise that I wished to break, and no need of my making one that I can not help keeping. It's all in our hearts."

" It will be very hard not to meet you, or hear from you," said Fedovsky, after an interval. " Would you like to have me leave New York ? "

" No ; stay here, if you can. I had rather not see you of my own free will, than not to be able to do it. And I will not write to you, either," she added. " My father would not allow it, and I do not wish to disobey him, or to deceive him. I shall only think of you — nothing more than that : but that will be every thing."

"But it may be a long time," he said. "How long will you wait?"

"As long as I live," Sallie answered.

They were now at the upper end of the park. By a common impulse they both reined in their horses.

"You shall not wait as long as that," Fedovsky said.

"Do not be anxious," she returned. "We love each other. Let us part here. Good-by, my love."

She stretched out her right hand, from which she had removed her glove. He took it and clasped it strongly He relinquished it abruptly, turned his horse and rode away. It had all passed in a moment, but the effect upon both of them was visible. As the young Russian passed Duffy, the groom, the latter stared at the strange expression of his face, which looked at him without seeing him. As for Sallie, her face was protected by her veil, and she moved on without turning her head.

Fedovsky rode back to the livery stable and left his horse there. Then he walked to the hotel, where Tom had his valise ready-packed, in preparation for their departure. It had been arranged that they were to be driven to the Grand Central Railway station in the hotel stage, and left there as if on their way to some place out of town. The trunks were to remain at the hotel until he either returned or sent for them ; and meanwhile, with an impulse to be rid once for all of any mortgage on the past, he paid his bill in the face of Tom's protests, and off they went.

Where they would bring up was a question that Fedovsky could not have answered. In his visit to the slums of New York he had not been given an opportunity to examine the abiding-places of that class of persons who do not combine rascality with poverty Such places are not a stimulating spectacle ; they are merely dull and depressing, and are consequently not recommended to the curiosity of sensation hunters. But to those who are compelled to occupy them they are not devoid of a certain interest and importance ; and now that the young Russian's lot was to be cast in these regions, he found his imagination awake.

Tom's early experiences of the city proved of convenience at this juncture. He knew of the existence of twenty-five cent hotels, and where they were to be found. To one of these they must needs go ; for the liquidation of their hotel bill had reduced their capital to a figure scarcely worth mentioning. They could lodge at the hotel for two and a half dollars a week : their board would probably cost them double that : and this divisor would go into their quotient a very limited number of times, indeed. Starvation is a hard word, and some people are inclined to pooh-pooh it altogether: but it is apt to loom large before the eyes of those who can calculate on their fingers the number of days to elapse before (barring a stroke of good luck) their means of buying any thing to eat will have been exhausted. But, of course, Fedovsky had no idea of starving : he meant to make a fortune, marry Sallie, and live happy ever after. And he was going to begin immediately!

Success seldom comes at the moment when we believe that we most want it ; and Fedovsky's experiences during the ensuing month or more were of quite an unsuccessful kind. This fact may be recorded ; but there is no necessity for us to travel the downward path step by step with him. Every day he went forth in the hopes of finding some employment, and every night he returned to his lodgings without having found any His money melted away with alarming rapidity ; and had not Tom found a position for himself as ostler in a livery stable, their state would soon have become desperate, indeed. But Tom's wages were barely sufficient for himself ; it was nearly an impossibility for two persons to subsist upon them in any fashion whatever. Fedovsky, moreover, felt that it would be better to starve promptly by himself than to help Tom to starve slowly. Accordingly, after awhile, he gave Tom to understand that he had actually been given a position as bookkeeper in a small shop down town, with a stipend of six dollars a week. By this ingenious expedient he expected to escape the necessity of refusing his former valet's alms, as well as of entering into any painful argument. As it turned out, however, he might have spared himself even this trouble.

Tom received the news with all his customary enthusiasm, and prognosticated an immediate and splendid turn of fortune. This engagement would immediately lead to another and a better, and in a short time they would both be fairly on the high-road to wealth. Fedovsky had the name and location of his supposed employer ready, in case he should be questioned about it ; but Tom, secure in the future, never thought of descending to mere details. In the course of the conversation that evening, moreover, he informed Fedovsky that he had again seen his brother, and had made an appointment to meet him the following day, to discuss a certain project which the latter had formed, and which, Tom surmised, would be likely to lead to the best results for all concerned. Fedovsky had his own opinion about that ; but he forbore to say any thing about it, being too much preocupied with his own prospects.

The next morning, Tom went off early to his stable. He had received leave of absence for the afternoon, to meet his brother, and would not return home till late. Fedovsky, for his part, dressed himself carefully, took his walking-stick and sauntered out of his hotel with the air of a gentleman who has a large business under his control, and is not obliged to hurry himself in order to keep in the van. No one would have supposed, to look at him, that he was on his last legs. His clothes appeared neat and fashionable : his linen was clean ; his boots were polished. His face was somewhat thinner and paler than before, and his gait had not its usual elasticity ; but ruddiness and activity are not the prerogative of millionaires.

As a matter of fact, the young Russian had lost hope, and every thing else, except the desire to appear decent, and like a gentleman, to the last. To-day, for the first time, he had decided to abandon the attempt to get employment. It was not in him to entreat, to plead, to vociferate, to carry his point and recommend himself by sheer audacity and persistence. At the first rebuff, he turned away ; had he staid longer, he might have been asked to stay permanently. He saw the defect in himself, but it was not one that he could remedy— especially on an empty stomach and with nothing in his pocket. So, to-day, instead of making the dreary rounds of shop after shop and office after office, he walked quietly along an east-side street until he came to the Battery, where he seated himself on a bench. It was a fine warm day of early summer. The Bay was blue and animated with shipping; the trees and grass around him were green; the sunshine lay brightly on all. It recalled to his mind his days the previous winter at Monte Carlo, under such different conditions. Was he really the same man ?

Hour after hour passed by, and the noon whistle, the signal to cease work, sounded from a thousand steam-pipes. Fedovsky had no work to pretermit ;

neither had he any luncheon to go to. But he took a biscuit from his pocket, with the careless air of a man who is hardly certain whether or not he feels an appetite, and nibbled at it until it was gone. Then he arose and strolled toward a fountain, where he drank two cups of water. Continuing his stroll, at a leisurely pace, he arrived at the west side of the town, and proceeded along the street that bounds the city there. Wharf after wharf was passed, with steamers and vessels lying moored, bound for lands which he would never see again. Here, too, was the ferry slip at which he had landed a few months before, full of sanguine anticipations. Bearing now towards the right, he emerged from a medley of small streets into Broadway, just at the Astor House; and, as he stood at the corner, he saw Fred Vanderblick descend the steps, with his straw hat on the back of his head, and a quill tooth-pick in his mouth. He had evidently just bolted another lunch. The young banker sprang across the street, dodging among the vehicles, and was soon lost on the opposite sidewalk. Apparently he was just as jolly and hearty as ever. Fedovsky wondered whether this friend had ever regretted his disappearance, or had taken any measures to discover his whereabouts. He had often speculated as to how the Vanderblick family had received Sallie's revelation of his fallen state. He had never learned any thing on the subject—as was but natural, insomuch as he had taken every precaution to keep out of the way of all his former acquaintances, and had not even looked into a newspaper for weeks.

He crossed over to the City Hall Park, and found a seat on another bench.   The benches were well patronized : the occupants were mostly subdued in demeanor and shabby of attire ; some dozed as they sat : others stared at nothing with lack-luster eyes ; all of them looked as if they would be the better for a square meal.   Most of them, probably, were failures in one way or another.   What were they waiting for ? Fedovsky fell to thinking of the Reign of Terror in the French Revolution : how the condemned prisoners sat in the prisons, waiting for the tumbril and the guillotine.   Were these people waiting for the river and the morgue ?

He sat among them, leaning forward on his knees, and with his hat tipped down over his brows, drawing figures in the sand with the tip of his cane. None of the others spoke to him.   He appeared too much of a swell to have any right there.   What business had a well-dressed, prosperous, aristocratic person with such as they ? Had he come to spy upon them and ridicule them ? Let him first find out what hunger meant !

Fedovsky had a very fair understanding of the sensation in question.   But there was something in his blood and breeding which prompted him to preserve an unruffled and immaculate front before the world to the last.   He was wearing his last clean shirt, and he was fastidiously careful to preserve the whiteness and smoothness of his collar

and cuffs. He might have gone to any one of a
dozen acquaintances, who might not have heard
of his misfortunes, and got himself invited to dinner or to spend the night. But he could not bring
himself to it. He had in his pocket the unused
visitors' cards of a couple of clubs. There was
nothing to prevent his going to one or other of
them and ordering all he wanted ; nothing, that is,
except himself. Or, again, there were his trunks at
the hotel up town. Why did he not go there, take
them out of the baggage-room, and live upon what
the nearest pawnbroker would give him for their
contents ? The obstacles in the way of this course
seemed trifling, and yet they were sufficient. It
would involve paying a fee of two or three dollars
at least for storage money, and a couple of dollars to a hack-driver to take the trunks to his
room. True, he might explain that he would pay
these sums as soon as he should have pawned something ; but that was an explanation that he could
not sacrifice his pride to make. But would he
rather starve to death than submit to so slight a
humiliation ? Well, at all events, he would not
make the submission.

After awhile he discovered that he had been
writing the name " Sallie " upon the ground with
his cane. He erased it hurriedly, the blood rushing
to his face as he did so. He got up, rather languidly, and continued his walk. Traversing back
streets, as before, he came at length to Washington
Square. Here were more benches, more green

trees and grass, and more undemonstrative sitters. He took his silent place among them. The sun went slowly toward the west. At six o'clock the whistles sounded again. New York was about to sit down to its dinner. Fedovsky took out a biscuit and ate it as slowly as he could ; then another. Then to a fountain once more. He drank as much as he could. Water costs nothing. Then he walked slowly back to his twenty-five cent inn. He would hear the result of Tom's interview : perhaps, after all, something might come of it. Tom had not returned when he arrived. He waited for him a long time, but still he came not. At last he went to bed, and lay half awake all night. In the morning, Tom had not appeared.

Fedovsky dressed himself, taking a long time over his toilet, partly from customary fastidiousness, but more from bodily weakness. At nine o clock he left his room, and having requested the attendant to tell Tom, in case of his return, that he had gone to the livery-stable, he took his way thither. It was a tedious journey and Fedovsky was suffering much pain. At the stable he learned that Tom had not been heard from since the previous morning. He lingered about there for an hour or two—in vain. He went back to the lodging-house : Tom was not there. It was noon. He dragged himself to the City Hall park, and lunched there: he was obliged to eat three biscuits this time. He hardly knew whether they relieved him or made him feel worse. He got back to the inn : but Tom was not there. What could have happened ? Could Tom have deserted him ? This brother was a thief. What if they had arranged something between them ? Fedovsky stopped short in this path of speculation. He could not bear to pursue it. He would rather think that some accident had happened. Yet, if Tom had been injured, he would surely have communicated the fact to Fedovsky, by some means : and if he had been killed, news of it would be in the papers. But there was no news of the kind.

The young Russian was more disheartened by this event than by any thing that had happened to him. It was like putting the last brick in the wall that shuts a man out from light and life forever. His mind now run on only the gloomiest ideas. And, in fact, he was at the end of his tether. He had in his pockets seven biscuits, and a five-cent nickel. He could no longer remain at his lodgings. That night, accordingly, he sat very late on his bench : and at last, when the park had been deserted by the latest straggler, he lay down upon it, with his head on his arm.

The night was warm and dry ; but Fedovsky felt cold. He closed his eyes : his thoughts wandered : strange fancies visited him—a sort of conscious delirium. Vera, Sallie and Tom were mingled in a fantastic dance. In a few minutes he would have been asleep.

Suddenly he was aroused with a start, and a sharp, jarring sensation, and a rough voice said :

"Get up, now, young fellow.　Can't have no loafers here ! "

It was a policeman, who had rapped on the soles of the homeless man's feet with his club.　As soon as Fedovsky comprehended the situation, he arose without a word and dragged himself away.　He came to another park, and, overcome with weakness, lay down as before.　Again he was rudely awakened, and driven on.　In this manner he spent the night.

The morning broke : the level beams of the eastern sun shone along the streets long before the traffic of the day began.　Fedovsky sat on a bench, with his arms folded.　He scarcely knew where he was : his brain acted sluggishly　He felt less pain than the day before, but a greater weakness.　By and by he remembered his biscuits, and, taking them out one by one, he ate them all.　He drank a cup of water, and felt a little refreshed.　But where was his next meal to come from ?　And could he endure another night in the streets such as he had just passed ?　He looked at his shirt-cuffs : they were soiled and dingy.　His boots, too, had lost their polish, and one of them was spattered with mud by a watering-cart.　A boot-black came along the path, with his box on his back.　He glanced at the boots.　" Shine ? "　Fedovsky nodded.　" How much ? " he asked, as the boy knelt before him and put his box in position.　" Nickel," replied the boy　" I can give you only three cents," returned the other.　The boy looked up at him, and after a moment ducked his head, in token of assent. Fedovsky put up his foot, and the operation began. When it was over, and the money paid, Fedovsky arose, and set out southward, in the direction of the East River ferries. He had two cents to pay his fare on a boat. But he had made up his mind what to do. He was resolved not to go more than half-way across the river. The broken down young nobleman made his way slowly along the crowded and sunny streets. It was beautiful weather ; the whole city seemed to be enjoying life. Life offers us so many enjoyable things,— so many means of enjoyment ! Surely, that human being must needs be very desperate who would voluntarily give up life altogether.

Fedovsky had made up his mind ; but he had plenty of time before him ; and his settled purpose had rendered him composed and indifferent. The secret knowledge that he was saying farewell to the world restored his dignity and self-respect. He trod the pavement with a free and leisurely step, and no longer avoided the fashionable thoroughfares. A man who is willing to surrender his life to preserve his respectability has a right to hold up his head with the most prosperous gentleman alive.

Leaving the little park behind the Reservoir, he proceeded eastward along West Fortieth Street ; and, by a sudden whim of memory, he recollected that his friend Mr. Williams had given his address as No. 15 on West Forty-first Street. This would place his residence at about the center of the Reservoir. Fedovsky smiled. The discovery was a confirmation of Tom's suspicions. The man must have been a swindler. Well, he could forgive him now. It was so easy to be a rascal ; and the young Russian knew, by experience, how numerous and powerful may be the attractions to rascality.

When he was a few rods west of Fifth Avenue, he saw a lady on horseback riding past the mouth of the street toward Central Park. He knew her at a glance. His heart gave a bound, and his eyes brightened. Involuntarily he quickened his step and raised his hand to attract her attention. But she passed on without regarding him. Had she seen him ? Who could tell ? But, at all events, it was better that she should pass him by. Nothing but pain could result from their meeting, and he, at least, had already suffered pain enough. To-morrow, perhaps, she would hear of something that had happened. If she were sorry, what more need he ask ?

He entered the avenue, and turned southward. He passed a couple of clubs, the cards of which were in his pocket ; he glanced up at the windows, but they were empty Was this accidental, or had the customary loungers betaken themselves into the background on the appearance of his once familiar and welcome figure ? Well, it was all over now.

He strolled on, leaving Madison Square on the left, and still following the avenue. A few blocks below, he saw three men approaching him,—Colo-

nel Jack Oakley, Dr. Warren Beale, and Judge
Farren. The doctor nodded to him, as he passed,
rather stiffly ; the judge apparently failed to see
him at all ; but the florid colonel stopped, and held
out his hand.

"Hello, count!" he said, "how are you ? Glad
to see you again. Was afraid you'd run off and
left us. Come back to stay, I hope ?"

"No ; I leave to-day."

"Oh, come, none of that ! Look here, Fedovsky," said the colonel, dropping his voice, and lay-
ing a kindly hand on the other's arm, "what you
want to do is to keep a stiff upper lip. You don't
know the American people ; what they want is to
see a man take his own part. There's been a lot
of rot talked about you in the club ; and Fred Vanderblick and I had words the other day about the
shabby way he's chucked you up. Well, fellows
will talk—but I can tell you that three-fourths of
the boys would back you up, if you'd turn round
and face it out. Half of 'em have been in a hole
themselves, as bad as you have. As I tell 'em,
you're as straight as a string. You ain't in debt ;
they haven't been able to find a gentleman or a
tradesman that you owe a cent to. And that's why,
if you want money, all you've got to do is to say so.
You may count on me for a hundred, for one,—
only say the word, that's all ! And if you want to
take hold and work a bit, there's a dozen chances I
know of myself ! Never say die !"

"I thank you heartily," replied Fedovsky, turning his grave eyes on the other's face. "I am glad I met you to-day, and know how you feel. You are a good fellow, and I shall remember it—as long as I live. But there are reasons why I had better go. As for money," he added, thinking of the two cents in his pocket, "I have all I need. When I get to the other side, I shall be all right—I hope."

"I hope so, too, my boy—I do indeed!" returned the colonel, again grasping the Russian's hand, and feeling, perhaps, a little the easier and more cordial because his offer of "a hundred" had not been snapped up. "I wish you'd stay here, and follow my advice : but, if you can get straight again by going to the other side, that may be the best thing after all. You'll come back again, of course?"

The count shook his head, with the ghost of a smile. "I think not," he said.

"Oh, yes, you will!" replied the colonel, unconscious of the ghostly nature of his prediction : "and at any rate, I expect to be over there before long! Well, good-by, in the meantime, old fellow: and good voyage to you!"

The two men parted, and the colonel swung along up the avenue, while the count continued his way in the opposite direction. Why had he not accepted the colonel's proposal? There can be no rational answer to such a question. But there can be little doubt that the purpose to take one's own life, once seriously formed, fascinates the will and can be turned aside only by causes beyond the intending suicide's control.

CHAPTER XIV

A PROFESSION.

THERE were, as has been remarked, many points of Fedovsky's story to which the inspector had listened with more evident interest than to others ; and two or three times he had scribbled down some hasty notes. The narrative having now been brought down to the hour of the adventure on Nassau Street, and there being nothing more to relate, he got up from his chair and paced up and down the room in silence, as was his habit when thinking deeply. The young Russian, meanwhile, remained seated, in a rather dejected frame of mind. The stimulus occasioned by the reminiscences called up by his tale, had now subsided, and was succeeded by a fit of depression. What a wretched failure his life had been! And how small seemed the chance that it could ever become any thing better !

The inspector resumed his seat. Fedovsky looked up, and met the eyes of the detective steadily regarding him.

" Young man," said the latter. " You ought to be able to make your way in the world. You have many advantages. Physically you are strong and active, and your appearance predisposes one in your favor. You are thoroughly educated and an accomplished linguist. You have mingled much in society, and know something about human nature. You have traveled, and are familiar with foreign countries and customs. More than that, you are a man of unusual intelligence : you have a clear mind, an excellent memory, you are accustomed to observe, and you possess a great deal of natural penetration and sagacity, when you choose to exercise it. How can a man like you fail to make a living ?"

"You can probably guess as well as I can, inspector," replied the other, with a sigh. "The fact is, I don't know what to go to work at. I am not especially interested in any thing. I suppose I could perform routine work in business, but there are plenty of men who can do that as well or better than I ; and it would give no opportunity for me to use whatever particular advantages I may possess. If I could only find some employment where such gifts and accomplishments as I have could be utilized to their full worth, I think I could get on. But what is there ? I can think of nothing."

"I have been considering that very question," the inspector answered, "and I don't know but I might find an answer to it."

"I would be profoundly thankful if you would tell me what it is," said Fedovsky.

"I agree with you that the routine of ordinary business would not give you a fair chance," the other continued. "You have become accustomed to change and movement, and to a certain amount of adventure. If you could be supplied with some definite aim and object, which would include such a life, you might do well."

" I believe I could : but—"

" Wait a moment ! There may be an obstacle. You are a nobleman in your own country, and you have the traditions and ideas of a gentleman. In this country, we believe that honest work, no matter of what kind, is good enough for any man. Are you yet American enough to take any stock in that idea ? "

" I certainly am ! " exclaimed Fedovsky, with energy.

" The work that I am thinking of, whatever it may be, or whatever may be thought of it, in other countries, is nothing to be ashamed of here. It is hard work, and it is honest work ; and it is not only honest, but its object is to help honest men to their rights, to secure the safety of property, and to bring rascals to their deserts. I speak confidently, for I know what I am talking about. The work is that to which I have devoted my life ; and I can say that there has never been a time when I have found cause to regret it ! " The inspector had spoken forcibly : he now suddenly changed his tone, leaned back in his chair, and added, as he lit a cigar, " How would you like to be a detective ?"

The question took Fedovsky at unawares, and startled him not a little. Had it been put to him by any other man than the one before him, he might have hesitated, or asked time for consideration. But there was something about Inspector Byrnes that had strongly attracted him, from the first moment of their meeting : he was, in his own person, the best argument that could be adduced in favor of his profession. So it was after only a moment's delay that Fedovsky gave his answer.

" If you think I can do it," said he, " I will do the best I can to warrant your good opinion. I should be glad to serve under you ; and if I fail, it will be the fault of my faculties, and never of my will."

The inspector smiled, and nodded his head. " So far, so good," he remarked. " But you don't yet know exactly what I want of you. I didn't contemplate sending you on the force in the ordinary way. You will have a great deal to learn, and after all, you would probably be no better than anybody else, if so good. But you are a special man, and you will be required for special work. I have no idea of sending you round the slums to pick up information about common rascals. You will be wanted for something much less commonplace, and, in a certain sense, much more difficult. In fact, I want you for a special case which no one except some such man as you could execute properly My intention is to put you on the Secret Service ; and it will be so secret, in this instance, that no one except you and myself will know that you belong to it."

Fedovsky's countenance, which, at the first

announcement of the inspector's scheme, had taken on an expression of resigned resolution, now brightened perceptibly.

"I should have better hopes of that," he said. "Is there any particular thing that you had thought of for me to do ?"

"I don't say but there is. Thanks to the criminals, there is never any lack of employment in our business. There are more things to do than there are men of the right sort to do them. What would you think of a trip to Europe ?"

"I should know my way about there, at any rate."

"Yes ; and you would have to do a good deal more than that. You would have to measure yourself against the cleverest and most dangerous gang of rogues that is to be found anywhere."

"But what have the American police to do with rogues in Europe ?"

"The rogues are in Europe, but they came from this country,—and I want you to apprehend them if possible !" added the inspector, letting his palm fall on the table, with a significant look.

"Do you believe I can do it, inspector ?" demanded he, looking the detective in the face with a gaze as searching as his own. "You know the conditions and the difficulties better than I do. Do you believe I can do it ?"

"You can, if you will."

"Then I will !" answered Fedovsky ; and the tone and look with which he said it satisfied the other that he had a man before him who would let

nothing stand in the way of keeping his word. It
was characteristic of the inspector, as of other
men who have achieved an honorable position by
their own innate force, to choose wisely the men
best qualified to co-operate with him, and to inspire
them with an enthusiasm to carry out his designs.
This faculty is sometimes called magnetism ; but
it is a combination of insight, tact and energy, and
is born with its possessor, not acquired by him.

Having thus come to an understanding with his
new lieutenant, the inspector proceeded to unfold
something of the matter he had especially in view.
There had lately been, it appeared, an attempt to
negotiate some forged bonds in Europe. The
forgeries had been executed in this country, and
the gang had then proceeded to Liverpool : but,
when all was ready, an unexpected hitch had
occurred. Another American rascal, acting independently, and with no knowledge of the larger
operators, had been concocting a small forgery of
his own : this had been detected by the European
police, and the man had been apprehended and
taken into custody. The authorities were therefore on the alert : and the managers of the larger
enterprise deemed it unsafe to act. The subordinates whom they had brought over to serve as
"layers-down" therefore found themselves without employment, and, money for their support not
being forthcoming in sufficient quantity, they
began to show symptoms of discontent and insubor-
dination. Finally, they received their tickets back

to New York ; where they engaged in new schemes with other parties, and were ultimately arrested by the exertions of the authorities.

"But there is not much gained by arresting subordinates, so long as the principals remain at large," the inspector observed. "There will always be men enough to do the physical part of the work : it's the planners and organizers that really make the mischief : and it's after them that I am sending you."

"How happens it that they have not been arrested already?" inquired Fedovsky. "Did the subordinates refuse to testify against them?"

"Their subordinates did not know who they were," was the reply. "The principals in a scheme are very seldom known to those who carry out their instructions : and most seldom of all in the case of the great forgers. Nobody really knows who they are : though there may be persons," added the inspector, stroking his chin, "who could give a shrewd guess at it."

"And what is your guess?" asked Fedovsky, with a smile.

"That is just what I am not going to tell you. I may believe that I could name correctly the men I want : or, I might say, the man I want : for there is probably one man at the bottom of it all. But my impression is not derived from actual knowledge or evidence of facts ; but from inference. Now inference is all very well to convince one's self : but it can not put the bracelets on a thief.   You must find the facts that prove my inferences, and then the work will be done."

" But why don't you tell me whom you suspect ? "

" Because your facts will be worth ten times as much if you get at them independently.   If you take your cue from me, and I happen to be wrong, you would go wrong too.   I might tell you, for instance, that you would not have to look far ; even among your own acquaintance, to find some traces of the man I am thinking of : but I shall not be more explicit.   If you work up the thing on your own account, you may still make a mistake : but if your investigations should lead you to the same conclusion that my deductions have led me—we should have the next thing to a certainty.   No : you must begin with no prepossession whatever, except a close scrutiny of one of the persons mentioned in your narrative."

" You can, at any rate, give me instructions how to go to work.   All I know now is, that a forgery was planned, but not executed, in England : and that the persons who did the work are there yet."

" Such fellows as we are after are not apt to remain long idle," replied the inspector, " and when that enterprise fell through, I made up my mind that we should hear of something new before long, and I didn't have long to wait.   I have reason to believe that a new scheme is already afoot, and that it is the heaviest of the kind that was ever undertaken.   If it accomplishes all that is expected of it, the profits will run into millions."

" How were you able to find that out ? " asked Fedovsky, in surprise.

" If I were like some of the detectives in French novels, I might leave you to think that I knew by intuition every thing that goes on in New York," was the answer: "but, as I am only a flesh-and-blood American, the explanation is simple enough. There is a class of persons in the city who, though not actually engaged in crime, are the acquaintances and companions of criminals, and are supposed by the latter to be trustworthy. I make it a point to know them and use them: they are my ' shadows '; they are not known to be such to one another, nor to any one else but myself. I meet one or other of them every night, at some appointed spot, and receive their reports. In this way I am kept informed of the movements and whereabouts of most of the noted criminals in America ; and if one of them leaves New York or elsewhere, I am on the watch for news of him. Some time ago I got information that several men, whom I knew to be forgers, had left New York in a transatlantic steamer. They landed in Europe ; and, by correspondence with the European authorities, I learned their addresses, and the aliases under which they passed. These men are not now at their addresses in England : neither have they returned to this country—at least, all of them have not. At the same time, I hear that certain swindling operations have been attempted upon some of our banking houses and financial institutions. For this reason,

I want to bring them to justice, as a number of our financiers are interested in the matter. They have been testing the quality of their forgeries and evidently they must be of unusual excellence. Having satisfied themselves of that, they will now proceed to operate on a gigantic scale. But you must be on the ground, and capture them in the very act !"

The inspector spoke with energy, and his listener's pulse quickened as he heard him. So aroused had he become, in fact, that he already longed to be at his work, and to prove that he could achieve all that was expected of him. " What shall I do first ?" he said.

" I can not foretell the contingencies that may arise," announced the inspector, " and you will often have to be guided by your own judgment at the moment. But there are some general hints that you may follow. You will travel, as you have hitherto done, in the style of a gentleman of wealth and leisure. You will inform yourself what banks have been swindled, and, by discreet inquiries, you will obtain a description, more or less accurate, of the personal appearance of the men supposed to be implicated in them. You may thus get on the track of the subordinates. That will be the easiest part of your work. You must be careful not to let any of these men suspect your real character and pur-pose. Your business will be to discover the person with whom they are in communication. He will be the middle-man, or go-between ; and he, and he alone, will be cognizant of the identity of the chief and ruler of the gang. If you can get at this chief, your work will be done, and you will have also solved a great problem. For up to this time, whatever our suspicions may be, he is, as a matter of fact, a mystery. No one can say with certainty, ' This is he.' He may turn out to be the very last person you would think of. But if you are patient, diligent and careful, you will find him."

" And until he is found, I am to make no arrests ? " Fedovsky inquired.

" Unless for some extraordinary reason—no ! to arrest one of the subordinates would be to give the alarm to the principal, and then the chance of capturing him would be hopeless. You have to deal with some of the shrewdest of men, and you must be shrewder than they."

" When am I to start ? "

" In a few days : after you have learned some of the technical details of our manner of work. You will proceed directly to London, and thence to the Continent."

" You have spoken very frankly to me, inspector," remarked the young count, with a smile. " How do you know that I am not myself in league with the forgers ? "

The detective also smiled. " Perhaps I know more about you than you imagine," he said quietly. " A great deal of what you have told me did not come to me as news. Since you disappeared from society life here, it has been a part of my business to work up your record. The reports brought to me coincide very well with your own version of your career, and neither does you any discredit. May I ask, by the way, whether you have made any thorough inquiry into the cause of the sequestration of your Russian estates, or any attempt to recover them ? "

" Nothing to speak of. By doing so, I might have lost the only other thing remaining to me—my personal liberty ; for I could have done nothing without going to St. Petersburg."

" Still, it might be worth while to bear the matter in mind," the inspector answered. " It appears that one, at least, of your agents was a rascal : and there is no telling but that somebody may have been telling lies about you to the authorities, with a view to getting hold of your property However, that is for you to consider. I will give you an address where you can find lodgings, and you will report here to me when notified. You will receive a regular salary, and when you start on your expedition, you will keep an account of your expenses, and draw upon me for them. I will see that your trunks are taken from the hotel, and brought to your rooms. I suppose they contain a wardrobe sufficient to supply you during your tour ? "

" More than sufficient."

" Very good. You will travel under your own name, and act in all outward respects as if you were exactly in the position you occupied before your loss of property took place. If you run across any of your acquaintances in this city, before you leave, you can tell them, if they are inquisitive, that you have been advised to look into the condition of your affairs abroad, and that you expect to be back here again in the spring. As regards this little affair of the bank messenger, you may possibly be called as a witness to the assault, but you need give yourself no further trouble about it. Thanks to you, Messrs. Vanderblick have not lost their bonds."

"Were Vanderblicks the owners?" exclaimed Fedovsky, with a start. He colored under the inspector's glance, and added, "Didn't I see something on the bulletins about their being concerned in a panic on the street?"

"There was such a report, I believe : and they seem to be on the wrong side of the market. There was an unexpected combination against them, and a very strong one. It is a matter one would sooner hear about than be mixed up in, apparently."

" A fortunate escape for me," thought Fedovsky : "but will it be serious enough to affect Sallie?" But as the inspector could not be expected to answer this question, the young Russian contented himself with expressing to him the thankfulness he felt at having been thus extricated from the jaws of an ignominious death : and after a few concluding words, the two men shook hands with heartiness, and parted. Fedovsky was conducted to his new lodgings ; and the inspector was left to the consciousness of having done a good thing, from a business as well as a philanthropic point of view.

In a few days afterwards Fedovsky had another long interview with the inspector, and receiving full instructions, shortly after left for the Continent.

CHAPTER XV

IN the winter of the same year, a stranger alighted at the Boehmische Bahnhof in Dresden, engaged a droschky, and was driven to the Bellevue Hotel. Having inscribed in the hotel register the name of Ivan Fedovsky, he was assigned a good room, had his trunks moved into it, dressed himself carefully, and came down-stairs to the *table d'hôte*.

It was then one o'clock in the afternoon: a clear, fine day, not too cold. The table was well attended; but after the soup had been served, another guest entered the room, sauntered down to a seat on the same side of the table as Fedovsky's, and a little distance below him. He had not noticed Fedovsky; but the latter recognized him immediately. He made no sign, however; but, during the course of the meal, he did a good deal of quiet thinking.

The company consisted largely of American and English visitors, many of whom were acquainted with one another, and kept up a running accompaniment of conversation to the clatter of dishes

and forks.   The stranger did not join in this talk ;
he seemed to be known to no one, and, beyond the
few words required by the courtesies of the table,
he ate his dinner in silence.   But he had taken the
precaution to fee the waiter on entering, and no
one was better served than he.

After the coffee had been brought on, and he had
swallowed a small cupful of it, he rose from the
table, and sauntered out.   In a moment, Fedovsky
followed his example.   When he reached the hall,
he saw the stranger, with his hat on, turning into
a passage which led to the covered terrace on the
Elbe.

This terrace ran the length of the hotel on the
river side, and was filled from end to end with
chairs and small square tables.   It was protected
by a glass covering from the cold air of winter ;
though in summer this was removed, and an awn-
ing substituted, to ward off the rays of the sun.
Immediately below the terrace the river flowed
along, sparkling in the sun, with many a ripple
and eddy.   The quaint old stone bridge, with its
many piers and arches, built solidly to enable it to
withstand the shock of the masses of ice driven
downward by the winter floods, spanned the
stream a few rods higher up the bank.   Across it,
two streams of people and vehicles were constantly
moving in opposite directions, those on one side
being bound for the Allstadt, and those on the
other for the Neustadt.   The hotel was situated in
the latter division of the city ; and looking across

the river, Fedovsky could see the large blocks of buildings looking down into the current on the Neustadt side. The stream here was between two and three hundred yards in breadth; and the whole scene was a bright and attractive one.

Meanwhile the stranger had seated himself at a table on the verge of the terrace, commanding a favorable view of the bridge, and of the course of the river beyond. He had just ordered a glass of cognac of the waiter, and was lighting a cigar. Fedovsky stepped up behind him, and laid his hand lightly on his shoulder.

"How do you do, Mr. Williams?" he said.

The other finished lighting his cigar, and flung away the match before he turned round. He then shifted his position in a leisurely manner, and glanced up with an inexpressive face at his accoster. But the next instant a look of recognition brightened his features, he rose, and took the count's hand with a smile.

"Well, I'm glad to see you," he exclaimed. "Let's see, it was in Monte Carlo, wasn't it? What have you been doing with yourself ever since?"

"I spent the summer in New York," replied Fedovsky. "I came back here a month or two ago."

"In New York, eh?" said the other, with a keen look, but still smiling. "Well, how is the old place looking? Sit down, and let's hear about it. Things move there quicker than they do here, don't they?"

"I liked it very well; in fact, I had some idea

of staying there permanently. I was obliged to come back here to attend to some business ; but I may return some day."

" Well, I don't know ; I'm always talking of going home ; but somehow or other I don't get there," said Williams. " If you want to sail in and do something, New York s the place ; but if you want to loaf and have a good time, it isn't bad over here. I recollect your speaking of making the trip when you were in Monte Carlo."

" I had had thoughts of asking you to give me some letters of introduction to some friends over there," remarked Fedovsky, "but you all disappeared so suddenly that I missed my opportunity "

Williams looked up with an easy laugh. " So we did, and that's a fact ! " said he. " I've often wondered what you must have thought of it, when you came to look us up the next day. But there was no help for it. She got a telegram that same night from her lawyers in Paris, obliging her to take the next train over there. There was something wrong about a certificate of income, and she had to be on the spot to sign the papers. I happened in the next morning and found her with her trunks packed, ready to start. I thought I might help her through : there was just time to stuff a change of clothes into a valise, and off we went. I dropped you a line from Paris afterwards, but I guess you must have left. It came back to me a couple of months later through the dead-letter office."

"Well, I hope the princess's journey was success-ful?" said Fedovsky.

"Oh, I guess so; she is pretty well fixed; though no doubt the prince's relatives would fire her out of the property if they found a chance."

"Where is she now?" inquired the other.

"I haven't got her address," was the reply, "but the last time I saw her, she told me she thought of passing the winter somewhere in Italy. Can't we manage it so as to go on there together, sometime, and look her up? She remembers you well."

"I'll think about it. I only arrived here this forenoon. Are you making a long stay?"

"I came last night, and my plans aren't set-tled—they seldom are. But it's my first visit to Dresden, and I suppose I must go the rounds. Are you busy this afternoon?"

"No, nothing in particular."

"How would you like to go round with me to the Police Bureau?"

"To the Police Bureau!" exclaimed Fedovsky, in surprise. "What is there to do there?"

"Well, there's a funny story about that," returned the other, flipping the ash from his cigar, "and as it shows the kind of risks a man may run in these European dynasties, without even knowing it, I'll tell it to you. The joke is on me, but I can afford to laugh at a good thing, even at my own expense. I have noticed, for the last few months, that the police have seemed to take an uncommon deal of interest in me, and I was puzzled to account for it. I'm a very quiet man, as you know, and all I want is to loaf about and enjoy myself.   But when I was in Paris (I have just come from there), I made up my mind that I was being followed about by a detective ; I questioned him, and at last I got at the truth.   I lost no time in going to headquarters, and getting myself set right ; and now that I have come to a strange place, I intend to take time by the forelock, and visit the police before they visit me."

"But I don't understand; what is the difficulty ?" Fedovsky inquired   He fancied that he had fairly good grounds for believing that Williams had something shady about him ; the positive manner in which Tom had declared that he was identical with the card-sharper who had swindled him in New York, and the fact that the address upon his card had turned out to be in the middle of the Reservoir, lending color to this impression.   When he ran across him unexpectedly in the hotel dining-room, he had resolved to accost him with a view to gaining more light upon the matter; for it might turn out that the man was in some way connected with the business that had brought him to Europe, and concerning which he had, thus far, been able to learn little that was of consequence.   Williams's proposal to go to police headquarters naturally surprised him, and he did not know what to think of it.   He doubted whether the man were in earnest.

" I hope," he said, " that if the police ask you for some New York address, you will give them a more reasonable one than you did me. If any one lives at No. 15 West 41st Street, it must be a water-nixie or a merman; and you don't look like either."

Williams looked puzzled; but presently his face cleared up. " Oh, you got caught on that, did you ? " he said, with his amused laugh. " Well, I should have told you about that before, but I never thought of it. No, I'm not a nixie, nor a merman ; and I don't live at No. 15 West 41st Street. But I ran out of my American visiting-cards last year, and I had some more engraved in London. I gave the fellow my address, written on a piece of note-paper ; and when the cards were sent to me, I found he had got it 41st Street, instead of 47th Street—which was what I wrote. I used to make the correction with a pen, as a general thing ; but I suppose the card I gave you hadn't been altered. I'm sorry I should have seemed to throw cold water on your attempt to look me up."

This explanation sounded so extremely probable, and was given in so frank and, at the same time, so careless a manner, that Fedovsky felt a trifle embarrassed. It was certainly a little absurd to have suspected an otherwise agreeable and in-telligent companion, because his "7" had been mis-taken for a "1," and because Tom had fancied there was a likeness between him and a person he had met several years before. Upon the whole, Fedov-sky felt as if he owed Mr. Williams an apology.

But some apologies are better thought of than uttered ; so he contented himself with looking as if he had never considered the matter as of any consequence, and renewed his inquiry as to what was taking his companion to the Police Bureau.

" Well, look here," said Williams, taking out his watch, " it's getting late, and there's no need of your hearing the story twice over.   Let's make our call on the superintendent now, and then you can listen to it once for all."

Fedovsky had no objection to offer : Williams called up the waiter and paid him : they left the terrace, entered a droschky, and told the driver to take them to the Bureau.   In a few minutes he drew up before a dark, square building in a narrow street ; and Williams, followed by the count, alighted.   A brief parley with the door-keeper ensued, and then they were conducted to a small sitting-room on an upper floor, where a gentleman in a dark broadcloth coat was tramping up and down, like a wild animal caged. He turned sharply upon the visitors, and scrutinized them from head to foot with a single quick glance.

He was himself a remarkable looking personage, about five feet nine inches in height, of light but powerful build, he was as sudden and unexpected in his movements as a cat. His head was of unusual size, very much developed above the ears and at the back : the top was broad and rather flat : the fore-head comparatively contracted, but prominent over the eyebrows. Thin hair, of a pale yellowish hue, curling tightly, covered his cranium : his eyes, restless and penetrating, were of the hazel variety, and changed under the influence of thought or emotion, from light green to bluish black. His manner was marked by a nervous impatience and imperiousness, modified by the instinctive courtesy of good breeding. This was Baron Lemcke, the famous chief of Secret Police of Saxony : a man of remarkable gifts of intellect and character : endowed with a subtlety that nothing seemed to elude, and with a knowledge so deftly used that it gave the impression almost of omniscience. Nothing seemed too obscure for him to penetrate it ; and yet this singular personage was occasionally misled and hoodwinked by the most obvious devices, and was known to have been guilty of the most astounding mistakes and indiscretions. In fact, the baron was a genius, with the incredible powers and not less incredible infirmities of genius; and those who knew him best were scarcely surprised when, a few years after the date of the present story, his reason forsook him, and he was confined, a hopeless maniac, in an insane asylum. His sad collapse explained many things that had been inexplicable in his career.

CHAPTER XVI.

A QUESTION OF IDENTITY.

"GOOD-AFTERNOON, Mr. Williams—good-afternoon, Count Fedovsky," said the baron, abruptly addressing his two visitors by name, as if he had been acquainted with them for years. He spoke English with scarcely a perceptible accent. "Be seated," he continued, motioning them to chairs, while he himself remained standing. "What can I do for you?"

"I called on a business matter, of importance to myself," said Williams, in his easy voice, seating himself, and throwing one leg over the other: "and as I ran across my friend the count, here, this morning, I thought I'd just bring him around. I wanted to know if you could give me a little information. I guess you can, if you've a mind to."

"What is it?" demanded the baron, with the same nervous rapidity.

"I want to know," continued the other, looking the chief in the face with a keen smile, "whether you happen to have received a circular containing a description of a fellow by the name of Willis, who is said to be traveling in these parts, and to be the sort of man you would be likely to feel a professional interest in ? "

"We are not in the custom of discussing professional matters with strangers," replied the baron, seating himself at a table, and drumming with his long fingers on a pile of papers.

" Well, as regards this particular matter, I don't know as I come under the head of a stranger," said Williams composedly. " I've been mixed up in it once or twice already, and I'm anxious to get done with it, as far as Saxony is concerned. I'm not in search of any private information ; but if you would trouble yourself to run your eye over that circular, and draw your own conclusions, I should feel obliged to you."

There was a short silence, during which the baron treated Williams to a searching and point-blank gaze, which the latter returned without winking. Then he abruptly turned aside and opened a drawer. " What name ? " he demanded.

"Willis—Henry Willis, I believe he calls himself," was the reply.

The baron took a paper out of the drawer, and glanced over it. Then he looked up at his visitor, this time with a peculiar expression. " Would you wish me to read it ? " he said.

" That's what I'd like, if it isn't too much trouble," returned Williams, crossing his other leg, and settling himself comfortably in his chair.

The baron read as follows : " Henry Willis. American. Five feet ten inches in height. Slender build.   Straight hair, brown mustache.   Good forehead, aquiline nose, gray eyes.   Speaks slowly, pleasant address, well educated.   Gives himself out to be a retired merchant, traveling for pleasure. This man once kept a gambling den on one of the thoroughfares in New York.   Has been arrested three times, but discharged.   Is now believed to be a forger, the principal of a gang who intend to work the Continental bankers.   Has a brown mole on left cheek, just above mustache.   Age about 36."

"Thank you, baron," said Williams, who had listened to this description with an amused smile. "Well, I call that pretty straight, don't you ?   Did you ever see any body that at all resembled Mr. Henry Willis ?"

Fedovsky barely suppressed an exclamation of bewilderment.   The description which the baron had just read applied minutely to Williams himself. Figure, features, bearing, every thing was identical. A photograph would not have been so exact.   It seemed impossible not to believe that Williams and Willis were one and the same man.   And yet here was Williams deliberately visiting the lion's den, and demanding to be confronted with the evidence of his own criminality !   Did he intend confession and surrender ?

The baron, also, was obviously perplexed, though he endeavored to disguise it.   He gave another glance at the paper, laid it down, and scratched his chin.   Then he rose, walked to the door, opened it, and said a few words in an undertone to some one outside. On resuming his chair, he said in a vivacious tone, and with a smile that lighted up his face pleasantly, " Well, now, Mr. Williams, have you any statement to make ?"

" Something of the sort will be in order, I expect," rejoined Williams, chuckling to himself, and extracting from an inner pocket a large russia-leather wallet, stuffed full of letters and other documents. " When I'm asleep, I sometimes dream that I am Henry Willis, sure enough ; but when I'm awake, I remember several things that lead me to doubt it again. I don't know that I ever met the gentleman, in the flesh ; but lately I've met a number of persons who took it for granted that I was he ; and once or twice I have found a good deal of trouble in persuading them there might possibly be some mistake. So now I take care to be provided against all contingencies. I came last from Paris ; had a good deal of fuss there ; the French are clever fellows, but a little quick in jumping at conclusions, as perhaps you may have noticed in the late war ! "

The baron nodded his head and smiled slightly. The victory of Sedan was not yet so distant an event that Germans did not enjoy being reminded how wrong a conclusion the French had jumped at in that instance.

" Now, I have here," added Williams, unslipping the elastic band of his wallet, and opening it, " a collection of arguments to show that I, and the fellow who looks like me, are two different people ; or, at any rate, that I am not he. First, here is my passport, which I had made out last week, so as to be up with the times. Then, here is a letter from the United States minister to France, who is a personal acquaintance of mine; then, here is a communication from my lawyers in New York, relative to some investments of mine in Western railroad stock; next, you see, is a note from Sir William Vernon Harcourt, the English Home Secretary, whose wife is an American girl, and a cousin of mine by marriage, asking me to escort Lady Harcourt to the Gallery in .the House of Commons— division on the Land Bill; here is a line from W W Story, the American sculptor in Rome, speaking about a dinner; I only show it you because the date—October 3d—is one of the days on which Mr. Henry Willis is said to have been in Vienna; here's a receipt from Brown Bros., of London, for the sum of ten thousand pounds sterling, deposited with them in November, ten days ago; and—well, in short, here s the wallet, and you may keep all the Willis you can find in it !"

He had passed the papers to the baron, one after the other, as he mentioned them; and he now put the wallet on the table, and turned to Fedovsky with an arch smile.

The baron examined the documents with an impassive demeanor. Nothing of his thoughts could be learned from the expression of his countenance. There was a certain indifference, indeed, in his manner, as if he did not consider the matter to be of much importance, any way. But if he seemed indifferent, Williams appeared absolutely unconcerned. He stretched out his long legs, took a pearl-handled penknife from his pocket, and pared his nails with Olympian serenity. He was evidently assured that there could be but one conclusion possible to the affair.

Presently the baron returned the papers to the wallet, and handed it back to Williams with a bow. "I don't think you need give yourself any uneasiness about Willis," he said. "Those papers would satisfy me. They are sufficient."

"Yes, that's all right; only I wanted to have the pleasure of hearing you say so," Williams replied. "I'm going to the bank to draw some money to-morrow, and I concluded it would be a wise thing to take you on my way."

"You carry a circular letter-of-credit, I presume?" said the baron.

"By the way, you may as well take a look at that too, while you are about it," Williams remarked, taking the letter from his pocket. "I bought it from Brown Bros. in London, at the time I made my deposit. I've only drawn on it once."

It struck Fedovsky that the baron examined this document with a good deal more care than he had expended upon the others. He scrutinized the engraved heading, the paper and the signature. But the examination seemed entirely to satisfy him, and he returned the paper to its owner with unmistakable cordiality.

" Are you acquainted with the banker—with Mr. Knoup ? " said he.

" No, sir, I never met him," replied Williams.

" He is an agreeable fellow," resumed the baron, "and will accept you at your own valuation ; but I should be glad to be the medium of your acquaintance, if you have no objection." As he spoke he took a fold of note-paper with the engraved heading of the Bureau upon it, and wrote a few lines, which he signed and passed over to Williams. It was an intimation that the writer knew the bearer, and was satisfied that he was all that he represented himself to be.

Williams read the note, seemed to hesitate a moment, and then, much to the surprise of both Fedovsky and the baron, he handed it back to the latter.

" I am just as much obliged to you, baron," he said, " but, under the circumstances, I guess I'd better not take it. After all, you don't know me. I didn't come here to ask favors of you ; I only wanted to show you that I was all right. But I have no right to ask you for your signature. I'll tell you what I would like you to do, though. I'd like to have you, and the count here, and Mr. Knoup, to take supper with me this evening. We shall be very quiet—a private room—and we'll have a good time. You're a busy man, of course, but you can't work all the time, and—what do you say ? "

" Thank you, Mr. Williams," said the baron, graciously. " It will be difficult ; but I think I must make the time for it. This evening, you say ?"

" At eight o'clock ; and I may depend on you too, count ?"

" I shall be very happy," Fedovsky replied.

" That's first rate ! Then I'll step round to the bank, and make sure of Mr. Knoup. Very glad to have met you, baron." He rose and held out his hand.

The baron grasped his hand and shook it cordially. " I shall not forget you," he said, smiling ; " my only hope is that I shall never mistake Mr. Willis for you. But I notice that there is one mark of identification which you seem to lack."

" What's that ?"

" The mole on your cheek. I see no signs of it."

" That's so," exclaimed Williams, laughing; " I'm glad you mentioned it. I haven't got a mole, sure enough. Why, that's a clean bill of health of itself, isn't it ?"

" The fact is, my dear sir," said the baron confidentially, " men of my profession depend very little on technical evidence to discriminate between an honest man and a rascal. I should know Willis the moment I set eyes on him ; and nothing would have given me confidence in him—not if he had produced the very same papers that you carry in your pocket. On the other hand, I never had an instant's doubt of you ; I would stake my reputation on your integrity anywhere. I admit, though," he added with another smile, " that I was somewhat interested in looking at your letter-of-credit. Perhaps you are not aware that Willis and his companions are wanted on suspicion of forging just such documents."

At this information, Fedovsky pricked up his ears. The conversation was turning in the direction of his own concerns. " I should have supposed that a letter-of-credit would be a particularly difficult thing to forge," he remarked. "As I understand, they bear special private marks, according to the sums they represent : and besides, there are the letters of identification, which are dispatched separately by the bank that issues credit to its correspondents. Then, again, when the drafts are sent in, the fraud would be detected at once."

" All that is true," said the baron, "and nevertheless there is little doubt that the thing will be tried. The banks on whom the forged credits are drawn are all in America ; so that ten days at least must elapse before the returning drafts can reach their destination. But ten days will be sufficient. I have here, " he continued, drawing a paper from a pigeon-hole, " a long dispatch from the chief of the Detective Bureau, in New York. He gives the names of Willis and eight or nine others believed to belong to his gang. He says the credits and the letters of identification were forged in America by a couple of experts, and handed over to Willis : Willis added the signatures and some other of the written entries. The two experts then re-turned to New York, in order to avert suspicion. Willis distributed the credits to the members of the gang, their instructions being to disperse to various principal cities in Europe, to travel rapidly, cashing drafts wherever possible, and finally to assemble in a rendezvous where the proceeds could be divided. As each of the credits is for a large amount, the aggregate is expected to reach four or five million francs. It is a big scheme; but for-tunately, the New York dispatch has put us on our guard, and we hope to nip the swindle in the bud."

"Have the thieves begun operations already?" Fedovsky inquired.

"No; but they have tested the quality of some of their forged paper, and I am sorry to say that they have uniformly been successful. The sums involved, however, were comparatively small. But the grand *coup* has not been attempted yet. Such things need very careful arrangements, and each member of the gang must keep in constant communication with headquarters. But, as I say, we hope to get our hands on them before they begin."

"I hope you'll nab my friend Willis, anyway," said Williams, humorously. "He's the head-center and captain of the whole crowd, is he?"

"That is our theory, at all events," the baron answered. "Events will show. He is a very myster-ious fellow, this Willis, and no responsible person has yet been found who could swear to his identity. Even the description I read to you just now may turn out to be founded on a mistake. Every attempt hitherto made to trace him down has failed. One might almost fancy that he is a will-o'-the-wisp—that no such man really exists. But we shall see! Whoever corners him will have a feather in his cap."

"If I listen to any more, I shall begin to have doubts of myself again," remarked Williams, with a comical pretense of uneasiness. "Come along, count! When we get the baron at supper to-night, we'll make him tell us what the detective methods are on this side of the water!"

"It will give me great pleasure," responded the baron: "but we do not pretend to be more clever than our confrères in New York."

"Inspector Byrnes is certainly very clever," Fedovsky said.

"'Till eight o'clock, then," Williams added, making a salute with his hat. The baron bowed, and Fedovsky followed the American out of the room.

"He is a very agreeable fellow, when you get inside of him," he observed, as they reached the sidewalk.

"He's agreeable enough," Williams assented, "but, for all that, if I were the King of Saxony, I'd have some one else at the head of my Detective Department."

"Why so?"

"Well, he doesn't know how to keep his mouth

shut. It's all very well to feel confidence in us : but however honest we may be, our tongues may be indiscreet, and for all he knows, we may repeat what he has told us all over town. However, that's his business. And so you know Inspector Byrnes, do you ? "

The question was carelessly put ; but it made Fedovsky feel that he, too, had not kept his mouth shut so closely as might have been advisable. He mumbled some indefinite reply (to which his companion appeared to pay no attention), and inwardly determined to be more cautious in future.

CHAPTER XVII.

A GERMAN BIER KELLER.

THE supper that evening was a very pleasant affair; and towards the latter part of it, the conversation turned on the anticipated raid of forgers. Gradually, Fedovsky found himself pairing off with Mr. Knoup, the banker; while Williams and the baron were similarly thrown together. Mr. Knoup was a lively and entertaining companion, and withal exceedingly well-informed : and he imparted to the count a good deal of useful knowledge as to the nature and management of the banking business in Europe, and the measures that were adopted to guard against fraud. Meanwhile, the baron, so far as Fedovsky could judge from the occasional sentences that fell upon his ears, was fulfilling his promise of acquainting Williams with the ways of European detectives.

Fedovsky had not been idle since his arrival on the Continent ; and although, in one sense, he was somewhat hampered by the fact that his instructions did not admit of his consulting, as an accredited officer, with the police of Europe, yet this independence had advantages of its own, and he was not, upon the whole, disposed to regret it. He was not obliged to weigh the conflicting opinions of various persons ; he was not liable to share the mistakes of others ; nor was he subjected to the rivalry of such as might desire to monopolize the credit of capturing the great unknown forger. He made his own observations, and drew his own conclusions. He had gained a general idea of what the thieves intended to do, and how they meant to do it ; he had acquired some personal knowledge (or so he imagined) about one or two of them ; but his efforts to trace the communication between these individuals and their superiors had not hitherto been successful ; and he had begun to think that some bold and perhaps perilous step was necessary to secure this result. Rather than fail, he was prepared to run any personal risk : the only risk he wished to avoid was that of letting the rogues slip through his fingers. But between these two contingencies it was difficult to steer.

The fact that the man to whom rumor pointed as the leader of the gang bore a strong resemblance to Williams interested him greatly, and he could not help thinking that it might, in some way, be turned to advantage. If the likeness were really so close that Willis could be mistaken for Williams, why might not Williams be mistaken for Willis ? In other words, might it not be possible to use the former as a sort of stalking-horse, by means of which to approach and discover the rest of the gang ? There appeared to be something in this idea, but the means of working it were still to seek. It occurred to Fedovsky that he himself might assume the guise of a shady character, and thus insinuate himself into the confidence of the genuine rascals. But that, again, might lead him into collision with the police, and compel undesirable explanations.

He would have liked to discuss the subject with Williams; but perceived that the discussion could not proceed far without giving Williams some suspicion of what he was driving at. No doubt Williams would be very glad to see his "double" captured and put out of the way; but it was doubtful how he would accept the revelation that his friend, Count Fedovsky, was the agent in the matter. He could be a very congenial companion, when he chose to be; but Fedovsky felt that there was another and harder side to his character, which might give trouble upon occasion. These easy, amiable men sometimes exhibit unsuspected depths.

While these reflections were passing through his mind, Mr. Knoup, whose Hebraic profile and soft voice and manner were revealed through the haze of fragrant cigar smoke that was enveloping the four friends, continued to enlarge upon the dangers and difficulties of the financial profession. "You have been long acquainted with Mr. Williams?" he said, with the intonation of one who has a heavy cold in his head, and is resigned to it.

"Not very long. I met him for the first time last winter."

" Ah ! He is a very charming gentleman—also very intelligent. It must be of great annoyance to him—this fellow Willis."

" I wonder if Willis is aware of the resemblance between them," said Fedovsky. " If he is, he might turn it to his advantage."

" How so, count ?" demanded Williams, suddenly turning to him.

" He might run up bills with unsuspecting tradesmen, who know you, for instance."

" Well, I guess we don't look so much alike but what you could tell the difference if you'd seen both of us. A mere description is never satisfactory, no matter how close it is. Anyhow, I should take it that Mr. Willis would find the likeness, such as it is, rather an inconvenience. It doubles the chance of his detection—eh, baron ? "

" It would have that effect," the baron assented. " People who see either of you would be struck by his similarity to the other ; and if it turned out not to be you, it would be certain to be he."

" That's it exactly Do you think your friend the inspector could make any thing of that suggestion, count ? "

" Really, I don't know," Fedovsky replied, not a little surprised by the question. But Williams seemed quite unconscious of having said any thing odd, and his face showed only his usual expression of good nature. " If I wasn't so infernally lazy," he remarked, " I would like to get on the trail of that fellow, and see if I couldn't run him down. I was always interested in detective work ; and since my talk with you this evening, baron, I see more in it than I ever did before."

" We should value very highly your co-operation," returned the baron smiling.

"Oh, yes, indeed, very highly," softly assented the banker.

" I suppose you think I'm losing my mind, don't you, count ? " said Williams, turning a humorous glance upon him.

" Not at all ! I feel an interest in such things myself ; and a criminal like Willis is enough to interest any body."

" Well, if I always felt as I do to-night, I would take service under the baron or under Inspector Byrnes, perhaps—right here on the spot," Williams said. " But I know myself, and that to-morrow I shall have a headache, and that'll be the end of it ! However, if any of you gentlemen ever come across Willis, just drop a line to me and I'll step in and give my evidence that he isn't me."

The party soon afterwards broke up, on the most cordial terms with one another; the banker pleading delicate constitution as a reason for retiring early, and the baron declaring that he had some official matters to attend to before going to bed. Williams and Fedovsky walked home together.

" Do you know," said the American, "I was more than half in earnest to-night. About doing a bit of amateur detective business, you know."

"I have no doubt it would be amusing," said Fedovsky.

"What would you say to taking a hand at it with me?" continued the other.

"I can't say that I'm fitted for that sort of thing," replied the count, conscious of some embarrassment. "I should probably hinder more than help you."

"Maybe you would. I was only joking, any way," said Williams. "But I'll tell you one thing that put it into my head. I believe I know who one of these fellows is. That is, I believe I could point out a man who has something to do with the forgeries."

"You could point him out?" Fedovsky exclaimed. "Who is he?"

Williams glanced at him, and laughed. "It is amusing, isn't it?" he said. "Yes, I believe I have spotted one of them; and I shouldn't wonder if he were pretty high up in the organization, too. I know he's an American, and I know he's a criminal, for I happened to see him once on trial in New York."

Fedovsky had begun to fear that he was betraying too much interest, and he now forebore to make any rejoinder; but Williams, without seeming to notice his silence, continued.

"It was while I was in business; and this fellow was arrested for forging the signature of our firm. The case was clear enough, but his lawyer got him off on some technicality. I don't forget such things, and I have borne him in mind ever since. I saw him again in Paris the other day, hanging round one of the banks,—a place at which, as I afterwards learned, they had tested some of their bogus paper. And I'm pretty sure that I caught a glimpse of him again last night, as I was driving to the hotel from the bahnhof."

"Do you know his name?" Fedovsky asked, in as indifferent a tone as he could assume.

"I'm not so good at remembering names as faces," Williams replied; "and besides, these fellows are always changing their patronymics. But what makes me think he is one of the Willis gang is, that when I saw him in Paris, he caught sight of me at the same moment; and he made a sort of sign of recognition to me, and started towards me as if he were going to speak to me. But when he got pretty close, he stopped short, with a very queer look, and then turned round and walked off. It didn't occur to me at the moment, but I thought afterwards that he must have mistaken me for Willis, and only found out his error at a nearer inspection."

"It certainly does look that way," said Fedovsky, who was impressed by the story, and could hardly decide what to think of his companion—whether he were in earnest or not. "Why didn't you mention it to the baron?" he added.

"Oh, the baron is a professional; and professionals, as perhaps you know, disregard the suggestions of amateurs on principle. If I were to tell

him that I considered so-and-so a suspicious character, he would make up his mind that, appearances
to the contrary notwithstanding, so-and-so must be
an honest man. Besides, whoever else solves the
mystery of these forgers, I would be willing to give
odds that our friend the baron does not. An independent guerrilla, like you or me, is much more
likely to hit the nail on the head."

They were walking along the Schloss strasse, and
had reached a point a little way above the Alt
Markt. On a corner of a narrow street to the left,
Williams halted.

" Look here," he said, " it's only about eleven
o'clock yet. Suppose we hunt up a *café* and have
a glass of beer before we turn in ? We shall sleep
the better for it."

Fedovsky offered no objection. Indeed, he had
been making a practice of frequenting such places,
for the sake of whatever information he might
chance upon there.

They turned down the narrow street, which
extended crookedly in a northern direction, and
presently reached the door of a beer saloon, or
" restauration," the windows of which were alight,
and whence proceeded a muffled sound of conversation. On entering, they found themselves in a
narrow and low-ceiled apartment, the atmosphere
foul with tobacco smoke and human exhalations,
and resonant with the gabble of fifty German
throats. The company were seated at numerous
small square tables, each man with a glass mug of

beer in front of him, holding about a pint. Waiters hastened about, bearing fresh mugs of beer in their hands, or carrying away empty ones. The floor of the saloon was of planks, strewn with sawdust. The outer room communicated, through a broad, low archway, with a similar apartment, lying at right angles to it.

With some difficulty, relieved by a five-groschen piece which Williams slipped into the hand of one of the waiters, a vacant table was secured for the new-comers, just on the further side of the arch-way, and commanding a view of both the rooms, though itself partly in shadow. Here the two friends seated themselves, Williams with his back against the wall. Beer was brought to them, and they lighted cigars.

"A queer idea these Germans have of enjoy-ment," Williams remarked, "taking this air into their lungs, and beer into their stomachs. And yet I suppose there must be a sort of fascination about it. I enjoy it, myself, occasionally."

"It might be well if Russians drank more beer," said Fedovsky; "it seems to be a calming bever-age, disposing one to philosophies; and philosophy is a thing that the inhabitants of Russia have need of."

"It's a sociable drink, too," rejoined the other; "nothing like a few schoppen of beer as a medium of acquaintance. Every body here seems to know every body else. We are the only strangers. Hullo!"

The exclamation was given in a different tone, and caused Fedovsky to look up at his companion. The latter had his eyes fixed on a distant corner of the room, with an expression as if he saw something unexpected, and not altogether welcome.

" What is the matter ?" inquired the Russian.

" We are not such strangers as I imagined," Williams replied ; " at least, I am not. I have just caught sight of somebody whom I have seen before."

" And whom you don't care to be recognized by, I should fancy."

" Well, that would depend. But it falls in rather oddly. We were just speaking about him."

" Not the baron, surely ?"

" No, not the baron ; but the man who, according to my assumption, the baron would be glad to meet."

" Ah, I think I understand—the man you saw in Paris at the bank? He is here, is he ?"

" Yes ; but don't turn round too suddenly ; if his attention is drawn to me, he will get up and go out. There is plenty of time. Shall we lay a plot to capture him ?"

" There would not be much use in that," replied Fedovsky, " unless there were some more definite evidence than has appeared yet."

" Probably you are right. You seem to understand these things. Still, it would be a good thing if we could devise some pretext for putting the police on his track."

" The police are not always grateful for outside assistance," Fedovsky said, being, indeed, rather anxious not to have Williams mixed up in the affair, if the man in question should really prove to be one of the forgers. " Besides, for all we know, they may already know about him, and only be waiting for an opportune occasion to arrest him. It is not uncommon for a criminal to slip through the hands of the police, merely because he was taken into custody too soon—at least, so I have heard."

" Well, if your authority dates from New York, it ought to be trustworthy," said the other, who, whether intentionally or by accident, seemed rather pertinacious in his allusions to Fedovsky's acquaintance with Inspector Byrnes. " And for my part," he added, " I am too lazy to think seriously of meddling in any body's business, least of all in a criminal's. But I wonder what the fellow is up to now ! "

At this juncture, Fedovsky changed his position in his chair, in such a way as to bring the further side of the room into view. His eyes traversed the confused medley of faces, and at first rested nowhere ; but, after a moment, he uttered an involuntary exclamation. It was under his breath, but Williams heard it

" You know him yourself, then, do you ?" he exclaimed, with an inquisitive smile.

Fedovsky bit his lip. He seemed fated to make blunders to-day. But Williams had conjectured rightly. He did know the man. The dark whiskers were gone, and a pair of spectacles concealed his eyes ; but there was no mistaking him. It was the thief whom he had attempted to arrest in the act of robbing the messenger boy in Nassau Street of his tin box of securities.

CHAPTER XVIII.

"ROBERT CECIL."

THERE was now no doubt in Fedovsky's mind that he had found one of the forgers—perhaps the semi-mythical Willis himself. He had never learned the name of the Nassau Street robber, and, although he had caught a glimpse of him in the gambling saloon where he had lost his thousand-dollar stake, he was not aware that he was the same man whom Tom had claimed as his brother. Yet such was the fact.

The young Russian now felt as if he were beginning to see the end of his long search ; and he was just casting about how he should get rid of Williams, in order to have a clear field for his operations against the forger, when Williams himself solved the problem by setting down his glass of beer and declaring that he felt ill.

" I know what's the matter with me, though," he observed. " It s that confounded old-time trouble of mine. It's apt to come on after I've been indulging in beer for a few days. I have some pills at home that will do all that can be done for me. Well, I'll have to bid you good-night. Don't stir on my account ; I can get home all right To-morrow morning I shall be better, and a more agreeable companion into the bargain. Goodnight ! "

He arose and walked out of the saloon, choosing (whether by chance or not) a moment for doing so when the suspected forger was looking another way. It occurred to Fedovsky that his abrupt departure might not be wholly due to liver complaint, but might also be connected with the presence of the forger. But he could not imagine what the connection could be, nor was it of much apparent consequence. His quarry was before him ; it only remained to pounce upon it.

Bold measures are sometimes the best. Something must be done at once, or the man might escape. Fedovsky got up from his table, and walked across the room as if intending to go out. But when he came within reach of the forger, he stopped, and looked at him with an earnest, yet doubtful air. Then, as if his uncertainty was dispelled, he laid his hand upon his shoulder, and met his upturned gaze of blank inquiry with a genial smile.

"How do you do, old fellow ! " he said in English; "don't you recognize me ? "

The man eyed him suspiciously for a moment, and shook his head. "To my knowledge, I never saw you before," he replied. "You've made a mistake."

This answer gratified Fedovsky, insomuch as it relieved him from his chief apprehension, which was that the man might recognize him as his assail-

ant in Nassau Street.   But that encounter had
evidently been too brief and confused for the
thief to have retained any memory of the count's
face, if indeed he had caught a fair glimpse of it
at all.   However, the count's appearance on that
occasion had been very different from what it was
now.

"Let me refresh your memory then," said he,
gayly. "My name is Fedovsky—Count Ivan Fedovsky at your service : and you are Mr. Robert Cecil of
Boston, United States, whom I met in London two
years ago."

The Russian's expectation was, of course, that
the man would disclaim the patronymic he had
bestowed upon him ; and it was his design there-
upon to enlarge upon the singularity of the resemblance, and, by one means or another, to engage him
in conversation.   For the rest, he would trust to
chance, and to such mother-wit as might come to
his aid.

But the subject of his experiment did not precisely fulfill his part of the programme. The fact
was (though Fedovsky was ignorant of it) that
Tom, the valet, had given him a good deal of information about the count on the night of the
gambling adventure in New York ; and he remembered the name and the information perfectly well.
As the count had been represented to him as a man
of great wealth, he had no reason to suppose that
the error as to "Mr. Robert Cecil" was other than
a genuine one ; and it flashed through his mind

that it might be worth his while to make the mis-
conception a basis for further acquaintance. Thus
it happened that a game at cross-purposes began of
rather a peculiar kind.

" I have heard of you before, count," said the
person whom he had addressed, " and, oddly
enough, it was through Mr. Cecil of Boston, who is
a friend of mine. My own name is "—he hesitated a
moment and then continued—" Charles Brown. I
have often been told that Cecil and I looked like
each other ; and that accounts for your mistake."

This audacious assertion amused Fedovsky ; but
though it confirmed him in his suspicions, he did
not understand exactly what Mr. Brown's object was
in making it. He was, of course, not aware that
the man's real name was Bolan. The imaginary
Robert Cecil meanwhile provided a topic of conversation.

" How was Cecil when you last saw him, Mr.
Brown ? " he inquired.

" He was in good health. But sit down, count,
and allow me to get some profit from your mistake. Are you making any long stay here ? "

" My movements are uncertain : I am here to-day
and gone to-morrow. The fact is, I am a little
disappointed that you are not the man I took you
for. I was badly in want of some advice, and
I fancied that you—that is, he—had been provi-
dentially sent to give it to me."

" Some advice, eh ? " said Mr. Brown, his pale

face assuming an inquisitive expression. " Our friend Cecil used to advise you, then ? "

" Yes, in his own line of business. You know what a remarkable head he had for business and finance ? "

" Certainly ! to be sure he had—wonderful ! " assented Brown, with an air as if he were recalling the ruling trait of an intimate friend.

" Whereas," continued Fedovsky, " I never could carry on the simplest transaction without falling into some absurd mistake or other. Well, it so happens that I have just called in some large investments that I had made—they were not bringing in what I expected of them—and I was looking out for something good to buy. Now Cecil would have been sure to know just the thing that will suit me. And meanwhile, here am I left with all this cash on my hands."

" That is to say, of course, you have deposited it at your banker's ? "

" Well, I suppose that is what I ought to do, in common prudence : half a million of francs is a considerable responsibility to take on one's own shoulders. But I only received the money this morning, in bonds and notes, and I have been so busy since then, doing nothing, that it is still on my hands. I think I'll take it round to-morrow, and ask Mr. Knoup what he thinks that I had better do with it."

" Ask Knoup, did you say ? " repeated Mr.

Brown, in a tone expressive of mingled surprise and compassion.

"Why not? He seems a very sensible fellow. and I don't know who would be more likely to give me good information on the subject."

"Knoup is all right, from his point of view," replied the other; "but his point of view is that of his own interests entirely, and therefore disregards those of other people. If you intrust your money to him, he will keep three francs of interest on it for every two francs that he gives you. It's none of my business; but, if I were in your shoes, I would let Knoup alone. Better keep the money in your trunk."

"You seem to have some knowledge of finance yourself, Mr. Brown?"

"Well, I ought to have! I was a stockholder in the Beacon Hill Bank for ten years, and a director for two. A man picks up a good bit of knowledge in that way."

"But, in that case," Fedovsky exclaimed, and then stopped short. "I have no right to make any such suggestion," he added.

"Not at all, sir," said Mr. Brown, courteously "If I can be of any assistance to you, command me! Any friend of Cecil's is a friend of mine!"

"Your extraordinary resemblance to him keeps making me forget that you are not he after all," the count remarked. "I was about to say that, considering your business training, you could probably advise me in the matter as well or better than Cecil himself."

"I don't say but what I might. I know Cecil often used to come to me when he struck any thing particularly intricate. But to be able to advise him, and to advise you, are two different things, count. I would be willing to accept the responsibility, for a friend ; but in the case of a stranger, it's another thing."

"If that is your only difficulty, you are too scrupulous," said the Russian. "Didn't you just say that any friend of Cecil's was a friend of yours? If you will favor me with any counsel, I will accept the responsibility of it, and be much indebted to you into the bargain. But of course, on the other hand, I don't want to tax your good nature beyond the proper limits."

"Oh, as far as that is concerned, advice is like politeness—it costs nothing ; and I should be happy to do you a good turn, if it comes in my way. How much did you say you had to invest?"

"About half a million francs, I believe."

"And it is in the form of negotiable securities?"

"Yes ; bonds and bank notes, and things of that kind."

"You don't carry them about your person, of course?"

"They are in my trunk at my room, just at present. I am stopping at the Bellevue."

"I shouldn't wonder, now," said Mr. Brown, meditatively, "if I knew just the thing for you to

do with that money It's what I'd do with it myself,
if I was investing."

" I am convinced there could not be a better
recommendation," returned Fedovsky, with a bow.

" Let me see, now ! " continued the other, still
apparently immersed in thought. " You haven't
got a list of those securities, have you ? "

" Indeed, I have nothing of the kind," exclaimed
Fedovsky, laughing. " I could only tell you in the
most general way of what they consist. As I said
before, I am a mere child in business matters. But
is it necessary you should know what they are ? "

" It might be desirable. You see, the transaction
I am considering will involve negotiations with a
third party, and he might want to know exactly
what he was dealing with. And it would simplify
things if I were able to tell him."

" It seems to me, then, that the simplest plan
would be for me to show you the securities themselves. That would be better than any list."

Mr. Brown emptied his glass of beer, and set it
down. " I had not thought of that ! " said he.

" Well, what do you say? Will you come up to
the hotel ? "

" I don't think I could manage that," replied
Brown ; "certainly not to-night—it's getting pretty
late. But may be I could arrange some way to
meet you to-morrow."

" Any time or place that you would appoint
would suit me," said Fedovsky. " I have no particular engagements ; and, to tell the truth, I feel

a little uneasy at having so much money in my possession."

"People are pretty honest here, I guess," observed Mr. Brown : "but half a million would be a good deal of a temptation to some folks, and it's as well to be on the safe side. I'll tell you how I'm fixed. You know, they built a new theater here a while ago, in place of the one that was burned down ; and I own some of the stock of it. They're getting out a new piece there now—to-morrow is the opening night—and I have to be round there in the afternoon to attend to some business. I shall be through by four o'clock. You come over there at that time, and bring your securities with you. If possible, I'll have the party I spoke of to meet you. At any rate, we can talk it over : I'll explain the investment to you, and you can take what action you see fit. How does that strike you ? "

"That will suit me perfectly, and I'm much obliged to you," said Fedovsky. "But how shall I get admission to the theater ? "

"This will do it," returned the other, taking out a note-book, and writing something on one of the leaves, which he tore out and passed over to his interlocutor. "Show that at the stage door, and you'll have no trouble. I'll be on hand, and conduct you to the office. Four o'clock sharp ! "

"I shall not forget," said Fedovsky. "You are sure it won't be too much trouble to you ? "

"None at all, count : I shall be glad of the

opportunity," Mr. Brown replied. " And now, as I am an early bird, I'll bid you good-night."

" I'll go with you as far as the corner," said the count, not to be outdone in politeness. They arose, and went forth together, and walked down the narrow street side by side, till they came to the main thoroughfare. " Good-night ! " said the count, making a courteous salute ; and turning on his heel, he walked swiftly towards the river.

He told himself, as he walked along, that this began to look a little like business. There was every reason to believe that Mr. Brown (as he called himself), was one of the forgers. He had struck up an acquaintance with him, which was a first and important step. In the second place, he had led Mr. Brown to suppose that he was in possession of a large sum of money in cash. Thirdly, he had arranged a meeting, at which the cash was to be produced. For the issue of the adventure, he must trust to his own readiness and resources.

It was evident, of course, that Mr. Brown intended in some way to possess himself of the cash in question; by strategy, if possible: if not, by violence. A theater, however, seemed a place so little suited to the latter method, that Fedovsky thought it more probable the former would be attempted. He would be prepared for either emergency As regarded the bonds and notes, he was already provided. Before leaving New York, he had been furnished with specimens of the paper which had

been forged during the last few years by the same
gang that was supposed to be now at work. The
aggregate amount of this bogus material did not,
indeed, approach the sum of half a million francs ;
but there was enough to answer the present purpose. All that was necessary was to seem to be
in possession of money enough to make it worth
while to rob him. If Mr. Brown should request to be
allowed the custody of the paper on any pretext,
it might be well to permit him to take it, and then,
when he attempted to get rid of it, to either arrest
him openly, or to force him, by threats of arrest,
to reveal the secrets of his accomplices. If,
on the other hand, he should meditate a forcible
seizure, Fedovsky felt confident that he could
defend himself. But, inasmuch as his own safety
was not the only thing at stake, but also (what was
of more importance) the success of the mission
with which he was charged, the young Russian
thought it would be prudent to secure an assistant
in the enterprise. In Dresden, however, there were
only two persons to whom he could apply—the
baron, and Mr. Williams. He had no hesitation in
deciding against the former. But Williams had,
in a manner, introduced him to Brown, and having
suggested the idea of opening a campaign against
him, seemed a more feasible ally ; and Fedovsky
determined to speak to him the next morning. He
need not confide his whole design to him, by any
means : it would be enough to have him within
hail in case of accidents.

But the next morning, on inquiring for Mr. Williams, he was informed that he had started that morning on a trip to Cologne, and would not return for three days. As the appointment with Bolan (*alias* Brown), could not be put off, there was nothing for it but to meet that astute individual alone ; and this Fedovsky prepared to do.

CHAPTER XIX.

AN APPOINTMENT.

THE following afternoon, Fedovsky put his bundle of bogus securities in his inside coat pocket, and in the hip-pocket of his trowsers a small but business-like revolver. He had never fired at a human being in his life, and did not expect to have to do so now ; but he knew that he was going to deal with a man who was a confirmed and probably a desperate criminal, and who was very likely supported by others of his kind. He would be at a disadvantage in any case, and he must have the means of acting decisively if need be.

He hoped, however, that Brown would not think it incumbent upon him to use violence. Fedovsky had played so successfully the part of the credulous and easy-going fool at their last night's interview, that it was probable Brown would depend upon his ingenuity alone to attain his object. In that case, the documents would be surrendered ; and as the count had a complete record of them, and the means of tracing them wherever they might be presented, there was no reasonable doubt of his being able to get a secure hold upon Brown. Such, at any rate, was his conviction ; and as the scheme was his own, he was naturally pleased with it.

The theater, a handsome new building, stood in the center of a square in immediate proximity to Fedovsky's hotel. On the bulletin-boards at the front door appeared the announcement of a new musical and spectacular drama, to be produced for the first time that evening. At this hour, however, there were no signs of life about the place. The box-office would not be open till five o'clock ; and the company had finished its final rehearsal and gone home to dinner. The stage door was in the rear of the building, and on walking round there, the count saw a man, wearing a cap ornamented with faded silver braid, indicating that he had some official connection with the establishment. To him Fedovsky showed the scrap of paper which Brown had given him the previous night. The man read it, glanced at the count, nodded, and unlocked the door. After admitting the visitor, the door was closed behind him. The adventure was now fairly begun.

The adventurer looked around him. He was at the end of a narrow corridor, which extended a dozen yards or so into the building, and then took a turn ; at the corner was a gas-jet, turned half on, and burning dimly. Upon the walls of the corridor were pasted some printed regulations for the guidance of the theater company. Fedovsky advanced along the corridor, until he reached the corner.

Here he found a short flight of steps, on ascending which he saw only darkness before him : and the silence was absolute.

There was nothing for it but to advance : and the young Russian had taken a step forward, feeling that the next step might land him in some ambush, when a door opened at some distance down the corridor, and there was a noise of some one coming forward. In a moment this some one came within the rays of the gas-jet, and turned out to be (as might have been expected) Mr. Brown.

He greeted Fedovsky effusively, grasping his hand and shaking it hard. "It's very good of you to come, my dear count," he said. " I was afraid you might forget ; but you're on time to a minute. Well, every thing looks well so far. The party I spoke to you about is here, and I imagine he is anxious to do business. By the way, did you happen to bring that stuff along with you ? "

There was a perceptible unevenness in the man's voice as he asked the question. Fedovsky answered with childlike manner, " Why, to be sure I did ! I've got the money in my pocket. You said the other party might want to see it, you know."

" Yes—yes, he might," responded the other hurriedly " I don't suppose it's of much consequence, any way ; but it's just as well to be ready. Now, let me lead you across here. It's dark, but there'll be a light directly. Come this way." He walked half a step in advance of the count, with his hand touching his elbow. It was perfectly dark, or so it seemed to Fedovsky, whose eyes were sti.l under the influence of the daylight out of which he had come. Once or twice Brown warned him to step up or down, or to turn to the right or left. After a minute or so of this sort of progress, he said, " Now, just stop where you are a moment, till I strike a light. Then we can see our way."

Fedovsky stood still, and heard Brown's steps walking away from him. From the sound, it seemed as if they were no longer in the corridor, but in an open space. There was an indefinable impression of space around him. Brown's footsteps were no longer audible. Fedovsky was a courageous fellow, and he was not a coward now. But darkness, silence and uncertainty are potent influences on a man's nervous system, and it may be admitted, without diminishing our respect for a worthy young gentleman, that he became aware at this moment that he had a heart. It thumped, in the cavity of his chest, with a vigor that was not only perceptible, but even audible. He stood erect, and pressed his lips together.

In an instant something from behind seized him round the throat, compressing the windpipe with intolerable force. He twisted himself violently to one side, but without shaking off the grip. He had heard of garotting, and had sometimes wondered that it was so uniformly successful; it had seemed comparatively easy to shake off such an assailant, but, like many other things, it turned out to be much easier in theory than in practice. The stoppage of the breath caused a dizziness in the brain, and he was being drawn backward with the whole strength of his assailant ; he felt as if he must succumb. Another tremendous effort to free himself was unsuccessful. The more he struggled the more terrible became the pressure. Nor could he unlock the hands that were clasped over his throat. To get out his revolver was equally impossible, and he could hardly have used it effectively even had it been in his grasp.

Meanwhile no word had been uttered by either antagonist. Fedovsky, of course, was for the time incapable of speech ; his enemy may have had his own reasons for being silent. Fedovsky could hear him breathing close to his ear, and gritting his teeth. It could be no one but Brown, and yet Brown had not seemed to possess the strength of this scoundrel. Perhaps there were more than one against him. What did they mean to do with him ?

At first he had taken it for granted that the object of the attack was robbery. But now it suddenly flashed upon him that Brown would not stop there. He was known to Fedovsky, and the latter, if his life were spared, would of course denounce him. No, his design must be to murder ! This conviction, which might have paralyzed a cowardly man, had the opposite effect upon the Russian. But he knew that in another moment he must lose consciousness. There was but a single chance left. He gave a gasp ; he ceased to struggle ; the rigidity left his limbs ; he hung limp in his adversary's arms. The latter perceived the change, but did not act at once upon it. He still kept the bone of his wrist upon Fedovsky's throat. But after a while (how long a while Fedovsky never knew), he allowed the limp body to slide to the floor. It fell there with a nerveless thump.

As the count lay there, controlling by a convulsive effort the gasping of his lungs, he realized that every thing depended upon what happened next. If his assailant robbed him before proceeding to kill him, there was a hope left ; but if he should take a fancy to put a bullet through his brain, or cut his throat, before helping himself to the bundle of bonds, then there was very little chance for escape.

The man was stooping above him, and passing the tips of his fingers over him, apparently to find out how he lay. As a matter of fact, Fedovsky was lying partly on his left side ; his left arm was under him, his right arm was thrown backward, and his left knee was drawn up. Having informed himself of these particulars, the thief and intending murderer knelt (as nearly as his victim could judge) on his right knee beside him, or in front of him, and threw back the right lapel of his coat, preparatory to searching the pocket.

Fedovsky had meanwhile advanced his right arm until he felt sure that it could not be many inches distant from the left leg of his antagonist, the foot of which was planted on the floor, in contact with the count's body. Then he silently drew in his breath for his effort. The instant before he made it, the other seemed to take the alarm, and made a hasty movement—what it was Fedovsky knew not, but, at any rate, it was too late. The young Russian thrust his right arm under the bent left knee of the thief, at the same moment gathering his own legs under him and springing to his feet. As he did so he felt a blow on the right side of his chest; it struck the thick bundle of papers in his pocket, and penetrating them, pricked his flesh, but there it stopped. The man was hurled backward, and fell heavily, but was immediately up again, and grappled with Fedovsky The latter, however, was now master of the situation. Throwing one arm around the fellow's neck, he caught him about the lower part of the body with the other, and, by a well-known wrestler's trick, lifted him off the floor and hurled him over his shoulder.

Then he faced about, waiting for the body to fall. After what seemed an unaccountably long interval he heard a crash, and thought he heard a groan, but both appeared to come from a great distance. Following this there was dead silence.

What did it mean? Fedovsky waited there in the darkness, and held his breath to listen ; but nothing occurred to enlighten him, nor could any conjecture of his solve the mystery He knew that he had thrown the man up in the air : by all the laws of nature and wrestling, he should have fallen a few feet behind him : it was impossible that he could so have fallen without an unmistakable concussion; and yet there had been nothing but that long-delayed and remote crash. The more he reflected upon it, the less probable did it seem that the noise had been occasioned by the fall of his antagonist. But if not, what could have become of him? He could not have remained suspended in the air.

"I could almost believe," said Fedovsky to himself, "that I had been wrestling with a phantom, and that having overcome it, it had taken to flight!"

The whole affair had come and passed so suddenly, and yet had been so intense and terrible while it lasted; and the circumstances amidst which it had taken place were so black and impenetrable, that the young man may be pardoned if, in default of any substantial explanation of the problem, he allowed his imagination too much scope. The truth was, that the inexplicable termination of the combat disturbed his nervous equipoise more than the combat itself had done. After remaining where he was for perhaps a minute, he came to the conclusion that the most sensible thing he could do was to get out of the theater. There was no telling what other goblins might be lying in wait for him. The difficulty now was, that he did not know which way to go. He took a step or two at a venture, and his foot struck against some light object, that rolled away. He could not repress a start and an exclamation; but, recovering himself, he stooped and laid hands upon the object, which proved to be his own hat, that had fallen off at the beginning of the struggle. He put it on, and walked forward cautiously, with hands outstretched. At length he came to a flat, upright surface, which could only be part of the scenery at the side of the theater stage. He felt along this until he came to an opening, through which he passed ; and by good luck at length reached the corridor by which he had entered. A minute more brought him to the corner where the gas-jet was still burning. By its welcome light, he took stock of his condition. He was in better order than might have been expected. There was a small rent in the breast of his coat, where the point of the knife had penetrated ; and the coat itself was dusty from the floor : but when he had brushed it and his hat, and pulled himself into shape a little, no one looking casually at him would have imagined what an experience he had just been having. Having satisfied himself of this, he walked up to the door, which was fastened by a spring lock that could be opened without a key from the inside, and stepped forth into the outer world. The doorkeeper was nowhere to be seen. But there was the open square ; there were people walking hither and thither upon their affairs : there was the arched bridge across the river : and above all, there was the sky, its clouds tinged with the ruddy hue of sunset. For the first time, Fedovsky fully realized what he had escaped, and inhaled the pure air that blew in his face with devout thankfulness.

He looked at his watch, and saw to his astonishment that it was only a quarter past four ; he had been less than fifteen minutes in passing through what seemed a large portion of his life. He walked across the square to his hotel, to change his dress. At the door some one passed him hurriedly ; in his preoccupation he did not notice who it was. But immediately he felt a touch on his arm, and turning, he confronted no less a personage than the baron.

" How do you do, my friend !" said this official, shaking him by the hand. " Ah, I see you also are a little pale from our entertainment of last night ! Well, now, I have a favor to request of you. I intended to include our friend, Mr. Williams, but he has run away for a few days. It is to join me this evening in my box at the theater. There is given a new piece which will be amusing : but there is also a particular reason why I desire your presence. It will be a favor to me, you understand. May I expect you ?"

" Thank you, baron, it will give me great pleasure."

" Ah, that is good. And it is possible it will be of good service as well. How is this—you have run against a nail? See the hole in your coat ! Pardon—we police, we see every thing. Till this evening then, M. le Comte ! I am in a hurry. Au revoir !"

"That happens very conveniently," said Fedovsky to himself, as he ascended the stairs to his room. "I shall be curious to see whether there are any traces this evening of my own and Mr. Brown's performance this afternoon!"

He took off his clothes, washed the wound in his chest, which was not more than quarter of an inch deep, and bled but little ; and put on evening dress. After this was done, he had still an hour at his disposal, and he employed it in writing his report to Inspector Byrnes. At six o'clock the report was nearly finished ; he locked it into the drawer of his table, put the key in his pocket, and betook himself to the theater.

CHAPTER XX.

A HOROSCOPE.

THE announcement of the new drama had evidently whetted the curiosity of the theater-going people in Dresden, for a steady stream of people was entering the doors, and when Fedovsky got inside, the auditorium seemed already nearly full. The royal box was decorated, and the king was expected to be present. After standing a while in the lobby, contemplating the scene, which was full of brilliance and liveliness, the young Russian made his way round to the box which the baron had designated.

The baron was already there, and received him cordially ; he wore a ribbon and a decoration in his button-hole, and made quite an imposing appearance. The only other person in the box was a middle-aged man with a rather inexpressive countenance, whom the baron introduced briefly as " Herr Klesmer," and took no further notice of.

After some preliminary chat, the baron said: " As I hinted to you just now, it is possible that you may do me a valuable service. Have you a good memory for faces ? "

"I generally remember my friends, if that's what you mean," said Fedovsky, smiling.

"Yes ; and your enemies too, perhaps?"

"He is a wise man who knows his own enemies, baron !"

"Ha ! very true ! Well, to come to the point, you have traveled a good deal in both Europe and America, and have seen many people ; and unless I am misinformed, you spent a good deal of time, while in New York, in exploring the shady side of that city—the haunts of the thieves—what they call the slums."

"I can hardly pretend to have done that, baron. I did spend a part of one evening in going about some low neighborhoods with a party of gentlemen; but we saw nothing worthy of record."

The baron shrugged his shoulders. "That may be a matter of opinion," he said; "at all events, you perceive that I have not been wholly ignorant of your movements, even on the other side of the Atlantic. Now, as our friend Mr. Williams was telling us yesterday, and as is generally known, there is a gang of American forgers at work over here ; but it is not generally known that there are also here other persons, who are not connected with that gang, but who nevertheless are doing some very dangerous work on their own account. One of these men—either an Englishman or an American—is at present in this city ; we are aware of some of his depredations, but till now we have been unable to identify him. I learned quite lately, however, from a source which I need not name, that this man, who speaks the German language like a native, has been passing himself off as a Saxon subject, and is actually engaged as a member of the company which is to act in the drama at this theater to-night."

" This is quite interesting, baron," observed Fedovsky, languidly lifting his opera-glass, and turning it upon a group of ladies in the dress-circle.

" That is not all," the baron continued. " I have reason to believe that this villain, no longer ago than this afternoon, and within this very house, robbed and perhaps murdered a wealthy foreigner, who had newly arrived here."

Fedovsky lowered his opera-glass, and polished the lenses with his handkerchief. " You are telling me an extraordinary story, my dear baron," he said. " Who was this wealthy foreigner ? "

" There are causes which prevent my naming him at present. All will come out in due time."

" But surely, if a man were robbed or murdered, or both, in this theater this afternoon, some traces must remain—"

" Quite so ! and that is the mysterious part of it. But the immediate point is this : The criminal who has been guilty of this wickedness will appear upon the stage this evening, and I shall be curious to know whether you will recognize him. If you do, and can connect him with any illegal transaction in America or elsewhere, it will simplify our operations ; for our evidence against him, though morally conclusive enough, is still lacking in a few technical points.

" What is the fellow's name ? " inquired the Russian.

" He has various aliases," was the reply, " but I have discovered that his real name is Bolan— Charles Bolan."

This information shed a flood of light into Fedovsky's mind. If Brown were Bolan, it accounted for the knowledge of the count which he had evinced in their first interview, and which had been ascribed to an acquaintance with the imaginary Robert Cecil.

But something still remained unexplained ; and that was, what had given rise to the report that somebody had been robbed and murdered in the theater that afternoon. Could the report have reference to any other incident than that in which he himself had played a principal part? It was impossible to believe so. And yet, where did the baron's information come from ? Certainly Fedovsky had said nothing about it ; and it was at least unlikely that his antagonist had turned informer. There might, to be sure, have been an unseen witness to the affray ; but how could a witness see in the dark, and why, if he could, had he not made his presence known ? Fedovsky was on the point of asking the baron at what hour that afternoon he had received the intelligence, when the entrance of the royal party caused a general

rising and commotion in the audience ; and immediately afterwards the curtain rose and the performance began.

It was a sparkling and amusing piece of work,
full of graceful costumes, attractive musical catches,
and glowing scenic effects—all of a description
with which the Parisian and New York publics are
familiar. The king laughed and applauded, and
chatted amiably with the lady who had the honor
of sitting beside him ; and the audience laughed and
applauded like the king. Fedovsky kept his eyes
upon the stage, but he was scarcely aware of what
was going on there. The baron, however, seemed
to be deeply interested in the performance : and
after a while he beckoned to Herr Klesmer, and
spoke to him in an undertone. Herr Klesmer
then got up, and softly left the box. He came
back in about ten minutes, and having whispered
in the baron's ear, resumed his seat. The curtain
went down on the first act.

"Very good, is it not?" Fedovsky observed.
"I can not say, though, that I recall any of the
faces on the stage."

"I was prepared to hear you say so," answered
the baron ; "the fact is, the person to whom I
wished to call your attention has not appeared."

"That is to say, he does not appear in the first
act?"

"The character appears, but not the performer."

"I beg your pardon?"

"My meaning is," said the baron, whose countenance betrayed some vexation, "that the character—that of *Zamiel* in the drama—has been assumed, at an hour's notice, by another actor. The man who had been cast for it can not be found."

"That is unfortunate, certainly," returned the count, with an air of sympathy; "though, after all, if he has just been committing a robbery and murder, one can hardly blame him for wishing to effect a temporary retirement."

"Your surmise would be correct," said the other, "were it not for the fact that he has no idea that he is suspected; and he would best consult his own safety by assuming his *rôle* of *Zamiel* as though nothing had happened."

"Then he has given you the slip altogether, has he?" inquired Fedovsky, who could not help being secretly amused at the baron's discomfiture.

"He will hardly succeed in doing that; I have already taken my measures to prevent it; it would have been a little more convenient if I could have carried out the original programme, but that is all." And he leaned back in his chair and began another confidential conversation with Herr Klesmer.

Meanwhile Fedovsky, having no Herr Klesmer to talk to, had recourse to his opera-glass, which he brought to bear upon the occupants of all the boxes and stalls that fell within his field of vision. Presently there was a little stir on the opposite side of the auditorium, and a lady, partially enveloped in a white opera-cloak, entered and took a seat in one of the smaller boxes. After a moment she removed the cloak, and appeared dressed in a low-necked dress of dark, steel-blue silk. Her arms and shoulders were perfect in form, and of a beautiful whiteness : her hair, of a reddish-gold color, was rippled above a face of singular and striking loveliness. It was the Princess Volgo-rouki.

What surprised Fedovsky most in this unexpected rencontre was the fact that it affected him so slightly. The woman who, during several years of his life, had been the chief thought and influence of his life, failed now to so much as quicken his pulses. She was even more beautiful than of old ; but her beauty had ceased to move him. When he last saw her, he had been ready to bind her to himself for life ; now, he debated whether it would be worth while to make the circuit of the lobby in order to converse with her. This was a great change, indeed, to have taken place in a year. But it was during that year that he had met and known Sallie Vanderblick ; and it was her clear eyes, brown hair, and pure and powerful nature that had wrought the miracle. Looking upon Vera, and thinking of Sallie, it rejoiced him to be so well convinced of the unrivaled supremacy of the latter in his heart. And yet Sallie was far from him, in distance as well as in hope ; whereas Vera, perhaps, could be his for the asking. But love scorns ease, and welcomes the hardships of laborious days.

As Fedovsky was sitting in the front of his box, and was in full view of the princess, it was not to be expected that she would remain long unconscious of his presence. He kept his eyes fixed upon her, awaiting the moment of recognition. During this interval, he recalled in memory the incidents of their last encounter at Monaco, her inexplicable behavior, and sudden and mysterious departure. He remembered, also, that it was Williams who had brought about their meeting ; and he could not but notice the coincidence of Williams and Vera again being present in the same city at the same time. The former, in his conversation with Fedovsky, had betrayed no knowledge of the fact : but that was not, perhaps, a certain indication that he was not aware of it. Possibly there was something between them. Well, Williams was a respectable man, and a wealthy one; Vera might do worse than marry him, if she were disposed to marriage. Nevertheless, this solution of the matter did not appear satisfactory to the young Russian. It seemed to him highly improbable that Vera would care to marry Williams. Yet what relation, other than one of the affections, could there be between them? But, after all, it was only a conjecture of his own that there was any relation between them whatever.

The princess, meanwhile, maintained a reposeful attitude in her box, whose only other occupant, at present, was her female companion. She seemed to feel no curiosity about the audience, and her pearl-mounted opera-glass lay on the shelf in front of her. Her eyes were fixed idly on the orchestra, to which one or two of the musicians had already returned, and were tuning their instruments and sorting their music scores in readiness for the next act. She held a blue fan, trimmed with swan's-down, moving it to and from her breast with a slow and lazy motion. Her expression was of mingled calmness and indifference. At length the orchestra struck up the prelude to the second act: the princess roused herself, looked across the theater, and saw Fedovsky. The fan's slow movement was arrested; their eyes met. For a moment she sat quite still, making no gesture or motion. Then she closed her fan, and, holding it in her right hand, let it drop backward until it rested on her shoulder. Fedovsky answered with a slight movement of his head.

He now turned to the baron. " There is a lady in a blue dress opposite us," he said. " I have an impression that I am acquainted with her. It was some years ago. If you can tell me her name, it may refresh my memory."

It was the baron's whim to know every thing and every body.

"You are to be congratulated," he said. " She is a Polish lady of high rank and great wealth. She travels under an incognito as Madame Kroneska. Her husband was executed for conspiracy six years ago; but her estates were restored to her by the emperor, on her personal solicitation.

She is a woman who would be apt to succeed in what she undertakes. She is somewhat eccentric, lives by herself, and sees very few people."

"It is rather a difficult position for an attractive woman."

The baron shrugged his shoulders. "Nothing has ever been said against her. She moves in some of the best society of Europe. Some day, of course, she may weary of respectability, and do something startling. But she is young yet, and still values her social position too much to imperil it."

"I think she must be the lady I know, though my acquaintance with her antedates the marriage you speak of," said Fedovsky. "With your permission, I will step over to her and find out. As your murderer seems to have vanished, you will not require my assistance during the next act."

He left the box, made his way round the auditorium, and was admitted to a seat beside "Madame Kroneska."

She gave him her hand, but there was no smile on her lips as she greeted him. "Are you satisfied with the baron's biography of me?" she inquired. Without waiting for his reply, she went on, "So you went to America after all, and—you came back again!"

"Yes; and perhaps I shall cross the ocean a third time before I am settled."

"I do not think I should like America," said she, with an abstracted air.

" I am sure you would not," returned Fedovsky.

She glanced at him quickly, and her eyes darkened. Then, with a resumption of her indifferent manner, she said, " And I· am sure that you will not like Europe."

" Why not ? I used to find it endurable. Has it changed so much in a year ? "

" There have been changes—yes ! " she answered, in a low tone. She opened her fan, and added, " Why don't you ask me the reason of my leaving Monaco without saying good-by to you ? "

" I saw Mr. Williams yesterday ; he spoke of you, and said something about——"

" Ah, yes. That was a reason for Mr. Williams. But there may be some reasons which the Mr. Williamses do not know about.. Never mind ! I avoided saying good·by to you. And now you have come back. Well, you will do as you choose."

" You almost give me to understand," said the count, smiling, " that you would have been better pleased if I had remained on the other side."

" Were you happy there ? "

The young man colored slightly. " Happy and unhappy—the way of the world," he answered.

" And have you been successful since you came here ? "

" Successful ? " he repeated. " In what way ? "

She gave him a singular smile. " You have at least escaped with your life," she said. " To that extent you have been successful."

This remark was so curiously apt, in view of the

impossibility of her knowing what had happened to him that afternoon, that Fedovsky was at a loss what to reply   She seemed to perceive his embarrassment, and smiled again.

" I have been studying astrology lately," she observed, "and I have cast your horoscope.   The stars tell me that this is a dangercus period for you.   You have undertaken to do something that you can not accomplish.   You have enemies, and they are plotting against you.   Abandon your enterprise and return before it is too late."

At this juncture the curtain rose on the second act.

CHAPTER XXI.

VERA turned away from him, and settling herself in her chair, fixed her eyes upon the
stage. Fedovsky did not know what to make of
her words and behavior : he could not but admit
that, if she had been acquainted with all the circumstances of his presence in Dresden, she could
not have spoken more to the point. Not only so,
but her allusion to dangers seemed to indicate a
more comprehensive knowledge of the situation
than he possessed himself. For although he was
plotting against the forgers, he had no reason to
suppose that they were aware of this fact, or were,
consequently, plotting against him. The reference,
to be sure, might be merely to his antagonist of
that afternoon : but, again, what insanity to imagine that Vera could know any thing about the
matter ! It was sufficiently inconceivable that the
baron should have been apprised of it ; but Vera
was out of the question.

The character of Zamiel, in the drama that was
enacting, though important, from an ethical point
of view, to the plot of the piece, and particularly
useful in the tableaux and dramatic culminations,

was not marked by any originality of conception
on the dramatist's part, and he had extremely little
to say for himself. The Satan of the spectacular
stage is generally a being whose speech smacks of
the shop, and who makes up for the conventionality
of his objects and utterances by the vividness of
his costumes and the abruptness of his appearances. So it was with the Zamiel of the present
affair. He materialized unexpectedly, and vanished in the same manner, generally with an ac.
companiment of red fire ; he spoke brief apothegms
in a deep bass voice, and posed, but never
walked. These limitations of visible action were
probably fortunate under the circumstances ; they
enabled the worthy human being who had under-
studied the satanic part to portray it, though at
such short notice, with comparative ease and
accuracy No hitch had occurred in the performance so far, and there was every prospect of a
prosperous continuance.

But a juncture had now arrived, toward which
the whole plot of the piece had been tending,
where a terrific struggle takes place between the
good and the evil principle (incarnated in the
forms of the Fairy Queen and Zamiel respectively)
to determine the fate of the lovers. The Fairy
Queen is first on the ground, and is in the act of
conducting the lovers to a haven of peaceful
security, when all of a sudden the ground yawns
at their feet, sulphurous flames belch forth, and in
the midst of them the mighty Zamiel shoots up-

ward out of the bottomless pit, and defies them to proceed. Such, at all events, are the stage directions.

Divested of the glamour of illusion, the bottomless pit was represented by the subterranean recesses underneath the stage, and the yawning of the earth by a trap-door arrangement. It may also be premised, for the benefit of those uninstructed in such mysteries, that the shooting upward of the arch-fiend is managed by the contrivance of a platform, which rises swiftly on the release of a catch, and forces the performer through the open trapdoor into the air. The trap-door instantly closes beneath him, he comes down upon it in an heroic attitude, and the trick is done.

Now, the Fairy Queen had appeared as aforesaid, and, holding above the lovers her protecting wand, had advanced with them as far as the center of the stage. The trap-door obeyed its cue, and opened ; but Zamiel, for some reason or other, delayed to appear. The Fairy Queen waited ; the lovers waited ; the audience, including the king, waited ; but it began to look as if his satanic majesty had been detained by some unavoidable engagement in his nether kingdom. It was very embarrassing ; and some of the more volatile of the spectators showed a disposition to titter.

Suddenly the suspense was ended, though in an unprecedented and amazing manner.

There was a smothered cry, coming no one knew whence ; but it had a strange and startling sound.

Upward into the air, out of the trap-door, hurtled a human figure, and fell back on the stage with a heavy jar. It moved—it struggled to its knees—it staggered to its feet, and stood, swaying from side to side, ghastly, soiled, tattered, its hair and face matted and smeared with blood, its eyes glaring and blinking in the light, its features quivering and contorted with terror and bewilderment — surely the great enemy of mankind, in all his protean disguises, never hit upon one so grotesque and eccentric as this.

The audience sat in stupefied silence for a moment, and then gave vent to an inarticulate roar of astonishment and dismay Several women shrieked and fainted. A number of men started to their feet ; then some murderous idiot in the· gallery yelled " Fire ! " with all his might. At that appalling cry, the whole great mass of spectators were on their legs, and faced about for a rush to the doors, which would have resulted in a calamity unfortunately too common in modern civilization.

But the panic was arrested almost as suddenly as it had begun. The royal box was situated in the center of the dress-circle, at the apex of the horseshoe curve ; and, as the audience faced round, it necessarily confronted this box. And in it they saw their good King Albert, who had fought valiantly in their behalf at Sedan, reclining comfortably in his chair, and apparently as far from sharing the alarm of his subjects as if he had been safely ensconced in his Japanese Palace up the river. And in the involuntary moment of silence that ensued, they heard him say, in German, to his companion, "Lend me thy lorgnette, Gretchen ; I I have never had an opportunity to see Zamiel in *deshabille* before !"

It was a triumph of common sense and presence of mind over blind fear and brute selfishness. The mob wavered, paused, broke out in confused murmurs and exclamations, followed by laughter and applause and cries of "Hoch ! hoch !" in compliment to his majesty, and, for the most part, resumed its seats. Meanwhile the baron had clambered from his box on to the stage, followed by the imperturbable Herr Klesmer, and, seizing the unkempt Zamiel by the collar, dragged him away behind the scenes. The Fairy Queen and the two lovers, though somewhat disorganized by the interruption, managed to regain their self-possession, and the performance proceeded in spite of the excited buzz of conversation that filled the theater.

During the tumult, Fedovsky and Vera had quietly retained their places. The apparition of the bloodstained man from the bowels of the stage had no doubt surprised them as much as it had the audience ; but to the count at least an explanation presently suggested itself. His wrestling match that afternoon with his unseen assailant (who, of course, could have been no other than Bolan), must have taken place near the middle of the stage ; and Bolan had previously opened the trap door with the purpose of throwing Fedovsky down there, after

choking and robbing him ; and he probably intended to go down there after him, finish him off
with a bludgeon, and conceal the body in the rub-
bish of the basement. The issue of the combat
had turned the tables upon the would-be assassin.
When Fedovsky flung him over his head, he must
have fallen through the trap-door, instead of on
the stage ; and coming in contact with the ground
more than fifteen feet below, had been completely
stunned by the crash. There he had lain undis-
covered for hours, until the noise of the performance had partially aroused him. Possibly some
vague recollection of his part in the drama had
visited his bewildered brain, and he had crawled
on the platform just at the moment when the exi-
gencies of the action demanded that it should be
sprung. The actor who had assumed his part,
being necessarily somewhat unpracticed in the
business, had been confused by discovering some
one on the platform before him ; the darkness and
the hurry had prevented investigation and explanation ; and thus the grotesque incident had come to
pass. The wretched Bolan had already received a
harrowing punishment for his crimes, and there
was every likelihood that the baron would not
allow his chastisement to stop there.

Having thus solved the matter to his own satisfaction, Fedovsky felt a curiosity to know how it had
affected Vera. She had leaned forward, on Bolan's
appearance, with parted lips, and a dilatation
of the eyes ; the alarm of fire had brought a color

to her cheek, but had seemed to restore rather than upset her composure. Finally, when Bolan was led away by the baron, she turned to Fedovsky with an arching of her eyebrows.

" The old proverb sometimes comes to pass," she said ; " he that diggeth a pit, shall fall therein."

" Do you know any thing about that man ?" demanded Fedovsky abruptly.

" I might as well ask you the same question," she replied. " But you need not answer it. I am aware of your dealings with him."

" How did you get your information ? "

She shrugged her shoulders. " I might say, as I proved to you just now, that I am an astrologist. Or I might say that I am a friend of the baron's."

" I should reply that neither the stars nor the baron know my affairs."

" And yet," she said with a smile, " they seem to be known ! " At the same time she rose, drew on her opera-cloak, and prepared to leave the box.

" You are going ? " said the count. " Tell me where I can see you ! "

" You had better not attempt to see me," was her reply. " If you are wise you will follow the advice I gave you a while ago. It would endanger both of us," she added in a more impassioned tone, " if I were to speak more plainly. The only chance for the success of your mission was its secrecy ; and the secret is out ! You have escaped once, but you will not escape a second time. Promise me that you will return."

"I can give you no promise, for I don't know what you mean," he answered. "You say you have discovered my secret. I say I will discover yours."

She looked at him, and, for a moment, seemed to hesitate. Then a cold, rigid expression came over her face, she bowed to him, took the arm of her companion, and turned away. His first impulse was to follow her; but he reflected that he could easily learn her address; and meantime he went back to his hotel.

As he passed the office, the clerk handed him a telegraphic envelope, evidently containing a dispatch from the New York Central office. He put it in his pocket, and went upstairs. He unlocked the door of his room, closed it behind him and locked and bolted it on the inside. He threw off his hat and coat, and, seating himself at his desk, unlocked the drawer in which he had placed his unfinished report. The drawer had also contained the package of bogus bonds and notes, with the hole pierced through them by Bolan's knife.

He opened the drawer. It was empty.

He started to his feet, and gazed about him, half expecting to find a thief in the room. But no one was there. He went to the door and examined the fastening. There were no signs of its having been tampered with. The windows were all fastened on the inside. He next subjected the lock of the desk drawer to a minute examination. It was a patent lock, and no other key than the one

made for it would open it. There was a slight
scratch, barely discernible, at the edge of the aperture ; but the lock itself worked freely as before.
Nevertheless, his room had been entered during
his absence, and his papers had been stolen. Those
papers contained a complete exposition of all that
he had done and intended to do with a view to capturing the forgers. His secret was out, indeed !
He sank into a chair, overcome with consternation;
and the last words of Inspector Byrnes rang in his
ears : "You will have to do with the cleverest and
most desperate criminals in the world !"

CHAPTER XXII.

FEDOVSKY was not long in perceiving that it would be useless to attempt to recover his papers. The report to Inspector Byrnes must already have been read : and the bogus material, being of no use to any one, was probably destroyed. Moreover, were he to apply to the police, he would not be able to conceal the true nature of his mission ; and although it was already known to the forgers (who, he could not doubt, committed the robbery), yet nothing was to be gained by giving further publicity to the facts. He had been egregiously outwitted, and he had nothing but his own carelessness and indiscretion to blame for it.

When he thought of the confidence that Inspector Byrnes had placed in him, and the disappointment this defeat would be to him, he felt ready to groan with mortification. He had not only failed, but he had failed before dealing a single effective blow toward his object. Nor did he know which way to turn to amend his position. He had begun to doubt whether Bolan really belonged to the gang of forgers whom he was pursuing. Had he been one of them, he would hardly have risked the larger objects which he and his accomplices were pursuing, by a robbery and murder that would be certain to be investigated. Mr. Williams must have been mistaken: and the baron must have been right. Bolan was following ends of his own, and acting independently of the others, and in endeavoring to entrap him, Fedovsky had simply been chasing a false clew.

He bethought him of the unopened dispatch in his pocket. With a heavy heart he took it out and broke the seal. It was from the inspector, as he had anticipated, and was expressed in the cipher agreed upon between them. Fedovsky referred to the key that he carried with him, and spelled it out.

After giving some directions on minor matters, the dispatch ran somewhat as follows: "You appear to be on the wrong track. Your confidence will be solicited by those least fitted to possess it. Think over every one you have met, and suspect those who have seemed least open to suspicion. Unless you strike soon, you will be too late. Look toward Italy: the dénoument will be there if anywhere."

"He knows more about this affair, sitting at his desk in New York, than I do here in the midst of them," said the young man to himself bitterly. "The only mistake he made was in sending me after them. How did it happen that he failed to know I was a fool? What will he say when he hears that I have failed?"

He got up and paced the floor in uncontrollable agitation.

"It would have been better for me if I had jumped into the river, as I intended," he exclaimed. "I have done more harm than good, and there is no chance of my ever remedying the matter. Vera was right—I may as well return before I make more blunders. And as for Sallie—well, at least I can congratulate myself on not having tied myself about her neck! May she never know what an escape I have had!"

There was a knock at the door. It was still early in the evening—barely nine o'clock. The knock was repeated. Fedovsky went to the door, and threw it open. A servant stood there, and said that there was a man below who wanted to see the count.

"What is his name?"

"He said it was Herr Bolan," replied the servant.

"Bolan!" repeated Fedovsky, in astonishment. "You must be mistaken." He paused, all manner of evil surmises running through his head. "Show him up," he said at length.

The servant retired. The count walked over to the table, took his revolver from his pocket, and laid it on the desk. He stood near the table, with the revolver convenient to his hand. Another knock at the door. "Come in!" said the count.

The door was pushed open, and a short, sturdy figure entered. It removed its hat from its head, and gazed earnestly at Fedovsky. The next moment, with a shout of joy, the two men ran together, and fairly hugged one another.

"Tom! Tom! can this really be you?" cried the count, shaking his old valet by both hands, while tears stood in his eyes. "I thought you were dead—I thought you had deserted me—but I never thought to see you here!"

"I might have died, sir," said Tom, in a voice that was by no means steady, "but it would take more than dying to make me desert you—I can tell you that! I've been looking for you these four months, and I'd never have given up the search, if it had lasted a hundred years. I served your father, and I served you; and there isn't nothing in this world is going to keep me away from you—not for long!"

"Where have you been? What became of you after you left me that day——"

"Ah! that was a day, sure enough! I was expecting to meet my brother, who was going to put me on to a good thing, he said: but I think it's just as well I didn't meet him, sir : for, from what I've heard since, I fancy he's no good. And no man that's a thief and a scoundrel is a brother of mine, whether he has the same name or not!"

"You did not meet him, then?"

"No, sir; not I. I went down to the Fulton Ferry that day, for it was in Brooklyn that we was to meet : there was a crowd aboard, and I got to the front, so as to be the first off when we reached

t'other side.   When the boat was within five foo'
of the slip, I jumped ; but my foot slipped on the
edge, and down I tumbled into the water.   The
current that was running underneath took me along
to the paddle-wheel, and there I got a bang on the
top of the head : that was the last I knew o:
any thing for a matter of six weeks or more."

"Six weeks !   You were not in the water all tha'
time ?"

"Not so far as I know, sir.   I was fished out
somehow, and the water emptied out of me ; and
as nobody knew who I was, or where I belonged,]
was carried to the hospital.   But that bang on the
head had knocked me silly—so they say ; and I was
as daft as a monkey.   What I may have done or
said of course I can't remember ; but I said nothing
that could help to identify me ; and they were for
sending me to the asylum, when one of the doctors
had the sense to take a look at my skull, where I
got hit, and he found a bit of the bone had been
knocked in, and was pressing on the stuff inside.
So he pried the piece out, and set it all smooth
again, and as soon as he done that, I came to
myself as right as a trivet ; and the first thing I
asked was, 'Who pulled me out of the water?'"

Here they both laughed, and Tom continued :

"Well, then the doctors and the other folks up
there, they made up a purse of twenty dollars, and
give it to me, and back I started to New York to
find you.   Well, sir, you took a deal of finding, and
that's a fact.   At last I thought I'd see if the police

didn't know any thing ; so I went up to the detective office, and they took me in to the inspector. Ah, sir ! He's a nice man, if ever there was one !"

"Quite right, Tom," assented the other, with a sigh. "Well, what did he say?"

"He asked me some pretty sharp questions ; and when he'd found out what I was and all about me, and had sized me up from top to bottom, he told me that I'd better stay where I was, for that you was gone to Europe, and you wouldn't be back till may be next spring. 'And as you seem to be a lively chap,' says he, 'I don't know but what I might find you some odd job to do here round the office.' Well, I thanked him hearty, but I told him I couldn't wait ; I'd have to go after you : and that I'd take the next steamer that started. 'And how are you going to get across?' says he. 'Ask a sailor that?' says I. 'I'll work my passage before the mast, to be sure. I ain't no first-cabin dude !' Well, he laughed, and told me to come again next day ; and next day I went, and he told me he'd got me a place as an assistant to the steward of one of the big steamers that goes to Havre ; it was to leave on the Saturday ; and he tipped me a five dollar bill, and said he, 'I guess your master will be glad to see you, Tom !' So I thanked him again, and off I went ; and to make a short story of it, sir, here I am ; and right glad I am to be here !"

"And right glad am I to have you here," said Fedovsky ; "though you have reached me at what is perhaps the most unfortunate moment of my life, and I am powerless to be of any use either to you or to any one else."

"It wasn't to have you of use to me that I came here, sir," said Tom, growing quite red in the face ; "the boot is on the other leg, if you please, sir. I may be conceited, but it's my idea that I can be of some use to you in this particular affair you re busy with."

"What affair are you talking about, Tom?" inquired the count, opening his eyes.

"Now, look here, sir," said Tom, leaning forward over the table, and assuming an expression of vast sagacity, "I was a fool in New York, and I know it. I didn't understand the way you ought to have carried on there, and I gave you bad advice. I see it now, and sorry I am for it. But in a thing of this kind, it's different ; I know my way about. You're doing something for Inspector Byrnes, ain't you ?"

"What put such an idea into your head ? What would I be doing for him ?"

"Well, two and two make four, that's all I can say ! Thinks I to myself, how does it happen that the inspector knows so much about the count over in Europe ? Then I heard something about a gang of American forgers out here ; and in hunting after you, I found that you had been wherever they had ; and altogether, I made up my mind that you was after them ; and I don't think you'll say I'm wrong."

"I don't know that I shall, Tom," said the other,

with a melancholy laugh. "Every body seems to know my business better than I do; and there's no reason why I should make it a secret from you. You are quite right; I am a member of the secret service, detailed to effect the arrest of the head of this forgery scheme; and I have succeeded so well that the whole gang know all about me and my designs, and have this evening entered my room during my absence, and stolen from my desk the report that I had just been writing to the inspector."

"They did, did they? And who might they be, sir?"

"I haven't the least idea! I thought I had identified one of them; he was no less a person than that brother of yours, Tom, whom you had such hopes of in New York. I had an interview with him this afternoon; he tried to garotte me, and I threw him down the trap-door in the stage of the theater; and now the baron has got him—the chief of police, that is. But though he's a thief, I don't believe he has any connection with the forgers."

"What brought you to think he had, sir?" Tom asked.

"Something that an acquaintance of mine told me—that Mr. Williams, by the way, whom you and I met last year in Monte Carlo."

"Oh, that cove!" said Tom, with a very distasteful air.

"You were mistaken about him," rejoined the

other with a smile. "He is not the same person as the swindler who cheated you in New York." And the count proceeded to relate the visit of himself and Mr. Williams to the baron's office, and what Mr. Williams had said and done there in support of his identity.

Tom listened closely and then shook his head.

"Do you believe all that, sir?" he said. "I don't; it's a pack of lies from beginning to end! Where did he get all those papers from, to prove he was Williams and not Willis! Ain't he a forger? and what's a forger good for, if not to do forgeries? All those papers was forgeries—letters, receipts, passports, letter-of-credit and all! Why, his game's plain enough—it stands to reason. And he was the one that got your desk opened this evening and walked off with your papers!"

"That is impossible, Tom. He is in Cologne at this moment."

"Is he? Then he must travel quick to get there; for I saw him not half an hour ago a quarter of a mile from where we are sitting!"

"What's that? You saw him?"

"As plain as I see you; and he wasn't up to any honest business either. I'll tell you how it was, sir. I got to this town about six hours ago, and I spent a couple of hours or so running about to find the hotel you was stopping at. When I found 'twas the Bellevue, I came and asked to see you, and they said you was out, but would be back later. So I waited around; and presently I saw a chap come along—a small, light chap, with a knowing face, and an expression like butter wouldn't melt in his mouth—and he went up and spoke to the porter there at the door. I didn't hear what he said; but the porter said, ' No, sir, the count has gone to the theater, and won't be back before nine.' Well, the chap went off, and thinks I, what does that fellow want with the count, I wonder. So having nothing better to do, I walked along after him; and he crossed the square, and turned down a side street, and whipped into a house there, with a big gable to it, and a milliner's shop underneath.

" There was a cigar store on t'other side of the street, and I went into it and bought a cigar and stood talking with the shopkeeper, and looking across at the door the fellow went in at. In about ten minutes, out he came again, though at first look I didn't recognize him. He had on a pair of black whiskers, and no overcoat, but only a dirty, old dress suit, like the waiters wear, and a napkin over his arm. He was carrying something under his napkin—a black box about a foot long and half as broad; it looked to be made of iron, with a shiny lacquer over it. Well, he trotted along, walking with them short steps the waiters use, as if he'd just run out to fill an order. I put after him, smoking my cigar, and looking in at all the shop windows, like I was out for a stroll to amuse myself. He got back to the hotel, and trotted right in past the porter, who just gave him a look, but didn't say nothing, supposing him to be one of the waiters that belonged there. I stood off near the bridge, about a hundred yards away, staring at the boats down in the river, but keeping an eye out on the door of the hotel just the same. And by and by out comes my man, just as he went in, with the box under his arm, and the napkin over it, and starts across the square towards the big covered archway that leads into the town. It was dark under there, but I hurried up, and wasn't more than fifty yards away when he went into it. Just in the middle of it, he met a man coming the other way, with a big overcoat on ; and they sort of run into each other, and stopped a moment close together, and then went on again, each his own way ; but the waiter fellow didn't have the box any longer. I turned right round then, and walked along toward the bridge ; and pretty soon the man in the overcoat passed me—he was walking fast—and I noticed two things about him : he had something under his overcoat, and he was your friend, Mr. Williams ! "

CHAPTER XXIII.

THE DISPATCH BOX.

AT this point in his narrative, Tom paused significantly, and looked steadily at the count. The latter kept silence for a considerable time, and appeared to be thinking deeply. Perhaps he was recalling the sentence in the inspector's dispatch —"Suspect those who have seemed least open to suspicion." At length he said, "Did you follow him, too?"

"You can go bail I did, sir," replied Tom, with a self-satisfied air. "He didn't go far, either— just across the bridge and into a hotel on the other side called the 'Stadt Cöln,' which means the City of Cologne, and is about as near to the real place as he has been, I fancy."

"Upon my word, Tom," said the count, after another pause, "you make out a pretty clear case. And now that I think it over, there are other reasons for believing that Williams is somehow connected with the case. There was a difference in his manner toward me from the moment I first mentioned Inspector Byrnes's name, and he alluded to it once or twice afterward. Then again, his setting me after that brother of yours — that was a very shrewd device to throw dust in my eyes, if you look at it in that way Your brother probably has nothing to do with the forgeries, and on the other hand, Williams may have had some grudge against him, as.well as against me : and thought, that by bringing us together, he could dispose of both of us. And it came near turning out so ! And yet I have my doubts about it, still !" added the count, in a lower tone, his mind reverting to a feature of the case that he scarcely ventured to scrutinize too closely.

" My idea is, that our first business should be to get hold of that dispatch-box, and find out what's in it," remarked Tom, with cheerful confidence.

" Perhaps so : but how is it to be done? We can not break into his room, as he has into mine, especially as we are not certain—"

" I'll risk the certainty ! " interrupted Tom, wagging his head sagaciously "All I ask is to get my fingers on the box. And I'll do it, too, before I'm many years older ! "

" The inspector intimates," said Fedovsky thoughtfully. "that we are to look toward Italy as the next scene of the drama. It would be worth something to know whether Williams intends going there. And perhaps, if we could be with him on the journey, we might have a better chance at that dispatch-box than while it is locked up in his room at the hotel."

" That's a good idea," Tom replied approvingly. " It stands to reason that he would want to leave town as soon as possible after this affair ; and if he does, we'll go on the same train with him. He doesn't know me : and as for you, sir, give me a pair of blue spectacles and a wig, and I can make you look so as you wouldn't know yourself in the looking-glass."

"I don't know about disguises," said Fedovsky, shaking his head. "They are liable to be found out, or at least suspected, and then they are worse than nothing."

"That would be very true if you had to talk to a man, and act like somebody else all through ; but if you only have to sit still and not look like yourself, it's as safe as a church, and saves more trouble than the multiplication-table. Yes, sir, that's a good scheme : and these fellows move so quick, that the sooner we get things ready, the better."

"All right, Tom, let us make a try for it, at all events !" exclaimed the count, throwing off his doubt and depression, and springing to his feet. "I was on the point of giving it all up, when you came in, and going back to New York with my tail between my legs. But now I'm determined to see the end of it : and nothing that man can do shall be left undone to succeed. My blunders have made the difficulties much greater than they were in the beginning ; but I shall trust in you to help me out : and we won't be beaten !"

"Ah, that's the way I like to hear you talk, sir," said Tom, rubbing his hands and grinning broadly. "That means business : and when you get your back up, as the saying is, there is nobody's going to stop your hitting the bull's eye. I can help here and there : and we won't be beaten, sure enough ! Now, what's the orders?"

" Go back to Williams's hotel," replied the count, "and find out whether he is about to leave, and if so, what railway station he means to leave by. Meanwhile I will pack my trunks, and have a droschky ready to start at a moment's-warning. We must go on the same train with him, if we are going at all, and never lose sight of him afterward. Come back to me the moment you have any definite information."

It was curious to see how, now that the young Russian's spirit was thoroughly aroused, he involuntarily took the command and acted on his own judgment and responsibility, instead of submitting to be led and advised by his servant, as heretofore. The latter rightly regarded the change as of good augury, and set off on his mission with cheerful confidence. When the Cossack blood grows warm, it can accomplish wonders, and obstacles only augment its energy and resources.

Into the details of the further events of that night it will be unnecessary to enter. Suffice it to say that Mr. Williams left his hotel at daybreak, accompanied by a trunk, a large valise, and a bundle of shawls and umbrellas, and was driven to a railway station in the Neustadt, in time to take an early train westward. He was met there by a small, capable-looking gentleman, who answered very well to Tom's description of the mysterious waiter ; and after some confabulation, Williams left him and his trunk on the train, and himself, with his valise and shawls, entered another hack, and was taken back across the river, and to the other side of the town, finally alighting at the Bohemian railway station a few minutes before the train started for the south. He got into a first-class carriage, which he had all to himself ; and evidently paid no attention to the fact that a slender, invalid gentleman, with a pair of dark spectacles and long, thin, flaxen hair, occupied the carriage next to his, in company with a stout personage with a red face and English mutton-chop whiskers, who asked the invalid for a light for his cigar ; and upon being informed by the latter that he carried no matches, and moreover objected to tobacco, replied defiantly, " You do, do you ? Well, I like it ! " and having borrowed a light from the guard, deliberately blew a cloud of smoke into the other's face. With that, the train drew out of the station, and hastened on its way.

When they were well on their way, flying along the beautiful banks of the Elbe, the invalid and the English gentleman put their heads together with an air of confidence and familiarity quite inconsistent with their late strangeness and disagreement.

" We couldn't have managed it better, sir," said Tom, with a chuckle. " He's in the next carriage, and he doesn't suspect us. The only question is whether he has the box in that valise, or whether he put it in the trunk that the other fellow has got."

"If the box has the value that we suppose," replied Fedovsky, "he certainly would not trust it out of his reach. It is in the carriage with him, if it be anywhere; and what we have to do is to get at it and examine it without his knowing that we have done so."

"Without his knowing!" repeated the other. "That won't be so easy. He's all alone. What's the matter with our getting into his carriage and tying him up, while we go through his things?"

"In the first place, he is probably armed, and would resist; and in the second place, and what is much more important, it is indispensable that he should have no suspicion that his baggage has been tampered with. Our object is not to rob him, but to determine whether he is in reality the man we believe him to be; and my hope is that the box contains conclusive evidence on that point. If it does not, there may at least be something to indicate where and how such evidence is to be obtained. But we must make no move to arrest him, until we are sure beyond the possibility of a doubt that we shall not be obliged to let him go again."

"And how do you mean to manage it, sir?" demanded Tom.

Fedovsky leaned forward, and in a low voice confided to his valet the plan he had formed. They debated the matter for some time, and having arranged every thing to their mutual satisfaction, they leaned back in their seats and awaited the time of action.

The train by which they traveled was an express, and stopped only at the principal stations on the route. The first station was upward of two hours from Dresden, and the one next following was nearly the same distance beyond. Presently the conductor came along, walking on the narrow foot-board that extends along the outside of most continental trains, and, holding on by the metal handles affixed to the sides of the carriage, put his head in at the window and requested to see their tickets. The tickets were shown, and he passed on.

"We will try it at the next station," said Fedovsky. "It will be as good a chance as any, and there is always the danger that he may leave the train at any point and so escape us. Have you the letter ready?"

"Here it is," said Tom, taking it out of his pocket, and glancing over the contents. "You have written it just about right, sir; just enough to draw him, and yet not so strong as to make him suspicious. It'll fetch him, if any thing will."

"Be prepared to jump out the moment the train arrives," added the count; "moments will be worth hours, and we have none to lose."

A little while longer, and a slight slackening of speed told that the train was nearing its first stop. Slower and more slowly it went, until it entered the station. Tom had his head out of the window, and was already beckoning to the guard to unlock the door. This was done, and the train had scarcely come to a standstill when he jumped out and disappeared into the refreshment room.

The doors of the other carriages were also unlocked ; and the invalid with the blue glasses saw the occupant of the next carriage step out and stand on the platform in front of his door, taking care, however, not to move more than a pace or two away from it. A minute passed, and then another. A third was almost gone when a railway porter came along the platform, looking carefully at one carriage after another, until he got to the one before which Mr. Williams was standing. He approached him, and handed him a sealed envelope. Williams glanced at the address, then at the porter, tore open the letter and read the contents. They appeared to be brief, but also interesting. Williams read them again, seemed to hesitate, then beckoned to the guard. The invalid, who had watched all this, heard him say in German : "Just look after my things for a moment ; I am going to step into the refreshment room. See that no one meddles with any thing."

The guard nodded, and Williams hurried away. Two minutes more passed. The passengers who had got out began to resume their places. The train was about to start.

There was only one minute left. Out of the refreshment room came leisurely the red-faced Englishman with the mutton-chop whiskers. He walked up to the guard, and put a silver thaler in his hand.

" The gentleman who occupies this carriage asked me to give you this," he said, "and to tell you that he has decided to stop over this train. You are to take out his baggage at the end of the route, and have it taken to the baggage office, where he will call for it when he arrives."

The guard had the money in his hand ; and seeing nothing of the occupant of the compartment in question, and there being no time at all left to weigh the matter, he very naturally slipped the thaler into his pocket, slammed the door and blew his whistle. The red-faced Englishman had in the meanwhile regained his own seat opposite the invalid, and the train moved on. A minute more, and it was a quarter of a mile away

The conspirators now had nearly two hours in which to carry out the remainder of their plot. With reasonable good luck, this was ample time.

" Did you have any difficulty with him ?" Fedovsky inquired

The fellow worked the trick to perfection, and then I tackled the guard, as you saw."

While Tom was delivering himself, Fedovsky was removing his wig and spectacles and overcoat, and appeared in a close-fitting knit jersey of a dark brown color, drawn over his vest, and displaying to advantage his active and symmetrical figure. The window of the compartment, when open at its widest, gave an aperture only about fifteen inches square. The train was now going at full speed, and was passing through a tract of woodland. Fedovsky put one leg out of the window, then the other, so that he sat upon the sill. Tom then put his hands beneath the other's arms, and let him slide downward and outward, until his feet rested upon the narrow platform outside. Fedovsky then turned round, grasped the handles, and was so far safe. He moved along to the window of the adjoining compartment, which fortunately happened to be open, and contrived to wriggle himself into it head foremost in a manner which, though not graceful, at all events got him there. Tom, who had watched the operation with intense anxiety and interest, now withdrew his head with a sigh, and awaited further developments.

Fedovsky, for his part, began his work without a moment's delay.

He had provided himself with a huge bunch of keys, of all sorts and conditions. The only article of baggage that Willis had brought with him, besides the bundle of shawls, was the large valise, and this was provided not only with straps, but with a lock. Fedovsky tried one key after another upon it without effect; at length he decided to wrench it open, but when he had unfastened the straps for that purpose, the valise opened of itself. It had not been locked at all.

What did it contain? Shirts, and other articles of underwear; a pair of slippers; toilet appliances; a box of excellent cigars; a railway novel or two; a tourists' map of Europe; a guide-book to Italy; —a number of such things as these, but of the iron dispatch-box, not a trace! No, it was absolutely not there. Here was another blunder, and this time a fatal one. Either the box was in the trunk, which had gone no one knew whither; or else Williams had nothing to do with it. The sweat started out on the count's forehead.

He closed and strapped the valise and flung it back upon the seat. In so doing, he dislodged the bundle of shawls, which fell to the floor of the carriage. He lifted it to restore it to its place, and was struck by its unaccountable weight. He felt of it, and fancied there was something solid in the pendently of one another, and each ring lettered round the edge. It was locked with a word, and could then be opened only by bringing the letters forming that word into line. There were four rings on this lock, and the word which opened it must therefore consist of four letters.

As the box was too strong to be broken open (even had such a course been desirable), there was nothing for it but to guess the word ; and Fedovsky proceeded accordingly to bring together all the collocations of four letters that he could think of. But none of them was the right one. He would not give up the task, and kept at it steadily for near half an hour, still with no result. Then he tried combining the letters at hap-hazard, but the lock was obstinate. Nothing throughout the affair had been so tantalizing as this. He had the secret literally at his very finger-ends, and he could not solve it. Time was passing, and the conductor might be expected on his rounds for the tickets at any moment. It would not do for Fedovsky to be discovered in that compartment. " I shall fail again," he said to himself despairingly. " It would have been better if I had staid in Dresden and had another interview with Vera. She may, after all, be a government spy, and be able to tell me just what I want to know."

As the thought passed through his mind, his fingers involuntarily moved the rings, until the letters spelled the name, " Vera." The box fell open. The secret was out !

The young man turned pale. He had succeeded, but his success had been purchased at the price of the fair repute of the woman he had once loved. If Vera's name was used as the shibboleth of a gang of thieves, it was asking too much of human charity to believe that she was not privy to their designs. Moreover, the discovery threw light on her past conduct, explaining many things that had seemed unaccountable. Yes, Vera was guilty ; and it must be through her that the truth would be attained, and justice done.

By and by Fedovsky manned himself, and examined the contents of the box. It held his report, as he had anticipated, and many other papers of value to the forgers, all of which he read, and of some of which he made copies. Then he replaced them, tied up the box in its bundle, and regained his own carriage five minutes before the guard appeared on his rounds.

CHAPTER XXIV

VERA.

A WEEK later, a young man, quietly but fash-
ionably dressed, and with the air of an idle
tourist taking a stroll to kill time, was walking along
a road immediately outside of the walls of Florence.
Presently he halted in front of a pretty villa, which
stood in a little garden, behind high walls, with
trees rising above its eaves.   In the midst of the
wall was an iron gate, curiously molded.   The
young man approached this gate, and rang a bell.

The gate was opened by a servant, who stared
inquiringly at the visitor.   The latter carelessly
uttered a few words, which seemed to have no
pertinence to the matter in hand, but which had
the effect of causing the servant to admit him
without hesitation. Passing by her while she refast-
ened the gate, he entered the house, and turned
into a room on the right of the hall.   A woman
was sitting there by an open window, with her back
toward him.   As his step sounded on the floor, she
turned languidly; then started to her feet, and
threw her arms apart with a sharp cry.

"Ivan Fedovsky! You!"

"Yes, Vera, here I am. I have followed you, you see."

She leaned back against the frame of the window and put her hand over her heart. Her eyes fixed themselves upon him waveringly ; she was manifestly much agitated. Her lips moved, but at first no audible words came from them.

"How did you pass the gate?" she asked at length.

"By using the password that is used by other persons who come here," he replied quietly.

"You don't know the password ! How could you have learned it ?"

"By the same means that I learned the names of Henry Willis and the other members of the gang, whose rendezvous is at this house, and who concoct here, with your assistance, their schemes of forgery."

She waved her hand with a gesture of negation, moved to a chair and sank down in it. "I know of no such men," she said, in a faint voice.

"You have known them for a long time. Without the shield of your supposed respectability—the protection your home and name have afforded them—they could not have carried out their designs. You are the repository of their secrets, and the guardian of their booty. I might have known it long ago, but I would not let myself believe it. But now all possibility of doubt has been removed, and therefore I am here."

His manner was so stern and composed, and his

words had such assurance of conviction, that the woman's resistance was shaken. "Even if I knew any thing of these men," she said, "it would not follow that I know any harm of them. I am not their confederate—if they are such men as you say."

"Vera," replied the count, sternly, "I did not come here to argue with you. I know of what I speak. But you are a woman, and I once loved you. A year ago, when I found you in danger and distress, I would have saved you, if you would have come with me. But even then you loved your shameful life too well to accept my offer. It is not that offer that I make to you to-day. But there is a chance that you may be rescued from final and open disgrace by revealing what may still remain obscure regarding your accomplices and their designs. Only, the revelation must be immediate and full."

"What right have you to make such a demand of me?"

"You already know by what right I demand it, for you have read the papers that were stolen from my desk in Dresden, and given to Henry Willis— or Williams, if he prefers to be known by that name. You know what other things occurred there; and you were a party to the plot by which it was sought to have me murdered by another friend of yours— Mr. Charles Bolan."

"It is false!" she cried, with passionate energy, half springing to her feet, and then sinking back in her chair. "It was he who planned that thing,"

she added, in a fainter voice : " I knew nothing of
it till afterwards. He distrusted and feared you,
and sought to put you out of the way by the hand
of a man whom he also wished to destroy. When
I heard it I threatened to betray him: and when,
afterwards, you came to me in the theater, I tried
by every means to induce you to give up your mission and return to America ; it was for your own
sake, not for theirs, that I did it. If they had
known I did it my own life would have been in
danger."

" What warrant can you give me of the truth of
what you say ? You told me a story in Monaco
about your marriage to a Russian prince. Is that
true, also ? "

" It was not true," she answered, bending down
her head. " But they forced me to tell it. I was
helpless against them."

" How could that be ? " asked the count, coldly.

" You misjudge me," she said, wiping the tears
from her eyes with her trembling fingers. " I am
not so vile as you suppose. That man whom your
father forced me to marry when I was parted from
you did not stop at robbing your estates. He engaged in other crimes, of which I was obliged
to be cognizant. At last, in connection with
others, he committed a great robbery,
amounting to over twenty thousand pounds.
He was arrested and convicted, but not
before he had disposed of the money. It was in-
trusted to me by his accomplices, and I was assisted

to escape. In time all the thieves were captured but one, and that is the man you met at Monaco. He knew my secret, and it gave him a power over me that I could not break. Whatever he commanded I was forced to do. By degrees—as we get used to every thing—I became accustomed to the life, and ceased to think or to regret. There was only one thing I could keep from degradation; and, whether you believe it or not, I did keep that. If I had gone with you to be your wife on that night when you asked me, at least I should not have had that to reproach myself with. I was the associate and the accomplice of thieves: but, as a woman, Ivan Fedovsky, I am pure!"

"I hope, and I believe that you are, Vera," said the count, gravely. "But it is not of this I came to speak. You must tell me every thing that you know of the plans and acts of these men in relation to the forgeries that are being perpetrated in this country and America ; and especially you must give such evidence as will enable me to convict Henry Willis of being the chief and the prime-mover of the crime."

Vera frowned. "And suppose I refuse?" said she.

"In that case I can do no more for you. You must take the consequences along with the rest."

"And what are the consequences to me? Do you think I find the life I have been leading so agreeable that I would exert myself greatly to continue it ? Do you not think I might find a

greater pleasure in disappointing a man who once
worshiped the ground on which I trod, and who
now comes here to insult and trample on me?"

"The love of my youth is still a sacred thing to
me, Vera," said the count, "though I have learned
since then to feel a deeper and higher love than
that. What you were I never shall forget; nor do
I blame you for what you are; doubtless you are
the victim of circumstances which were too strong
for you. But, however that may be, you would not
now wish, yourself, that there should be any closer
relations between us. We have grown far apart,
and nothing on this side of the grave could bring
us together again. I am not subject to you, as I
once was, but I have for you every honorable feeling that a man can entertain for a woman; and in
so far as I can help and protect you without
betraying justice, I am earnest and resolved to do
so."

"Well, I suppose I must thank you," she replied,
with one of her peculiar smiles. "You are very
upright and correct; though perhaps"—and here
she flashed a strange glance at him out of her dark
eyes—"I might yet find the means, if I chose to
take the trouble, to make you forget, for a few
hours at least, the blameless young lady who, as I
gather from your words, is fortunate enough to
possess your regard. But no matter: you are in
search of information: though really, you appear
to know so much, that I hardly see how you can
expect me to increase your knowledge." She

paused, and pressed her hands over her forehead. "I have always looked forward to some such ending as this," she said, in a sort of broken voice that touched Fedovsky deeply. "And I'm not sure but that I'm glad of it. One gets tired of suspense and excitement and all this lying and trickery. And yet they have treated me very fairly, all things considered. Are you going to be married, Ivan?"

"I have no great expectation of it," he replied, taken aback by the suddenness of the question.

"Well, I hope you will be, and that you will be happy. You and I might have been happy, if things had been a little different. But, as you say, it would be impossible now. I am destined to the shadows!" She bent her head, and was sunk for a few moments in somber meditation. "By the way," she said, rousing herself, and in a lighter tone, "you have been rather poor the last year, have you not? There was a report that your estates had been confiscated. Did you ever inquire into that matter."

The count shook his head. "One does not throw one's self into the arms of the bear to find out whether he has strength to crush," he replied.

"A little curiosity is sometimes very useful, however," she answered. "If you had made inquiries, you would perhaps have learned things that would have surprised you. What should you say if I told you that the letters you received announcing the confiscation were nothing but a practical joke of some acquaintances of mine—Signor Strogello and a few others—who thought that if they could only persuade you that you had lost the estates it might afterwards be possible to persuade the Russian government to hand them over to them, as your appointed heirs and assigns ?"

" I should say that—I doubted it."

" Oh, well, you are very incredulous. It is true, nevertheless. It was a great scheme, but only the first part of it succeeded—the part that concerned you. The government refused to be entrapped, and the estates are still yours whenever you choose to go and claim them. I make you a present of this information as a wedding gift. So, you see, in the midst of your happiness and prosperity you will have to remember me ! "

" Is this really true, Vera ?" began the count ; but she interrupted him.

" It is really true, but I must trouble you not to thank me. I am merely putting my house in order previous to vacating it, and getting rid of the lumber that is no longer of any use to me. And now you want evidence against Henry Willis, do you ? "

Fedovsky gave a sign of assent.

" Well, I hate him ! He has tyrannized over my life. He has shut me out from amendment. He has made me what I am. I have been his slave, and he has been my ruin. And now I have a chance to be avenged. Is it not natural that I should use it ?"

She spoke with flashing eyes and flushed cheeks, and a passionate gesture of the hands. She had never looked so beautiful and so dangerous.

"It would be strange, indeed, if you did not," said Fedovsky.

She broke into a laugh. "Well, I like to be strange," she replied, "and I mean to be so just this once more! I will tell you nothing about Henry Willis. He was my accomplice—he confided in me—and I will not betray him. You may capture him, if you can, and I hope you will, and"—she clinched her teeth together—"and give him his deserts! But you shall never say that I helped you to do it. I am going away; and that burden, at least, I will not carry on my soul!"

She rose as she spoke, and made a sign of farewell. Fedovsky had also arisen, not understanding what she was going to do. She bowed down her face, and pressed her hands over her mouth. The count noticed a movement in her throat, as if she were swallowing. Then he understood, and sprang forward to prevent her. But it was too late. As he held her on his arm, with her head on his shoulder, she turned her face upwards towards him, and smiled that strange smile once more. She closed her eyes, and sighed; and there was the scent of almonds in her breath.

*　　*　　*　　*　　*　　*

The evidence which Fedovsky had already accumulated was sufficient for his purposes, and the papers and other articles that were discovered in

Vera's house were hardly needed to confirm it.
Willis was arrested the next morning at his hotel,
and, on being confronted with the facts against him,
he broke down, and made a complete and circum-
stantial confession, detailing his whole career from
the beginning, and fatally implicating all his accomplices, all of whom were also captured, and made to
serve their several penalties. This confession was
afterwards reduced to writing, and a copy of it is
preserved in the secret archives of the New York
Central office. It is considered to be the most
remarkable document of the kind in existence ; but
in no respect is it more remarkable than in the
manner in which it confirms all the theories and
anticipations formed by Inspector Byrnes regarding the case. His analysis and prognostication
were justified in every essential particular ; and by
his instrumentality and foresight a scheme of robbery on a scale unexampled in modern times was
nipped in the bud, and its organizers forever broken
and scattered.

It would need another volume to tell how
Fedovsky recovered his estates ; how he returned
to New York to make his personal report to the
inspector, and to hand in his resignation as an
officer of the secret service ; how he searched for
Sallie Vanderblick, and found her at last teaching
in a public school at a salary of six hundred dollars
a year—her father having failed, and partially lost
his reason, and Fred being employed as a clerk in
the firm of the man who had been chiefly instru-

mental in his father's ruin.　Fedovsky and Sallie were married, and enjoy as much happiness as can ever fall to the lot of human beings,—a happiness in which the faithful Tom fully shares.　Sallie is fond of saying that they owe it all to Inspector Byrnes. Her husband is by no means behind her in his acknowledgment of this indebtedness ; but a memory sometimes occurs to his mind which he never speaks of to his wife : the memory of a woman who was passionate, generous, sinful and unfortunate ; and his prayer of gratitude for blessings received is coupled with the name of Vera.

THE END.

Illustrated, Fine-Art, and other Volumes.

Abbeys and Churches of England and Wales, The: Descriptive, Historical, Pictorial. Series II. 21s.

Adventure, The World of. Fully Illustrated. In Three Vols. 9s. each.

Africa and its Explorers, The Story of. By Dr. ROBERT BROWN, F.L.S. Illustrated. Complete in 4 Vols., 7s. 6d. each.

Animals, Popular History of. By HENRY SCHERREN, F.Z.S. With 12 Coloured Plates and other Illustrations. 7s. 6d.

Arabian Nights Entertainments, Cassell's Pictorial. 10s. 6d.

Architectural Drawing. By R. PHENÉ SPIERS. Illustrated. 10s. 6d.

Art, The Magazine of. Yearly Vol. With 14 Photogravures or Etchings, a Series of Full-page Plates, and about 400 Illustrations. 21s.

Artistic Anatomy. By Prof. M. DUVAL. *Cheap Edition.* 3s. 6d.

Astronomy, The Dawn of. A Study of the Temple Worship and Mythology of the Ancient Egyptians. By Prof. J. NORMAN LOCKYER, C.B., F.R.S., &c. Illustrated. 21s.

Atlas, The Universal. A New and Complete General Atlas of the World, with 117 Pages of Maps, in Colours, and a Complete Index to about 125,000 Names. List of Maps, Prices and all Particulars on Application.

Bashkirtseff, Marie, The Journal of. *Cheap Edition.* 7s. 6d.

Bashkirtseff, Marie, The Letters of. 7s. 6d.

Battles of the Nineteenth Century. An Entirely New and Original Work. Illustrated. Vol. I., 9s.

Beetles, Butterflies, Moths, and Other Insects. By A. W. KAPPEL, F.E.S., and W. EGMONT KIRBY. With 12 Coloured Plates. 3s. 6d.

"Belle Sauvage" Library, The. Cloth, 2s. each. A list of the Volumes post free on application.

Biographical Dictionary, Cassell's New. *Cheap Edition,* 3s. 6d.

Birds' Nests, Eggs, and Egg-Collecting. By R. KEARTON. Illustrated with 16 Coloured Plates. 5s.

Birds' Nests, British: How, Where, and When to Find and Identify Them. By R. KEARTON. With an Introduction by Dr. BOWDLER SHARPE and upwards of 130 Illustrations of Nests, Eggs, Young, etc., from Photographs by C. KEARTON. 21s.

Breech-Loader, The, and How to Use It. By W. W. GREENER. Illustrated. New and enlarged edition. 2s. 6d.

Britain's Roll of Glory; or, the Victoria Cross, its Heroes, and their Valour. By D. H. PARRY. Illustrated. 7s. 6d.

British Ballads. With Several Hundred Original Illustrations. Complete in Two Vols., cloth, 15s. Half morocco, *price on application.*

British Battles on Land and Sea. By JAMES GRANT. With about 600 Illustrations. Four Vols., 4to, £1 16s.; *Library Edition,* £2.

Butterflies and Moths, European. With 61 Coloured Plates. 35s.

Canaries and Cage-Birds, The Illustrated Book of. With 56 Facsimile Coloured Plates, 35s. Half-morocco, £2 5s.

Captain Horn, The Adventures of. By FRANK STOCKTON. 6s.

Capture of the "Estrella," The. A Tale of the Slave Trade. By COMMANDER CLAUDE HARDING, R.N. 5s.

Cassell's Family Magazine. Yearly Vol. Illustrated. 7s. 6d.

Cathedrals, Abbeys, and Churches of England and Wales. Descriptive, Historical, Pictorial. *Popular Edition.* Two Vols. 25s.

Cats and Kittens. By HENRIETTE RONNER. With Portrait and 13 Full-page Photogravure Plates and numerous Illustrations. £2 2s.

Chums. The Illustrated Paper for Boys. Yearly Volume, 8s.

Cities of the World. Four Vols. Illustrated. 7s. 6d. each.

Civil Service, Guide to Employment in the. Entirely New Edition. Paper, 1s. Cloth, 1s. 6d.

Clinical Manuals for Practitioners and Students of Medicine. A List of Volumes forwarded post free on application to the Publishers.

Colour. By Prof. A. H. CHURCH. With Coloured Plates. 3s. 6d.

Commons and Forests, English. By the Rt. Hon. G. SHAW-LEFEVRE, M.P. With Maps. 10s 6d.

Cook, The Thorough Good. By GEORGE AUGUSTUS SALA. 21s.

Cookery, A Year's. By PHYLLIS BROWNE. 3s. 6d.

Cookery Book, Cassell's New Universal. By LIZZIE HERITAGE. With 12 Coloured Plates and other Illustrations. Strongly bound in Half-leather. 1,344 pages. 6s.

Cookery, Cassell's Shilling. 110*th Thousand.* 1s.

Cookery, Vegetarian. By A. G. PAYNE. 1s. 6d.

Cooking by Gas, The Art of. By MARIE J. SUGG. Illustrated. 2s.

Cottage Gardening, Poultry, Bees, Allotments, Etc. Edited by W. ROBINSON. Illustrated. Half-yearly Volumes, 2s. 6d. each.

Count Cavour and Madame de Circourt. Some Unpublished Correspondence. Translated by A. J. BUTLER. Cloth gilt, 10s. 6d.

Countries of the World, The. By ROBERT BROWN, M.A., Ph.D., &c. *Cheap Edition.* Profusely Illustrated. Vol. 1., 6s.

Cyclopædia, Cassell's Concise. Brought down to the latest date. With about 600 Illustrations. *Cheap Edition.* 7s. 6d.

Cyclopædia, Cassell's Miniature. Containing 30,000 subjects. Cloth, 2s. 6d. ; half-roxburgh, 4s.

David Balfour, The Adventures of. By R. L. STEVENSON. Illustrated. Two Vols. 6s. each.

Part 1.—Kidnapped.   Part 2.—Catriona.

Defoe, Daniel, The Life of. By THOMAS WRIGHT. Illustrated, 21s.

Diet and Cookery for Common Ailments. By a Fellow of the Royal College of Physicians, and PHYLLIS BROWNE. 5s.

Dog, Illustrated Book of the. By VERO SHAW, B.A. With 28 Coloured Plates. Cloth bevelled, 35s. ; half-morocco, 45s.

Domestic Dictionary, The. Illustrated. Cloth, 7s. 6d.

Doré Bible, The. With 200 Full-page Illustrations by DORÉ. 15s.

Doré Don Quixote, The. With about 400 Illustrations by GUSTAVE DORÉ. *Cheap Edition.* Bevelled boards, gilt edges, 10s. 6d.

Doré Gallery, The. With 250 Illustrations by DORÉ. 4to, 42s.

Doré's Dante's Inferno. Illustrated by GUSTAVE DORÉ. With Preface by A. J. BUTLER. Cloth gilt or buckram, 7s. 6d.

Doré's Dante's Purgatory and Paradise. Illustrated by GUSTAVE DORÉ. *Cheap Edition.* 7s. 6d.

Doré's Milton's Paradise Lost. Illustrated by DORÉ. 4to, 21s. *Popular Edition.* Cloth gilt or buckram gilt, 7s. 6d.

Dorset, Old. Chapters in the History of the County. By H. J. MOULE, M.A. 10s. 6d.

Dressmaking, Modern, The Elements of. By J. E. DAVIS. Illd. 2s.

Earth, Our, and its Story. By Dr. ROBERT BROWN, F.L.S. With Coloured Plates and numerous Wood Engravings. Three Vols. 9s. each.

Edinburgh, Old and New. With 600 Illustrations. Three Vols. 9s. each.

Egypt: Descriptive, Historical, and Picturesque. By Prof. G. EBERS. With 800 Original Engravings. *Popular Edition.* In Two Vols. 42s.

Electric Current, The. How Produced and How Used. By R. MULLINEUX WALMSLEY, D.Sc., etc. Illustrated. 10s. 6d.

Electricity in the Service of Man. Illustrated. *New and Revised Edition.* 10s. 6d.

Electricity, Practical. By Prof. W. E. AYRTON. 7s. 6d.

Encyclopædic Dictionary, The. In Fourteen Divisional Vols., 10s. 6d. each ; or Seven Vols., half-morocco, 21s. each ; half-russia, 25s.

England, Cassell's Illustrated History of. With upwards of 2,000 Illustrations. *Revised Edition.* Complete in Eight Vols., 9s. each ; cloth gilt, and embossed gilt top and headbanded, £4 net the set.

English Dictionary, Cassell's. Giving definitions of more than 100,000 Words and Phrases. *Superior Edition*, 5s. *Cheap Edition*, 3s. 6d.

English Literature, Library of. By Prof. HENRY MORLEY. Complete in Five Vols., 7s. 6d. each.

English Literature, The Dictionary of. By W. DAVENPORT ADAMS. *Cheap Edition.* 7s. 6d.

English Literature, Morley's First Sketch of. *Revised Edition.* 7s. 6d.

English Literature, The Story of. By ANNA BUCKLAND. 3s. 6d.

English Writers. By Prof. HENRY MORLEY. Vols. I. to XI. 5s. each.

Etiquette of Good Society. *New Edition.* Edited and Revised by LADY COLIN CAMPBELL. 1s.; cloth, 1s. 6d.

Fairway Island. By HORACE HUTCHINSON. *Cheap Edition.* 3s. 6d.

Fairy Tales Far and Near. Re-told by Q. Illustrated. 3s. 6d.

Fiction, Cassell's Popular Library of. 3s. 6d. each.

THE AVENGER OF BLOOD. By J. MACLAREN COBBAN.	THE SNARE OF THE FOWLER. By Mrs. ALEXANDER.
A MODERN DICK WHITTINGTON. By JAMES PAYN.	"LA BELLA" AND OTHERS. By EGERTON CASTLE.
THE MAN IN BLACK. By STANLEY WEYMAN.	LEONA. By Mrs. MOLESWORTH.
A BLOT OF INK. Translated by Q. and PAUL M. FRANCKE.	FOURTEEN TO ONE, ETC. By ELIZABETH STUART PHELPS.
THE MEDICINE LADY. By L. T. MEADE.	FATHER STAFFORD. By ANTHONY HOPE.
OUT OF THE JAWS OF DEATH. By FRANK BARRETT.	DR. DUMÁNY'S WIFE. By MAURUS JÓKAI.
	THE DOINGS OF RAFFLES HAW. By CONAN DOYLE.

Field Naturalist's Handbook, The. By the Revs. J. G. WOOD and THEODORE WOOD. *Cheap Edition.* 2s. 6d.

Figuier's Popular Scientific Works. With Several Hundred Illustrations in each. Newly Revised and Corrected. 3s. 6d. each.

THE HUMAN RACE. MAMMALIA. OCEAN WORLD.
THE INSECT WORLD. REPTILES AND BIRDS.
WORLD BEFORE THE DELUGE. THE VEGETABLE WORLD.

Flora's Feast. A Masque of Flowers. Penned and Pictured by WALTER CRANE. With 40 Pages in Colours. 5s.

Football, The Rugby Union Game. Edited by REV. F. MARSHALL. Illustrated. *New and Enlarged Edition.* 7s. 6d.

For Glory and Renown. By D. H. PARRY. Illustrated. 5s.

France, From the Memoirs of a Minister of. By STANLEY WEYMAN. 6s.

Franco-German War, Cassell's History of the. Complete in Two Vols. Containing about 500 Illustrations. 9s. each.

Free Lance in a Far Land, A. By HERBERT COMPTON. 6s.

Garden Flowers, Familiar. By SHIRLEY HIBBERD. With Coloured Plates by F. E. HULME, F.L.S. Complete in Five Series. 12s. 6d. each.

Gardening, Cassell's Popular. Illustrated. Four Vols. 5s. each.

Gazetteer of Great Britain and Ireland, Cassell's. Illustrated. Vols. I. and II. 7s. 6d. each.

Gladstone, William Ewart, The People's Life of. Illustrated. 1s.

Gleanings from Popular Authors. Two Vols. With Original Illustrations. 4to, 9s. each. Two Vols. in One, 15s.

Gulliver's Travels. With 88 Engravings by MORTEN. *Cheap Edition.* Cloth, 3s. 6d.; cloth gilt, 5s.

Gun and its Development, The. By W. W. GREENER. With 500 Illustrations. 10s. 6d.

Heavens, The Story of the. By Sir ROBERT STAWELL BALL, LL.D., F.R.S., F.R.A.S. With Coloured Plates. *Popular Edition.* 12s. 6d.

Heroes of Britain in Peace and War. With 300 Original Illustrations. Two Vols., 3s. 6d. each; or One Vol., 7s. 6d.

Highway of Sorrow, The. By HESBA STRETTON and ******** 6s

Hispaniola Plate (1683-1893). By JOHN BLOUNDELLE-BURTON. 6s.

Historic Houses of the United Kingdom. Profusely Illustrated. 10s. 6d.

History, A Foot-note to. Eight Years of Trouble in Samoa. By ROBERT LOUIS STEVENSON. 6s.

Home Life of the Ancient Greeks, The. Translated by ALICE ZIMMERN. Illustrated. *Cheap Edition.* 5s.

Horse, The Book of the. By SAMUEL SIDNEY. With 17 Full-page Collotype Plates of Celebrated Horses of the Day, and numerous other Illustrations. Cloth, 15s.

Horses and Dogs. By O. EERELMAN. With Descriptive Text. Translated from the Dutch by CLARA BELL. With Photogravure Frontispiece, 12 Exquisite Collotypes, and several full page and other engravings in the text. 25s. net.

Houghton, Lord: The Life, Letters, and Friendships of Richard Monckton Milnes, First Lord Houghton. By Sir WEMYSS REID. In Two Vols., with Two Portraits. 32s.

Household, Cassell's Book of the. Complete in Four Vols. 5s. each. Four Vols. in Two, half-morocco, 25s.

Hygiene and Public Health. By B. ARTHUR WHITELEGGE, M.D. 7s. 6d.

Impregnable City, The. By MAX PEMBERTON. 6s.

India, Cassell's History of. By JAMES GRANT. With about 400 Illustrations. Two Vols., 9s. each. One Vol., 15s.

Iron Pirate, The. By MAX PEMBERTON. Illustrated. 5s.

Island Nights' Entertainments. By R. L. STEVENSON. Illustrated. 6s.

Kennel Guide, The Practical. By Dr. GORDON STABLES. 1s.

Khiva, A Ride to. By Col. FRED BURNABY. *New Edition.* With Portrait and Seven Illustrations. 3s. 6d.

King George, In the Days of. By COL. PERCY GROVES. Illd. 1s. 6d.

King's Hussar, A. Edited by HERBERT COMPTON. 6s.

Ladies' Physician, The. By a London Physician. *Cheap Edition, Revised and Enlarged.* 3s. 6d.

Lady Biddy Fane, The Admirable. By FRANK BARRETT. *New Edition.* With 12 Full-page Illustrations. 6s.

Lady's Dressing-room, The. Translated from the French of BARONESS STAFFE by LADY COLIN CAMPBELL. 3s. 6d.

Letters, the Highway of, and its Echoes of Famous Footsteps. By THOMAS ARCHER. Illustrated. 10s. 6d.

Letts's Diaries and other Time-saving Publications published exclusively by CASSELL & COMPANY. (*A list free on application.*)

'Lisbeth. A Novel. By LESLIE KEITH. 6s.

List, ye Landsmen! By W. CLARK RUSSELL. 6s.

Little Minister, The. By J. M. BARRIE. *Illustrated Edition.* 6s.

Little Squire, The. By Mrs. HENRY DE LA PASTURE. 3s. 6d.

Llollandilaff Legends, The. By LOUIS LLOLLANDLLAFF. 1s.; cloth, 2s.

Lobengula, Three Years With, and Experiences in South Africa. By J. COOPER-CHADWICK. *Cheap Edition,* 2s. 6d.

Locomotive Engine, The Biography of a. By HENRY FRITH. 3s. 6d.

Loftus, Lord Augustus, The Diplomatic Reminiscences of. First and Second Series. Two Vols., each with Portrait, 32s. each Series.

London, Greater. By EDWARD WALFORD. Two Vols. With about 400 Illustrations. 9s. each.

London, Old and New. Six Vols., each containing about 200 Illustrations and Maps. Cloth, 9s. each.

Lost on Du Corrig; or, 'Twixt Earth and Ocean. By STANDISH O'GRADY. With 8 Full-page Illustrations. 5s.

Medicine, Manuals for Students of. (*A List forwarded post free.*)

Modern Europe, A History of. By C. A. FYFFE, M.A. *Cheap Edition in One Volume,* 10s. 6d. Library Edition. Illustrated. 3 Vols., 7s. 6d. each.

Mount Desolation. An Australian Romance. By W. CARLTON DAWE. *Cheap Edition.* 3s. 6d.

Music, Illustrated History of. By EMIL NAUMANN. Edited by the Rev. Sir F. A. GORE OUSELEY, Bart. Illustrated. Two Vols. 31s. 6d.

National Library, Cassell's. In 214 Volumes. Paper covers, 3d.; cloth, 6d. (*A Complete List of the Volumes post free on application.*)

Natural History, Cassell's Concise. By E. PERCEVAL WRIGHT, M.A., M.D., F.L.S. With several Hundred Illustrations. 7s. 6d.

Natural History, Cassell's New. Edited by Prof. P. MARTIN DUNCAN, M.B., F.R.S., F.G.S. Complete in Six Vols. With about 2,000 Illustrations. Cloth, 9s. each.

Nature's Wonder Workers. By KATE R. LOVELL. Illustrated. 3s. 6d.

New England Boyhood, A. By EDWARD E. HALE. 3s. 6d.

New Zealand, Picturesque. With Preface by Sir W. B. PERCEVAL, K.C.M.G. Illustrated. 6s.

Nursing for the Home and for the Hospital, A Handbook of. By CATHERINE J. WOOD. *Cheap Edition.* 1s. 6d.; cloth, 2s.

Nursing of Sick Children, A Handbook for the. By CATHERINE J. WOOD. 2s. 6d.

Ohio, The New. A Story of East and West. By EDWARD E. HALE. 6s.

Oil Painting, A Manual of. By the Hon. JOHN COLLIER. 2s. 6d.

Old Maids and Young. By E. D'ESTERRE KEELING. 6s.

Old Boy's Yarns, An. By HAROLD AVERY. With 8 Plates. 3s. 6d.

Our Own Country. Six Vols. With 1,200 Illustrations. 7s. 6d. each.

Painting, The English School of. *Cheap Edition.* 3s. 6d.

Painting, Practical Guides to. With Coloured Plates:—

MARINE PAINTING. 5s.	WATER-COLOUR PAINTING. 5s.
ANIMAL PAINTING. 5s.	NEUTRAL TINT. 5s.
CHINA PAINTING. 5s.	SEPIA, in Two Vols., 3s. each; or in One Vol., 5s.
FIGURE PAINTING. 7s. 6d.	
ELEMENTARY FLOWER PAINTING. 3s.	FLOWERS, AND HOW TO PAINT THEM. 5s.

Paris, Old and New. A Narrative of its History, its People, and its Places. By H. SUTHERLAND EDWARDS. Profusely Illustrated. Complete in Two Vols., 9s. each; or gilt edges, 10s. 6d. each.

Peoples of the World, The. In Six Vols. By Dr. ROBERT BROWN. Illustrated. 7s. 6d. each.

Photography for Amateurs. By T. C. HEPWORTH. *Enlarged and Revised Edition.* Illustrated. 1s.; or cloth, 1s. 6d.

Phrase and Fable, Dr. Brewer's Dictionary of. Giving the Derivation, Source, or Origin of Common Phrases, Allusions, and Words that have a Tale to Tell. *Entirely New and Greatly Enlarged Edition.* 10s. 6d.

Picturesque America. Complete in Four Vols., with 48 Exquisite Steel Plates and about 800 Original Wood Engravings. £2 2s. each. *Popular Edition*, Vols. I. & II., 18s. each. [the Set.

Picturesque Canada. With 600 Original Illustrations. Two Vols. £6 6s.

Picturesque Europe. Complete in Five Vols. Each containing 13 Exquisite Steel Plates, from Original Drawings, and nearly 200 Original Illustrations. Cloth, £21; half-morocco, £31 10s.; morocco gilt, £52 10s. POPULAR EDITION. In Five Vols., 18s. each.

Picturesque Mediterranean, The. With Magnificent Original Illustrations by the leading Artists of the Day. Complete in Two Vols. £2 2s. each.

Pigeon Keeper, The Practical. By LEWIS WRIGHT. Illustrated. 3s. 6d.

Pigeons, Fulton's Book of. Edited by LEWIS WRIGHT. Revised, Enlarged and supplemented by the Rev. W. F. LUMLEY. With 50 Full-page Illustrations. *Popular Edition.* In One Vol., 10s. 6d.

Planet, The Story of Our. By T. G. BONNEY, D.Sc., LL.D., F.R.S., F.S.A., F.G.S. With Coloured Plates and Maps and about 100 Illustrations. 31s. 6d.

Pocket Library, Cassell's. Cloth, 1s. 4d. each.

A King's Diary. By PERCY WHITE.
A White Baby. By JAMES WELSH.
The Little Huguenot. By MAX PEMBERTON.
A Whirl Asunder. By GERTRUDE ATHERTON.

Poems, Aubrey de Vere's. A Selection. Edited by J. DENNIS. 3s. 6d.

Poets, Cassell's Miniature Library of the. Price 1s. each Vol.

Pomona's Travels. By FRANK R. STOCKTON. Illustrated. 5s.

Portrait Gallery, The Cabinet. Complete in Five Series, each containing 36 Cabinet Photographs of Eminent Men and Women. 15s. each.

Portrait Gallery, Cassell's Universal. Containing 240 Portraits of Celebrated Men and Women of the Day. With brief Memoirs and *facsimile* Autographs. Cloth, 6s.

Poultry Keeper, The Practical. By L. WRIGHT. Illustrated. 3s. 6d.

Poultry, The Book of. By LEWIS WRIGHT. *Popular Edition.* 10s. 6d.

Poultry, The Illustrated Book of. By LEWIS WRIGHT. With Fifty Coloured Plates. *New and Revised Edition.* Cloth, gilt edges (*Price on application*). Half-morocco, £2 2s.

Prison Princess, A. By Major ARTHUR GRIFFITHS. 6s.

"Punch," The History of. By M. H. SPIELMANN. With upwards of 160 Illustrations, Portraits, and Facsimiles. Cloth, 16s.; *Large Paper Edition*, £2 2s. net.

Q's Works, Uniform Edition of. 5s. each.

Dead Man's Rock.	The Astonishing History of Troy Town.
The Splendid Spur.	"I Saw Three Ships," and other Winter's Tales.
The Blue Pavilions.	Noughts and Crosses.

The Delectable Duchy.

Queen Summer; or, The Tourney of the Lily and the Rose. With Forty Pages of Designs in Colours by WALTER CRANE. 6s.

Queen, The People's Life of their. By Rev. E. J. HARDY, M.A. 1s.

Queen Victoria, The Life and Times of. By ROBERT WILSON. Complete in Two Vols. With numerous Illustrations. 9s. each.

Queen's Scarlet, The. By G. MANVILLE FENN. Illustrated. 5s.

Rabbit-Keeper, The Practical. By CUNICULUS. Illustrated. 3s. 6d.

Railways, Our. Their Origin, Development, Incident, and Romance. By JOHN PENDLETON. Illustrated. 2 Vols., 24s.

Railway Guides, Official Illustrated. With Illustrations, Maps, &c. Price 1s. each; or in cloth, 2s. each.

LONDON AND NORTH WESTERN RAILWAY.	GREAT EASTERN RAILWAY.
GREAT WESTERN RAILWAY.	LONDON AND SOUTH WESTERN RAILWAY.
MIDLAND RAILWAY.	LONDON, BRIGHTON AND SOUTH COAST RAILWAY.
GREAT NORTHERN RAILWAY.	SOUTH-EASTERN RAILWAY.

Railway Guides, Official Illustrated. Abridged and Popular Editions. Paper covers, 3d. each.

GREAT EASTERN RAILWAY.	LONDON AND SOUTH WESTERN RAILWAY.
LONDON AND NORTH WESTERN RAILWAY.	

Railway Library, Cassell's. Crown 8vo, boards, 2s. each. (*A List of the Vols. post free on application.*)

Red Terror, The. A Story of the Paris Commune. By EDWARD KING. Illustrated. 3s. 6d.

Rivers of Great Britain: Descriptive, Historical, Pictorial. THE ROYAL RIVER: The Thames, from Source to Sea. 16s. RIVERS OF THE EAST COAST. *Popular Edition*, 16s.

Robinson Crusoe, Cassell's New Fine-Art Edition of. 7s. 6d.

Romance, The World of. Illustrated. Cloth, 9s.

Royal Academy Pictures, 1895. With upwards of 200 magnificent reproductions of Pictures in the Royal Academy of 1895. 7s. 6d.

Russo-Turkish War, Cassell's History of. With about 500 Illustrations. Two Vols. 9s. each.

Sala, George Augustus, The Life and Adventures of. By Himself. In Two Vols., demy 8vo, cloth, 32s.

Saturday Journal, Cassell's. Yearly Volume, cloth, 7s. 6d.

Science Series, The Century. Consisting of Biographies of Eminent Scientific Men of the present Century. Edited by Sir HENRY ROSCOE, D.C.L., F.R.S. Crown 8vo, 3s. 6d. each.
> **John Dalton and the Rise of Modern Chemistry.** By Sir HENRY E. ROSCOE, F.R.S.
> **Major Rennell, F.R.S., and the Rise of English Geography.** By CLEMENTS R. MARKHAM, C.B., F.R.S., President of the Royal Geographical Society.
> **Justus Von Liebig: His Life and Work.** By W. A. SHENSTONE, F.I.C.
> **The Herschels and Modern Astronomy.** By MISS AGNES M. CLERKE.
> **Charles Lyell: His Life and Work.** By Professor T. G. BONNEY, F.R.S.

Science for All. Edited by Dr. ROBERT BROWN. Five Vols. 9s. each.

Scotland, Picturesque and Traditional. A Pilgrimage with Staff and Knapsack. By G. E. EYRE-TODD. 6s.

Sea, The Story of the. An Entirely New and Original Work. Edited by Q. Illustrated. Vol. I. 9s.

Sea Wolves, The. By MAX PEMBERTON. Illustrated. 6s.

Shadow of a Song, The. A Novel. By CECIL HARLEY. 5s.

Shaftesbury, The Seventh Earl of, K.G., The Life and Work of. By EDWIN HODDER. *Cheap Edition.* 3s. 6d.

Shakespeare, The Plays of. Edited by Professor HENRY MORLEY. Complete in Thirteen Vols., cloth, 21s. ; half-morocco, cloth sides, 42s.

Shakespeare, Cassell's Quarto Edition. Containing about 600 Illustrations by H. C. SELOUS. Complete in Three Vols., cloth gilt, £3 3s.

Shakespeare, The England of. *New Edition.* By E. GOADBY. With Full-page Illustrations. 2s. 6d.

Shakspere's Works. *Édition de Luxe.*
> "King Henry VIII." Illustrated by SIR JAMES LINTON, P.R.I. (*Price on application.*)
> "Othello." Illustrated by FRANK DICKSEE, R.A. £3 10s.
> "King Henry IV." Illustrated by EDUARD GRÜTZNER. £3 10s.
> "As You Like It." Illustrated by ÉMILE BAYARD. £3 10s.

Shakspere, The Leopold. With 400 Illustrations. *Cheap Edition.* 3s. 6d. Cloth gilt, gilt edges, 5s. ; Roxburgh, 7s. 6d.

Shakspere, The Royal. With Steel Plates and Wood Engravings. Three Vols. 15s. each.

Sketches, The Art of Making and Using. From the French of G. FRAIPONT. By CLARA BELL. With 50 Illustrations. 2s. 6d.

Smuggling Days and Smuggling Ways. By Commander the Hon. HENRY N. SHORE, R.N. With numerous Illustrations. 7s. 6d.

Social England. A Record of the Progress of the People. By various writers. Edited by H. D. TRAILL, D.C.L. Vols. I., II., & III., 15s. each. Vol. IV., 17s.

Social Welfare, Subjects of. By Rt. Hon. LORD PLAYFAIR, K.C.B. 7s. 6d.

Sports and Pastimes, Cassell's Complete Book of. *Cheap Edition.* With more than 900 Illustrations. Medium 8vo, 992 pages, cloth, 3s. 6d.

Squire, The. By Mrs. PARR. *Popular Edition.* 6s.

Standishs of High Acre, The. A Novel. By GILBERT SHELDON. Two Vols. 21s.

Star-Land. By Sir R. S. BALL, LL.D., &c. Illustrated. 6s.

Statesmen, Past and Future. 6s.

Story of Francis Cludde, The. By STANLEY J. WEYMAN. 6s.

Story Poems. For Young and Old. Edited by E. DAVENPORT. 3s. 6d.

Sun, The. By Sir ROBERT STAWELL BALL, LL.D., F.R.S., F.R.A.S. With Eight Coloured Plates and other Illustrations. 21s.

Sunshine Series, Cassell's. 1s. each.
> (*A List of the Volumes post free on application.*)

Thackeray in America, With. By EYRE CROWE, A.R.A. Ill. 10s. 6d.

The "Treasure Island" Series. *Illustrated Edition.* 3s. 6d. each.

Treasure Island. By ROBERT LOUIS STEVENSON.	**The Black Arrow.** By ROBERT LOUIS STEVENSON.
The Master of Ballantrae. By ROBERT LOUIS STEVENSON.	**King Solomon's Mines.** By H. RIDER HAGGARD.

Things I have Seen and People I have Known. By G. A. SALA. With Portrait and Autograph. 2 Vols. 21s.

Tidal Thames, The. By GRANT ALLEN. With India Proof Impressions of Twenty magnificent Full-page Photogravure Plates, and with many other Illustrations in the Text after Original Drawings by W. L. WYLLIE, A.R.A. Half morocco. £5 15s. 6d.

Tiny Luttrell. By E. W. HORNUNG *Popular Edition.* 6s.

To Punish the Czar: a Story of the Crimea. By HORACE HUTCHINSON. Illustrated. 3s. 6d.

Treatment, The Year-Book of, for 1896. A Critical Review for Practitioners of Medicine and Surgery. *Twelfth Year of Issue.* 7s. 6d.

Trees, Familiar. By G. S. BOULGER, F.L.S. Two Series. With 40 full-page Coloured Plates by W. H. J. BOOT. 12s. 6d. each.

Tuxter's Little Maid. By G. B. BURGIN. 6s.

"Unicode": the Universal Telegraphic Phrase Book. *Desk or Pocket Edition.* 2s. 6d.

United States, Cassell's History of the. By EDMUND OLLIER. With 600 Illustrations. Three Vols. 9s. each.

Universal History, Cassell's Illustrated. Four Vols. 9s. each.

Vision of Saints, A. By Sir LEWIS MORRIS. With 20 Full-page Illustrations. Crown 4to, cloth, 10s. 6d. *Non-illustrated Edition*, 6s.

Wandering Heath. Short Stories. By Q. 6s.

War and Peace, Memories and Studies of. By ARCHIBALD FORBES. 16s.

Westminster Abbey, Annals of. By E. T. BRADLEY (Mrs. A. MURRAY SMITH). Illustrated. With a Preface by Dean BRADLEY. 63s.

White Shield, The. By BERTRAM MITFORD. 6s.

Wild Birds, Familiar. By W. SWAYSLAND. Four Series. With 40 Coloured Plates in each. (Sold in sets only; price on application.)

Wild Flowers, Familiar. By F. E. HULME, F.L.S., F.S.A. Five Series. With 40 Coloured Plates in each. (In sets only; price on application.)

Wild Flowers Collecting Book. In Six Parts, 4d. each.

Wild Flowers Drawing and Painting Book. In Six Parts, 4d. each.

Windsor Castle, The Governor's Guide to. By the Most Noble the MARQUIS OF LORNE, K.T. Profusely Illustrated. Limp Cloth, 1s. Cloth boards, gilt edges, 2s.

Wit and Humour, Cassell's New World of. With New Pictures and New Text. 6s.

With Claymore and Bayonet. By Col. PERCY GROVES. Illd. 5s.

Wood, Rev. J. G., Life of the. By the Rev. THEODORE WOOD. Extra crown 8vo, cloth. *Cheap Edition.* 3s. 6d.

Work. The Illustrated Weekly Journal for Mechanics. Vol. IX., 4s.

"Work" Handbooks. Practical Manuals prepared *under the direction of* PAUL N. HASLUCK, Editor of *Work*. Illustrated. 1s. each.

World Beneath the Waters, A. By Rev. GERARD BANCKS. 3s. 6d.

World of Wonders. Two Vols. With 400 Illustrations. 7s. 6d. each.

Wrecker, The. By R. L. STEVENSON and L. OSBOURNE. Illustrated. 6s.

Yule Tide. Cassell's Christmas Annual. 1s.

ILLUSTRATED MAGAZINES.

The Quiver. Monthly, 6d.

Cassell's Family Magazine. Monthly, 6d.

"Little Folks" Magazine. Monthly, 6d.

The Magazine of Art. Monthly, 1s. 4d.

"Chums." Illustrated Paper for Boys. Weekly, 1d. ; Monthly, 6d.

Cassell's Saturday Journal. Weekly, 1d. ; Monthly, 6d.

Work. Weekly, 1d. ; Monthly, 6d.

Cottage Gardening. Weekly, ½d. ; Monthly, 3d.

CASSELL & COMPANY, LIMITED, *Ludgate Hill, London.*

𝕭ibles and 𝕽eligious 𝖂orks.

Bible Biographies. Illustrated. 2s. 6d. each.
 The Story of Moses and Joshua. By the Rev. J. TELFORD.
 The Story of the Judges. By the Rev. J. WYCLIFFE GEDGE.
 The Story of Samuel and Saul. By the Rev. D. C. TOVEY.
 The Story of David. By the Rev. J. WILD.
 The Story of Joseph. Its Lessons for To-Day. By the Rev. GEORGE BAINTON.
 The Story of Jesus. In Verse. By J. R. MACDUFF, D.D.

Bible, Cassell's Illustrated Family. With 900 Illustrations. Leather, gilt edges, £2 10s.

Bible Educator, The. Edited by the Very Rev. Dean PLUMPTRE, D.D. With Illustrations, Maps, &c. Four Vols., cloth, 6s. each.

Bible Manual, Cassell's Illustrated. By the Rev. ROBERT HUNTER, LL.D. *Illustrated.* 7s. 6d.

Bible Student in the British Museum, The. By the Rev. J. G. KITCHIN, M.A. *New and Revised Edition.* 1s. 4d.

Biblewomen and Nurses. Yearly Volume. Illustrated. 3s.

Bunyan, Cassell's Illustrated. With 200 Original Illustrations. *Cheap Edition.* 7s. 6d.

Bunyan's Pilgrim's Progress. Illustrated throughout. Cloth, 3s. 6d.; cloth gilt, gilt edges, 5s.

Child's Bible, The. With 200 Illustrations. *150th Thousand.* 7s. 6d.

Child's Life of Christ, The. With 200 Illustrations. 7s. 6d.

"Come, ye Children." Illustrated. By Rev. BENJAMIN WAUGH. 3s. 6d.

Conquests of the Cross. Illustrated. In 3 Vols. 9s. each.

Doré Bible. With 238 Illustrations by GUSTAVE DORÉ. Small folio, best morocco, gilt edges, £15. *Popular Edition.* With 200 Illustrations. 15s.

Early Days of Christianity, The. By the Very Rev. Dean FARRAR, D.D., F.R.S. LIBRARY EDITION. Two Vols., 24s.; morocco, £2 2s. POPULAR EDITION. Complete in One Volume, cloth, 6s.; cloth, gilt edges, 7s. 6d.; Persian morocco, 10s. 6d.; tree-calf, 15s.

Family Prayer-Book, The. Edited by Rev. Canon GARBETT, M.A., and Rev. S. MARTIN. With Full page Illustrations. *New Edition.* Cloth, 7s. 6d.

Gleanings after Harvest. Studies and Sketches by the Rev. JOHN R. VERNON, M.A. Illustrated. 6s.

"Graven in the Rock." By the Rev. Dr. SAMUEL KINNS, F.R.A.S., Author of "Moses and Geology." Illustrated. 12s. 6d.

"Heart Chords." A Series of Works by Eminent Divines. Bound in cloth, red edges, One Shilling each.

MY BIBLE. By the Right Rev. W. BOYD CARPENTER, Bishop of Ripon.

MY FATHER. By the Right Rev. ASHTON OXENDEN, late Bishop of Montreal.

MY WORK FOR GOD. By the Right Rev. Bishop COTTERILL.

MY OBJECT IN LIFE. By the Very Rev. Dean FARRAR, D.D.

MY ASPIRATIONS. By the Rev. G. MATHESON, D.D.

MY EMOTIONAL LIFE. By the Rev. Preb. CHADWICK, D.D.

MY BODY. By the Rev. Prof. W. G. BLAIKIE, D.D.

MY GROWTH IN DIVINE LIFE. By the Rev. Preb. REYNOLDS, M.A.

MY SOUL. By the Rev. P. B. POWER, M.A.

MY HEREAFTER. By the Very Rev. Dean BICKERSTETH.

MY WALK WITH GOD. By the Very Rev. Dean MONTGOMERY.

MY AIDS TO THE DIVINE LIFE. By the Very Rev. Dean BOYLE.

MY SOURCES OF STRENGTH. By the Rev. E. E. JENKINS, M.A., Secretary of Wesleyan Missionary Society.

Helps to Belief. A Series of Helpful Manuals on the Religious Difficulties of the Day. Edited by the Rev. TEIGNMOUTH SHORE, M.A., Canon of Worcester. Cloth, 1s. each.

CREATION. By Harvey Goodwin, D.D., late Bishop of Carlisle.

THE DIVINITY OF OUR LORD. By the Lord Bishop of Derry.

MIRACLES. By the Rev. Brownlow Maitland, M.A.

PRAYER. By the Rev. Canon Shore, M.A.

THE ATONEMENT. By William Connor Magee, D.D., Late Archbishop of York.

Holy Land and the Bible, The. By the Rev. C. GEIKIE, D.D., LL.D. (Edin.). Two Vols., 24s. *Illustrated Edition*, One Vol., 21s.

Life of Christ, The. By the Very Rev. Dean FARRAR, D.D., F.R.S LIBRARY EDITION. Two Vols. Cloth, 24s. ; morocco, 42s. CHEAP ILLUSTRATED EDITION. Cloth, 7s. 6d. ; cloth, full gilt, gilt edges, 10s. 6d. POPULAR EDITION (*Revised and Enlarged*), 8vo, cloth, gilt edges, 7s. 6d. ; Persian morocco, gilt edges, 10s. 6d. ; tree-calf, 15s.

Moses and Geology ; or, The Harmony of the Bible with Science. By the Rev. SAMUEL KINNS, Ph.D., F.R.A.S. Illustrated. *New Edition.* 10s. 6d.

My Last Will and Testament. By HYACINTHE LOYSON (Père Hyacinthe). Translated by FABIAN WARE. 1s. ; cloth, 1s. 6d.

New Light on the Bible and the Holy Land. By B. T. A. EVETTS, M.A. Illustrated. 21s.

New Testament Commentary for English Readers, The. Edited by Bishop ELLICOTT. In Three Volumes. 21s. each. Vol. I.—The Four Gospels. Vol. II.—The Acts, Romans, Corinthians, Galatians. Vol. III.—The remaining Books of the New Testament.

New Testament Commentary. Edited by Bishop ELLICOTT. Handy Volume Edition. St. Matthew, 3s. 6d. St. Mark, 3s. St. Luke, 3s. 6d. St. John, 3s. 6d. The Acts of the Apostles, 3s. 6d. Romans, 2s. 6d. Corinthians I. and II., 3s. Galatians, Ephesians, and Philippians, 3s. Colossians, Thessalonians, and Timothy, 3s. Titus, Philemon, Hebrews, and James, 3s. Peter, Jude, and John, 3s. The Revelation, 3s. An Introduction to the New Testament, 3s. 6d.

Old Testament Commentary for English Readers, The. Edited by Bishop ELLICOTT. Complete in Five Vols. 21s. each. Vol. I.—Genesis to Numbers. Vol. II. — Deuteronomy to Samuel II. Vol. III.— Kings I. to Esther. Vol. IV.—Job to Isaiah. Vol. V.—Jeremiah to Malachi.

Old Testament Commentary. Edited by Bishop ELLICOTT. Handy Volume Edition. Genesis, 3s. 6d. Exodus, 3s. Leviticus, 3s. Numbers, 2s. 6d. Deuteronomy, 2s. 6d.

Plain Introductions to the Books of the Old Testament. Edited by Bishop ELLICOTT. 3s. 6d.

Plain Introductions to the Books of the New Testament. Edited by Bishop ELLICOTT. 3s. 6d.

Protestantism, The History of. By the Rev. J. A. WYLIE, LL.D. Containing upwards of 600 Original Illustrations. Three Vols. 9s. each.

Quiver Yearly Volume, The. With about 600 Original Illustrations. 7s. 6d.

Religion, The Dictionary of. By the Rev. W. BENHAM, B.D. *Cheap Edition.* 10s. 6d.

St. George for England ; and other Sermons preached to Children. By the Rev. T. TEIGNMOUTH SHORE, M.A., Canon of Worcester. 5s.

St. Paul, The Life and Work of. By the Very Rev. Dean FARRAR, D.D., F.R.S. LIBRARY EDITION. Two Vols., cloth, 24s. ; calf, 42s. ILLUSTRATED EDITION, complete in One Volume, with about 300 Illustrations, £1 1s. ; morocco, £2 2s. POPULAR EDITION. One Volume, 8vo, cloth, 6s. ; cloth, gilt edges, 7s. 6d. ; Persian morocco, 10s. 6d. ; tree-calf, 15s.

Shall We Know One Another in Heaven ? By the Rt. Rev. J. C. RYLE, D.D., Bishop of Liverpool. *Cheap Edition.* Paper covers, 6d.

Searchings in the Silence. By Rev. GEORGE MATHESON, D.D. 3s. 6d.

"Sunday," Its Origin, History, and Present Obligation. By the Ven. Archdeacon HESSEY, D.C.L. *Fifth Edition.* 7s. 6d.

Twilight of Life, The. Words of Counsel and Comfort for the Aged. By the Rev. JOHN ELLERTON, M.A. 1s. 6d.

Educational Works and Students' Manuals.

Agricultural Text-Books, Cassell's. (The "Downton" Series.) Edited by JOHN WRIGHTSON, Professor of Agriculture. Fully Illustrated, 2s. 6d. each.—Farm Crops. By Prof. WRIGHTSON. -Soils and Manures. By J. M. H. MUNRO, D.Sc. (London), F.I.C., F.C.S. —Live Stock. By Prof. WRIGHTSON.

Alphabet, Cassell's Pictorial. 3s. 6d.

Arithmetics, Cassell's "Belle Sauvage." By GEORGE RICKS, B.Sc. Lond. With Test Cards. (*List on application.*)

Atlas, Cassell's Popular. Containing 24 Coloured Maps. 2s. 6d.

Book-Keeping. By THEODORE JONES. For Schools, 2s. ; cloth, 3s. For the Million, 2s. ; cloth, 3s. Books for Jones's System, 2s.

British Empire Map of the World. By G. R. PARKIN and J. G. BARTHOLOMEW, F.R.G.S. 25s.

Chemistry, The Public School. By J. H. ANDERSON, M.A. 2s. 6d.

Cookery for Schools. By LIZZIE HERITAGE. 6d.

Dulce Domum. Rhymes and Songs for Children. Edited by JOHN FARMER, Editor of "Gaudeamus," &c. Old Notation and Words, 5s. N.B.—The words of the Songs in "Dulce Domum" (with the Airs both in Tonic Sol-fa and Old Notation) can be had in Two Parts, 6d. each.

Euclid, Cassell's. Edited by Prof. WALLACE, M.A. 1s.

Euclid, The First Four Books of. *New Edition.* In paper, 6d. ; cloth, 9d.

Experimental Geometry. By PAUL BERT. Illustrated. 1s. 6d.

French, Cassell's Lessons in. *New and Revised Edition.* Parts I. and II., each 2s. 6d. ; complete, 4s. 6d. Key, 1s. 6d.

French-English and English-French Dictionary. *Entirely New and Enlarged Edition.* Cloth, 3s. 6d. ; superior binding, 5s.

French Reader, Cassell's Public School. By G. S. CONRAD. 2s. 6d.

Gaudeamus. Songs for Colleges and Schools. Edited by JOHN FARMER. 5s. Words only, paper covers, 6d. ; cloth, 9d.

German Dictionary, Cassell's New (German-English, English-German). *Cheap Edition.* Cloth, 3s. 6d. *Superior Binding*, 5s.

Hand and Eye Training. By G. RICKS, B.Sc. 2 Vols., with 16 Coloured Plates in each Vol. Cr. 4to, 6s. each. Cards for Class Use, 5 sets, 1s. each.

Hand and Eye Training. By GEORGE RICKS, B.Sc., and JOSEPH VAUGHAN. Illustrated. Vol. I. Designing with Coloured Papers. Vol. II. Cardboard Work. 2s. each. Vol. III. Colour Work and Design, 3s.

Historical Cartoons, Cassell's Coloured. Size 45 in. × 35 in., 2s. each. Mounted on canvas and varnished, with rollers, 5s. each.

Italian Lessons, with Exercises, Cassell's. Cloth, 3s. 6d.

Latin Dictionary, Cassell's New. (Latin-English and English-Latin.) Revised by J. R. V. MARCHANT, M.A., and J. F. CHARLES, B.A. Cloth, 3s. 6d. *Superior Binding*, 5s.

Latin Primer, The First. By Prof. POSTGATE. 1s.

Latin Primer, The New. By Prof. J. P. POSTGATE. 2s. 6d.

Latin Prose for Lower Forms. By M. A. BAYFIELD, M.A. 2s. 6d.

Laws of Every-Day Life. By H. O. ARNOLD-FORSTER, M.P. 1s. 6d. *Special Edition* on Green Paper for Persons with Weak Eyesight. 2s.

Lessons in Our Laws; or, Talks at Broadacre Farm. By H. F. LESTER, B.A. Parts I. and II., 1s. 6d. each.

Little Folks' History of England. Illustrated. 1s. 6d.

Making of the Home, The. By Mrs. SAMUEL A. BARNETT. 1s. 6d.

Marlborough Books:—Arithmetic Examples, 3s. French Exercises, 3s. 6d. French Grammar, 2s. 6d. German Grammar, 3s. 6d.

Mechanics and Machine Design, Numerical Examples in Practical. By R. G. BLAINE, M.E. *New Edition, Revised and Enlarged.* With 79 Illustrations. Cloth, 2s. 6d.

Mechanics for Young Beginners, A First Book of. By the Rev. J. G. EASTON, M.A. 4s. 6d.

Books for Young People.

"Little Folks" Half-Yearly Volume. Containing 432 4to pages, with about 200 Illustrations, and Pictures in Colour. Boards, 3s. 6d.; cloth, 5s.

Bo-Peep. A Book for the Little Ones. With Original Stories and Verses. Illustrated throughout. Yearly Volume. Boards, 2s. 6d.; cloth, 3s. 6d.

Beneath the Banner. Being Narratives of Noble Lives and Brave Deeds. By F. J. Cross. Illustrated. Limp cloth, 1s. Cloth gilt, 2s.

Good Morning! Good Night! By F. J. Cross. Illustrated. Limp cloth, 1s., or cloth boards, gilt lettered, 2s.

Five Stars in a Little Pool. By Edith Carrington. Illustrated. 6s.

The Cost of a Mistake. By Sarah Pitt. Illustrated. *New Edition.* 2s 6d.

Beyond the Blue Mountains. By L. T. Meade. 5s.

The Peep of Day. *Cassell's Illustrated Edition.* 2s. 6d.

Maggie Steele's Diary. By E. A. Dillwyn. 2s. 6d.

A Book of Merry Tales. By Maggie Browne, "Sheila," Isabel Wilson, and C. L. Matéaux. Illustrated. 3s. 6d.

A Sunday Story-Book. By Maggie Browne, Sam Browne, and Aunt Ethel. Illustrated. 3s. 6d.

A Bundle of Tales. By Maggie Browne (Author of "Wanted—a King," &c.), Sam Browne, and Aunt Ethel. 3s. 6d.

Pleasant Work for Busy Fingers. By Maggie Browne. Illustrated. 5s.

Born a King. By Frances and Mary Arnold-Forster. (The Life of Alfonso XIII., the Boy King of Spain.) Illustrated. 1s.

Cassell's Pictorial Scrap Book. Six Vols. 3s. 6d. each.

Schoolroom and Home Theatricals. By Arthur Waugh. Illustrated. *New Edition.* Paper, 1s. Cloth, 1s. 6d.

Magic at Home. By Prof. Hoffman. Illustrated. Cloth gilt, 3s. 6d.

Little Mother Bunch. By Mrs. Molesworth. Illustrated. *New Edition.* Cloth. 2s. 6d.

Heroes of Every-day Life. By Laura Lane. With about 20 Full-page Illustrations. Cloth. 2s. 6d.

Bob Lovell's Career. By Edward S. Ellis. 5s.

Books for Young People. *Cheap Edition.* Illustrated. Cloth gilt, 3s. 6d. each.

The Champion of Odin; or, Viking Life in the Days of Old. By J. Fred. Hodgetts.	Bound by a Spell; or, The Hunted Witch of the Forest. By the Hon. Mrs. Greene.

Under Bayard's Banner. By Henry Frith.

Books for Young People. Illustrated. 3s. 6d. each.

Told Out of School. By A. J. Daniels.	*The Palace Beautiful. By L. T. Meade.
Red Rose and Tiger Lily. By L. T. Meade.	*Polly: A New-Fashioned Girl. By L. T. Meade.
The Romance of Invention. By James Burnley.	"Follow My Leader." By Talbot Baines Reed.
*Bashful Fifteen. By L. T. Meade.	*A World of Girls: The Story of a School. By L. T. Meade.
*The White House at Inch Gow. By Mrs. Pitt.	Lost among White Africans. By David Ker.
*A Sweet Girl Graduate. By L. T. Meade.	For Fortune and Glory: A Story of the Soudan War. By Lewis Hough.
The King's Command: A Story for Girls. By Maggie Symington.	

Also procurable in superior binding, 5s. each.

"Peeps Abroad" Library. *Cheap Editions.* Gilt edges, 2s. 6d. each.

Rambles Round London. By C. L. Matéaux. Illustrated.

Around and About Old England. By C. L. Matéaux. Illustrated.

Paws and Claws. By one of the Authors of "Poems written for a Child." Illustrated.

Decisive Events in History. By Thomas Archer. With Original Illustrations.

The True Robinson Crusoes. Cloth gilt.

Peeps Abroad for Folks at Home. Illustrated throughout.

Wild Adventures in Wild Places. By Dr. Gordon Stables, R.N. Illustrated.

Modern Explorers. By Thomas Frost. Illustrated. *New and Cheaper Edition.*

Early Explorers. By Thomas Frost.

Home Chat with our Young Folks. Illustrated throughout.

Jungle, Peak, and Plain. Illustrated throughout.

The "Cross and Crown" Series. Illustrated. 2s. 6d. each.

Freedom's Sword: A Story of the Days of Wallace and Bruce. By Annie S. Swan.

Strong to Suffer: A Story of the Jews. By E. Wynne.

Heroes of the Indian Empire; or, Stories of Valour and Victory. By Ernest Foster.

In Letters of Flame: A Story of the Waldenses. By C. L. Matéaux.

Through Trial to Triumph. By Madeline B. Hunt.

By Fire and Sword: A Story of the Huguenots. By Thomas Archer.

Adam Hepburn's Vow: A Tale of Kirk and Covenant. By Annie S. Swan.

No. XIII.; or, The Story of the Lost Vestal. A Tale of Early Christian Days. By Emma Marshall.

"Golden Mottoes" Series, The. Each Book containing 208 pages, with Four full-page Original Illustrations. Crown 8vo, cloth gilt, 2s. each.

"Nil Desperandum." By the Rev. F. Langbridge, M.A.

"Bear and Forbear." By Sarah Pitt.

"Foremost if I Can." By Helen Atteridge.

"Honour is my Guide." By Jeanie Hering (Mrs. Adams-Acton).

"Aim at a Sure End." By Emily Searchfield.

"He Conquers who Endures." By the Author of "May Cunningham's Trial," &c.

Cassell's Picture Story Books. Each containing about Sixty Pages of Pictures and Stories, &c. 6d. each.

Little Talks.
Bright Stars.
Nursery Toys.
Pet's Posy.
Tiny Tales.

Daisy's Story Book.
Dot's Story Book.
A Nest of Stories.
Good-Night Stories.
Chats for Small Chatterers.

Auntie's Stories.
Birdie's Story Book.
Little Chimes.
A Sheaf of Tales.
Dewdrop Stories.

Illustrated Books for the Little Ones. Containing interesting Stories. All Illustrated. 1s. each; cloth gilt, 1s. 6d.

Bright Tales & Funny Pictures.
Merry Little Tales.
Little Tales for Little People.
Little People and Their Pets.
Tales Told for Sunday.
Sunday Stories for Small People.
Stories and Pictures for Sunday.
Bible Pictures for Boys and Girls.
Firelight Stories.
Sunlight and Shade.
Rub-a-Dub Tales.
Fine Feathers and Fluffy Fur.
Scrambles and Scrapes.
Tittle Tattle Tales.

Up and Down the Garden.
All Sorts of Adventures.
Our Sunday Stories.
Our Holiday Hours.
Indoors and Out.
Some Farm Friends.
Wandering Ways.
Dumb Friends.
Those Golden Sands.
Little Mothers & their Children.
Our Pretty Pets.
Our Schoolday Hours.
Creatures Tame.
Creatures Wild.

Cassell's Shilling Story Books. All Illustrated, and containing Interesting Stories.

Bunty and the Boys.
The Heir of Elmdale.
The Mystery at Shoncliff School.
Claimed at Last, & Roy's Reward.
Thorns and Tangles.
The Cuckoo in the Robin's Nest.
John's Mistake.   [Pitchers.
The History of Five Little
Diamonds in the Sand.
Surly Bob.

The Giant's Cradle.
Shag and Doll.
Aunt Lucia's Locket.
The Magic Mirror.
The Cost of Revenge.
Clever Frank.
Among the Redskins.
The Ferryman of Brill.
Harry Maxwell.
A Banished Monarch.
Seventeen Cats.

"Wanted—a King" Series. *Cheap Edition.* Illustrated. 2s. 6d. each.

Great Grandmamma. By Georgina M. Synge.
Robin's Ride. By Ellinor Davenport Adams.
Wanted—a King; or, How Merle set the Nursery Rhymes to Rights. By Maggie Browne. With Original Designs by Harry Furniss.
Fairy Tales in Other Lands. By Julia Goddard.

The World's Workers. A Series of New and Original Volumes. With Portraits printed on a tint as Frontispiece. 1s. each.

John Cassell. By G. Holden Pike.
Charles Haddon Spurgeon. By G. Holden Pike.
Dr. Arnold of Rugby. By Rose E. Selfe.
The Earl of Shaftesbury. By Henry Frith.
Sarah Robinson, Agnes Weston, and Mrs. Meredith. By E. M. Tomkinson.
Thomas A. Edison and Samuel F. B. Morse. By Dr. Denslow and J. Marsh Parker.
Mrs. Somerville and Mary Carpenter. By Phyllis Browne.
General Gordon. By the Rev. S. A. Swaine.
Charles Dickens. By his Eldest Daughter.
Sir Titus Salt and George Moore. By J. Burnley.

Florence Nightingale, Catherine Marsh, Frances Ridley Havergal, Mrs. Ranyard ("L. N. R."). By Lizzie Alldridge.
Dr. Guthrie, Father Mathew, Elihu Burritt, George Livesey. By John W. Kirton, LL.D.
Sir Henry Havelock and Colin Campbell Lord Clyde. By E. C. Phillips.
Abraham Lincoln. By Ernest Foster.
George Müller and Andrew Reed. By E. R. Pitman.
Richard Cobden. By R. Gowing.
Benjamin Franklin. By E. M. Tomkinson.
Handel. By Eliza Clarke.   [Swaine.
Turner the Artist. By the Rev. S. A.
George and Robert Stephenson. By C. L. Mateaux.
David Livingstone. By Robert Smiles.

*** The above Works can also be had Three in One Vol., cloth, gilt edges, 3s.*

Library of Wonders. Illustrated Gift-books for Boys. Paper, 1s.; cloth, 1s. 6d.

Wonderful Balloon Ascents.
Wonderful Adventures.
Wonderful Escapes.

Wonders of Animal Instinct.
Wonders of Bodily Strength and Skill.

Cassell's Eighteenpenny Story Books. Illustrated.

Wee Willie Winkie.
Ups and Downs of a Donkey's Life.
Three Wee Ulster Lassies.
Up the Ladder.
Dick's Hero; and other Stories.
The Chip Boy.
Raggles, Baggles, and the Emperor.
Roses from Thorns.

Faith's Father.
By Land and Sea.
The Young Berringtons.
Jeff and Leff.
Tom Morris's Error.
Worth more than Gold.
"Through Flood—Through Fire;" and other Stories.
The Girl with the Golden Locks.
Stories of the Olden Time.

Gift Books for Young People. By Popular Authors. With Four Original Illustrations in each. Cloth gilt, 1s. 6d. each.

The Boy Hunters of Kentucky. By Edward S. Ellis.
Red Feather: a Tale of the American Frontier. By Edward S. Ellis.
Seeking a City.
Rhoda's Reward; or, "If Wishes were Horses."
Jack Marston's Anchor.
Frank's Life-Battle; or, The Three Friends.
Fritters. By Sarah Pitt.
The Two Hardcastles. By Madeline Bonavia Hunt.

Major Monk's Motto. By the Rev. F. Langbridge.
Trixy. By Maggie Symington.
Rags and Rainbows: A Story of Thanksgiving.
Uncle William's Charges; or, The Broken Trust.
Pretty Pink's Purpose; or, The Little Street Merchants.
Tim Thomson's Trial. By George Weatherly.
Ursula's Stumbling-Block. By Julia Goddard.
Ruth's Life-Work. By the Rev. Joseph Johnson.